A
COUSINLY
CONNEXION

A
COUSINLY
CONNEXION

Sheila Simonson

Walker and Company
New York

First published in the United States of America in 1984 by the Walker Publishing Company, Inc.

Published simultaneously in Canada by John Wiley & Sons Canada, Limited, Rexdale, Ontario.

Library of Congress Cataloging in Publication Data

Simonson, Sheila, 1941-
    A cousinly connexion.

    I. Title.
PS3569.I48766C6   1984   813'.54   84-11962
ISBN 0-8027-0802-1

Printed in the United States of America

10 9 8 7 6 5 4 3 2 1

1

At eighteen jane Ash fell in love with Edward Wincanton, an ensign in the Royal Navy. The youngest son of a local squire, Wincanton did not seem to Jane's father a suitable match for his only daughter, and after some thought, for he was inclined to indulge her, Mr. Ash refused his consent to the match. Jane wept. Ensign Wincanton, his leave up, returned to his ship. Life went on.

Unlike several of her favourite heroines, Jane did not go into a decline or join the navy in the guise of a cabin boy or sit mindless in a ruined tower twining jonquils into her tangled locks. As she was a sensible girl and fond of her father and brothers she very soon entered again into their ordinary country pursuits, and if she occasionally sighed without apparent cause or read the naval news with more eagerness than might have been expected in a female of tender years her family were careful to take no notice.

In the course of the next six years the Nation continued their sanguinary struggle with the French, Ensign Wincanton progressed in rank and fortune, and, as might have been expected, Jane continued the even tenor of her ways. She danced and sketched and pic-nicked and was presented by her aunt, Lady Meriden. She even enjoyed a modestly successful London Season in her aunt's household, and received three very eligible marriage proposals and several ineligible ones. She refused the gentlemen kindly and returned to Walden Ash older and somewhat wiser, content to play hostess in her father's house. There she was reasonably happy and, indeed, scarcely remembered her first love.

Just after her twenty-fourth birthday, however, Ensign Wincanton—now Captain Wincanton of H.M.S. *Bonheur* and suitably enriched with prize-money—returned to Sussex. Waterloo had brought Europe peace at last, and Captain Wincanton retired. Europe might be at peace. Jane was besieged.

The captain, much bluffer and heartier than the lovesick lad who had vowed eternal devotion to her, had a fancy to settle down to a snug piece of land and the life of a country gentleman. If only his dear Jane—his lodestar, the figurehead of his soul's barque—could be persuaded to keep his little nest for him. At that—he was in her withdrawing room as he said it—he clasped her hand and raised it to his full lips, and Jane made an interesting discovery. He was a very silly man.

Which, as she told her companion Miss Goodnight later, served her well for cherishing romantical daydreams.

"Oh, Jane, do not say so!" Miss Goodnight cried. "So handsome a young man and so sincerely attached to you. Six years...."

"But, Goody, he snorts so."

"Jane! Miss Ash!"

"Indeed he does. And I find I don't like a red face and gooseberry eyes—if I ever did. And if he says to me one more time, 'Stap me, Miss Jane, you're in high bloom today,' I'll ... I'll—"

"Jane!"

"I'll stap him," Jane muttered. "Why must Papa change his mind now! It passes wonder. I shall have to find some means of escape soon. Perhaps I could enter a convent."

Miss Goodnight moaned. A worthy lady—Jane's mother's remote cousin—she had little of her charge's liveliness, but she was kindhearted and Jane did not often mind explaining to her what was serious, what a jest. Now, however, Jane merely shook her head in exasperation and ran off to corner her father. If, as she suspected, he was twitting her, she meant to put a period to his levity. If not...it did not bear thinking on.

She found him inclined to laugh at her.

"Is he not the man you expected him to be, Jane?"

"No! That quarterdeck voice...."

"His manners are perhaps a trifle bluff, my dear, but I find him very good-natured and willing to learn. He was most interested in my mangel-wurzels."

Jane sighed. Her father's agricultural experiments were his obsession, and Captain Wincanton had struck a shrewd blow if he had had the wit to admire them. In general Jane supported her father's efforts to improve his estate and the lot of his tenants, but it is difficult for those not directly concerned to feel enthusiasm for the more exotic root crops. Many a time had Jane's eyes glazed at the mention of mangel-wurzels. She could not help but feel that Captain Wincanton was playing unfairly.

When her father went on to remind her of her advancing age—four-and-twenty, very nearly on the shelf—and, with a meaningful sigh, that he could not wait forever to dandle her children on his knee, she

2

recommended that he dandle young Master Thomas Ash as much as he liked and reminded him that her sister-in-law Joanna was increasing again.

"A daughter-in-law is not a daughter," he said with a look of reproach. Jane began to feel decidedly ill-used.

She bore with Captain Wincanton's attentions—and her father's sighs and her brothers' sly looks—as politely as she could, but several weeks of nautical ardour had begun to oppress her naturally lively spirits when, one morning, she received a summons from her father to join him at once in the bookroom.

She excused herself from a very boring recital of her sister-in-law's latest symptoms and went in to him directly.

"What is it, Papa? If Edward has called again—"

"No. No, it is not that." He looked very grave. A much crossed letter lay open before him. "My dear, your Aunt Louisa writes that Meriden has died and his heir also—young Harry—within a week of each other."

Jane sat down abruptly. "Oh, my poor aunt. But, sir—"

"There is also some sort of scandal," her father interrupted. "I cannot have misread ... that is, do see if you can decipher this word."

"Deal?" Jane said doubtfully, studying the word at which her father was pointing. "Duet?"

"I believe it must be 'duel.' Harry has been killed in a duel."

"Good God, sir, surely not." But, with a sinking feeling, Jane realised that it was altogether too possible. The Honourable Henry had been as wild a buck as Society could boast, causing even his doting stepmama to deplore his rackety ways. Harry dead. Jane could not believe it possible.

Mr. Ash peered again at the crossed lines. "Louisa speaks of the new heir—that will be the second son, the military one—as most disobliging, and she appears to think she will be cast out from Meriden Place with her children. Tsk." He set the letter down. "I do not scruple to say, Jane, that my sister is as hen-witted a woman as it has been my misfortune to know. Her marriage portion was substantial and tied to her children, so I cannot believe the new baron, however unfeeling, has the power to do any such thing, even if he wished to make a further scandal. No doubt Louisa's nerves are a little overset."

Jane preserved her gravity. Lord Meriden had not been a considerate spouse, but to lose one's husband and a son—even a stepson—at one blow might overset the most stolid of females, and Aunt Louisa was far from moderate in her sensibilities.

"I fear we should go to her at once." Mr. Ash frowned. "I do not like it, but she cannot rely on Meriden's sister."

"Indeed not." Jane shuddered. Lady Brackhurst was parrot-faced and stone-hearted and the two ladies cordially despised each other. Nevertheless her aunt would need counsel and comfort from some near relation. So many children, too—five in the schoolroom still, though Maria must soon turn eighteen, and one in leading strings. Only the Honourable Vincent, the youngest stepson, was of age. Horrible.

"I cannot myself stay above a day or so," her father was saying, "but I am afraid your visit may extend for some time. Jane, my dear, I am sorry. Shall you dislike it too much? Perhaps Miss Goodnight...."

"I shall certainly take her, and I shall stay as long as my aunt needs me."

"You are a very good girl," Mr. Ash said affectionately and gave her a hearty kiss. "I don't know how we shall get on without you."

Jane smiled. "I'm sure I don't either, sir. Joanna will order everything you most dislike for dinner, but truly, Papa, there is nothing else to be done. I'll pack at once."

"Jane?"

"Yes."

"I had forgot." He looked genuinely troubled. "What of Edward Wincanton?"

Jane's eyes widened, and she was hard put not to burst into laughter. Of course. To be set down in West Dorset must put her beyond her importunate suitor's reach.

"Dear Papa, only show him your new seed drill and I'm sure he will forget that his heart is broken."

2

SOMEWHAT EARLIER IN the same month William Tarrant, lately Captain Tarrant of the Fighting 95th, rode out from his windswept East Riding manor to pay a call on his friend, Julian Stretton, also late of the Rifles.

Tarrant, a Peninsular veteran, had sold out at the beginning of the short-lived Peace, prospects for promotion then seeming dim, and had returned to his native Yorkshire to take up life on the small estate left him by his father and, not incidentally, to resume enjoyment of his interrupted marriage.

Julian Stretton had not sold out and might, but for the luck of a minor wound taken at Toulouse, have ended up in North America with so many of the other Peninsular soldiers. Instead he had spent his convalescence with Will and Margaret Tarrant and had liked the country and the company so well that he had invested his prize-money and a small inheritance in the adjoining estate with an eye to settling there when he, too, decided to sell out. Will thought he was mad, for, with the sum Julian had expended on the small bankrupted estate, his friend could easily have purchased the majority he had been breveted to before Orthez. It was all very well for Will, still a captain at thirty-five, to be settling down at home, but Julian was only seven-and-twenty and his friends looked for Great Things from him.

What Julian lacked was ambition. And possibly connexions, although he had certainly had his lieutenancy by purchase. What maddened Will, resigned to his own mere competence, was that Julian's military talents would surely be wasted on a farmer. If his friend was not ambitious, he did possess in generous sum the magic combination of cool intelligence and raw luck that took him, repeatedly, to the right place at the right time. Will confidently expected to see him a general officer at forty like the Peer.

But dreams of glory, however vicarious, do not always lead where one wishes them to lead, and Will's prophecy was destined to fail.

Pronounced fit by the army surgeons, Julian had rejoined his regiment in Kent just as the news came of Bonaparte's escape from Elba and Julian had been sent directly to Belgium, where the 95th was one of the few Peninsular regiments to fight in the sanguinary battle of Waterloo. The English victory at Waterloo had finished the Corsican monster forever, but it also put paid to Julian Stretton's brilliant prospects and very nearly to Julian as well.

The rumours and counterrumours of the Hundred Days had driven Will in his Yorkshire retreat to pacing restlessly back and forth, biting the heads off his servants, his friends, his infant son, and even his gentle wife so that finally, in exasperation, she suggested that he see for himself what was happening. Thus it was that he joined the hundreds of English civilians in Brussels.

Unlike so many of them, he did not fly to Antwerp at the first rumour of cannonfire. He watched grimly as the baggage trains, the first deserters, the first of the wounded entered the city. He was there when the Duke of Brunswick's body was brought in by his black-clad dragoons after Quatre Bras, and there the next afternoon when the first wounded survivors of the Scots Greys straggled past, then more wounded, an unending parade. Though his heart sank, he held fiercely to his faith in the Duke, but when it became at last clear that Wellington had truly done the trick, that even the splendid Imperial Guard were in full retreat before Bluecher's Prussians, Will had neither time nor thought for celebration. He found Julian.

His friend lay in one of the hastily rigged field hospitals in immediate peril of losing one leg and very probably both if he should survive the loss of a great deal of blood. Will and Julian's bâtman Thorpe formed an instant alliance against the weary army surgeons, for both were certain that Julian would prefer death to the half-life of a legless cripple. Spiriting him off to Will's quarters in a quiet Bruxellois household, they had, by dint of round-the-clock care and Thorpe's highly unorthodox remedies, nursed him through the worst dangers of infection. Why he had not developed gangrene in the terrible wounds on his left leg, Will did not know, for Julian had lain in the field through the first night after the battle with only the sketchiest of treatment. The fact that Julian lived and kept both limbs amazed Will afterwards. At the time he was far too busy and tired, and melancholy from the deaths of other friends he could not help, to feel anything but a desire to leave Belgium as soon as possible. Within the month, Julian was pronounced strong enough to risk the sea voyage home. They sailed direct to Scarborough, for Will would not subject the sick man to more jolting on the rough roads than necessary. Even so, the wounds tore open again, and Julian Stretton returned to Yorkshire in a very sorry state.

In all this travail it had not occurred to either Will or Thorpe to ask the help of the Stretton family, nor had Julian's father made inquiries after his son. Will was not surprised. Julian had never spoken of his connexions, and Will could only suppose there had been a falling-out. There was certainly indifference. So Will did not apply for help, though he could have used it.

The expedition, especially the sea voyage home, had cost Will a pretty sum, more than a small landowner could easily afford. But, as he told his Margaret, "I'd have sold the house and the lands if I had to. I should've been with them, Peggy. Such losses! It is worse even than Badajoz. There has never been anything like it. My poor friends—not one in five of them left!"

If Margaret rejoiced that her husband had escaped such universal slaughter, she was too wise to say so. Indeed, when she saw Julian transformed from the vigorous young man who had left them to a gaunt, pain-wracked ghost, she felt only appalled relief that Will was with her and whole and sound.

"For, my dear," she said to Will, tears in her eyes, "even if Julian regains some of his former strength, there is no saying he will ever have the use of his legs."

"No, no," Will had replied with forced heartiness. "He'll come about. Always has before. Wiry devil. He don't look it now, Peggy, but he'll rally." He refused to meet her eyes.

Despite their doubts—expressed and denied—the patient did rally and was so much improved in another month, at least in his own mind, as to remove to his own house. Will could not like it. Julian was not able to walk, but Thorpe had somewhere unearthed a wheeled invalid chair, and Julian contrived to get about in that. When Will had last visited him early in the week, he had been trying to walk on crutches, amid much grumbling from Thorpe who did not think he was ready. And the attempt had not met with notable success. Now Will rode to Whitethorn—for so Julian's house was called—with some misgivings as to his friend's progress.

The housekeeper—a brisk, plump woman of middle age who kept the house and its sparse furnishings in sparkling order—led Will out to the garden that lay beyond a low terrace.

"He's been there all morning." She sniffed. "Foolishness. He'll fall in the rosebushes, and then where'll we be? Talk sense to him, Mr. Tarrant."

Will promised meekly to do so and ventured down the neat gravelled path which led to the rose garden. Most of the roses were overblown brown cabbageheads, but here and there late bloomers thrust their brave colours into the breeze. Will did not spare a glance for the flowers. Round a turn in the path he stopped short. Perhaps fifty paces ahead, his back to Will, Julian was walking. True, he leaned heavily on the crutches, but he was making his legs work for him.

Slow, even steps. So great was his concentration that he had apparently not heard Will's crunching tread at all, for he continued without hesitation. Step, step, lurch, as the crutches came forward. Step, step, lurch. He had shed his coat and waistcoat on a stone bench, and in spite of a brisk east wind, sweat moulded the thin cambric shirt to his back.

Will's jaw ached. He found he had been gritting his teeth against what must have been an excruciatingly painful exercise. He let out his breath harshly.

Julian's head snapped up. "Thorpe, I told you to go away. By God—" He turned and, wobbling towards the nearest rosebush, nearly fulfilled the housekeeper's prophecy. Will was beside him in three strides.

"You damn fool, you'll fall and break that leg!"

Julian shook his head and laughed, gasping from his efforts. "Don't natter, Granny," he managed after a moment.

Grim-faced, Will steered him to the bench and sat him down. "How long have you been at it?"

"An hour." He took an unsteady breath. "What time is it?"

"Noon."

"Oh."

"Nearer three hours, I'll lay odds," Will said, resigned. "At least put your coat on, man. You're shivering and don't trouble to think up a sharp answer."

Julian closed his mouth.

"You might consider my feelings before you work yourself into a fever and wind up sticking your spoon in the wall after all my pother. Damn your selfish hide, I've not so many friends left I can spare you."

"Sneck up, Will." Julian rubbed his hands over his face and grinned at Will sidelong. "Listen to that. I'll turn into a proper Yorkshireman yet."

He picked up the brown stuff coat and poked one arm into a sleeve. "Here, help me into this."

Will obeyed. "How's that?"

"You'd not make your mark as a gentleman's gentleman but I suppose it'll have to do. How does Peggy go on?"

As Margaret was increasing again and, indeed, due to commence labour at any moment, Julian had chosen his subject shrewdly. Diverted, Will entered into a lengthy analysis of the perils of paternity to which, owing to his protracted absences on duty, he was not yet accustomed. In fact he was given to moments of unreasonable anxiety when he imagined Margaret perishing in childbirth, but he was a sensible man and, as she had borne one child without much difficulty, he generally talked himself out of despair. Julian was content to let him ramble and to sit very quiet.

After perhaps five minutes of fears and imaginings, Will broke off with a self-conscious laugh. "I beg your pardon, old man. What are you at to let me go prosing on and on?"

"Matrimony has been the ruin of you," Julian said lightly.

Will flushed and grinned like a youth of twenty.

"How is the heir?"

"You should see him now, Ju. Young Will is walking as steady as a seasoned trooper."

"A splendid example to me."

Will fumbled in the pockets of his greatcoat. "I forgot. Peggy said I should give you this." He extracted a clumsy packet and handed it over. "Now what have I done to send you into the whoops?"

Julian shook his head, speechless.

"It's pork jelly," Will explained.

Julian spluttered.

"Why, damn it, man, she's *concerned*."

At that his friend sobered. "I know, but if what you say is true, she had much better save her concern for herself. Tell her I thank her for it." He smiled. "I'll place it in my collection along with Mrs. Bradford's essence of veal knuckle and Thorpe's liniments and my cousin Georgy's bog-oak walking stick. Have I showed you that?"

Will shook his head ruefully. "Lord, I might've known you'd be fussed beyond bearing. It's a wonder you don't wish me in Jericho."

"Oh, not so far. Scarborough, perhaps. Will, don't get up yet."

"I only stopped by to see how you did."

9

"And to bring Peggy's placebo. Tell me, do I eat it or rub it in?"

"I wish you will be serious, Ju. This parade-ground drill is all very well but you're worn to the bone, man. Try it on later."

"That's just what I can't do," Julian snapped. "If I wait until later, the leg will tighten like wet rawhide. It pulls, Will. Do you remember poor Whitney? They might as well have chopped his leg off after Salamanca. It was never any good to him again. I won't be tied to a Bath chair for the rest of my days. My God, if I lived to be seventy-seven that'd be fifty years of sitting."

Will didn't speak.

"It's the devil," Julian muttered.

Will threw up his hands in mock surrender. *"Basta!* I'll stop jobbing at you, but I wish you'd come back to us for a while at least."

"And try my hand at midwifery," Julian interrupted acidly. "Do *you* try for a little common sense. I'm very well suited here and"—he took a breath, catching at his temper with visible effort—"I think I'm already sufficiently in your debt—and Peggy's."

Will stiffened and felt his neck go red.

"No, you don't want to talk about it," Julian said shortly. "I know that well enough, but let me speak my piece."

Will made to rise.

"And don't turn tail and run. I can't chase after you."

Will sat back stiff as a pillar.

"That I owe you my life and rather more is beside the point," Julian went on in a dogged voice. "The fact is I was too devilish sick in Brussels to think, or I'd not have let you squander the ready at the rate you did."

Will shifted. He caught a glimpse of his friend's face, which was white under the fading tan and set in grim lines.

"I wish you will give me an accounting of that little sea excursion you took me on. There's no reason for you to bear the cost of that."

Will got up. "You'll oblige me by not mentioning the matter again if we are to continue friends."

"Very dramatic. When did you take to reading novels?"

Will shook his head. "Don't try me, Ju," he said softly, and after a moment Julian lowered his eyes.

"Help me to the chair." Julian's voice was flat with exhaustion. "Let's go in. I'm cold." And, indeed, he was shivering again.

"Damned fool," Will murmured, uneasy but determined.

Julian did not reply.

As they reached the house, however, they were forestalled by Mrs. Bradford, the housekeeper, from the admirable intention of puffing a cloud and taking a glass or two of claret.

"There's a person here to see you, Mr. Stretton. I knew you wouldn't want him out there." She nodded at the terrace window through which Will had just trundled the chair. "But he's come from Lunnon and he's mortal impatient to see you, sir. I've put him in the library."

Julian swore under his breath. "What sort of 'person'?"

Mrs. Bradford, looking rather dubious, handed him a card.

"Leak and Horrocks." He stared at it. "Oh. Probably a clerk from my father's man of business."

Will grunted. A trifle late for his lordship to be making anxious paternal gestures.

Apparently Julian thought so, too, for he shrugged and jammed the card in his pocket. "Some tedious legal nonsense. No need for you to go off without trying my claret, Will." He gave the chair a sharp thrust and rolled down the corridor that led to the interior rooms. "A new pipe. Best so far."

Will followed him.

As they negotiated the library door, a young man with butter-yellow hair and a spotty complexion sprang to his feet and looked uncertainly from one man to the other.

Julian put a hand to his bedraggled neckcloth as if he were suddenly conscious of presenting a slovenly appearance and said briskly, "Mr. Crofts? I'm Julian Stretton. Mrs. Bradford informs me that your business is of some moment. I trust that's so."

"I ... er, yes." The boy's voice squeaked, and he cleared his throat. "That is, yes, sir, if you are Major the Honourable Julian Alexander St. John Stretton." He seemed doubtful.

Julian's mouth quirked. "The same."

"I have the sad duty, sir, to inform you of Lord Meriden's death."

Will felt his stomach knot. Julian, he noticed, had gone very still. After a moment, his friend said mechanically, "I'm sorry to hear it. Apoplexy, I collect? Rather sudden, was it not?"

"Yes sir." The boy was in obvious misery, his chin wobbling, but Will perceived that some other emotion—fear? no, excitement—was working in him also. At last he went on in a rapid breathless voice, "That is, I apprehend I should say, 'yes, my lord.' "

"What!"

The boy jumped.

Julian pushed himself forward, his knuckles white on the chair wheels. "Tell me."

"Ow, dear, Mr. Horrocks warned me you might not have heard the tragic news, but I thought he was bamming me. *Every*body knows. Ow, sir—my lord, that is, I'm that sorry."

"Stop blethering," Will roared.

Far from wishing to flee—his first impulse—Will was now consumed with curiosity. An entire division under Soult would not have driven him from the library. Julian a lord? Impossible.

"Explain yourself, Crofts," Will demanded.

The clerk closed his eyes and took a gulp of air. "The Honourable Henry Stretton, sir, has been dead these two weeks. His lordship was so stunned, what with his grief and the scandal—"

"Scandal?" Will interposed. Julian had neither spoken nor moved.

"Mr. Henry Stretton was killed in a duel, sir."

"Oh, dear God," Julian whispered. "Not Harry, too. They're none of them left."

The silence extended. After a long time, Crofts ventured timidly, "But, my lord, it's not true, you know. They're not all gone. There's the Honourable Vincent and Miss Maria and Miss Drusilla and Mr. Felix...."

"His lordship was not referring to his half brothers and sisters," Will said shortly.

"Her ladyship—"

"A very good kind of woman, no doubt. Ju ...?" He gripped his friend's shoulder.

"I ... yes. In a moment. Will, don't leave me."

"No, I'll not leave," Will said comfortably, his voice at odds with the glare he sent the clerk. "Mr. Crofts, go out and desire Mrs. Bradford to bring in a tray. Tell her the brandy. Snap to it!" This last in a parade-ground voice that had been his major military asset. Crofts fled.

Will went over to a bookshelf and stared hard at a leatherbound copy of the *Moral Discourses* of Epictetus, left behind by a previous inhabitant. When he thought his friend had been silent too long, he said with calculated bluntness, "Shouldn't have thought you'd take it hard, Ju. Shock, of course. Not close to this brother, was you?"

"I can't remember what he looked like," Julian said dully.

Will cursed silently and comprehensively. He knew very well what the trouble was, for he had himself felt the same dazed emptiness Julian's voice betrayed—after Waterloo, when he had found name after name of men he had known and loved better than his own brothers on the lists of the dead.

Will had supposed that Julian's physical suffering had at least pre-occupied his mind sufficiently to save him from that ordeal of loss, but he saw now that his friend had been spared nothing and that the shock of this absurd melodrama—for Will could not think of the death of such an indifferent parent, such a feckless brother, as anything other—had merely plunged Julian three months back into a far more bitter tragedy.

"Julian? Ju, old friend—"

"I'm sorry," Julian said quietly. He took a shaky breath. "You're right, of course. I doubt if I saw Harry above three times since I first went abroad. He wrote me once in Portugal. I believe I lit a cheroot with the letter."

"Come, that's more the thing. Shall I go find that rabbity clerk?"

There was a clatter outside. Julian shook his head. "Unnecessary, I think. He has just dropped my best decanter on the parquet."

He cocked his head towards the door, the ghost of a grin on his face. "Mrs. Bradford is beating him with her chain. How edifying. Perhaps you should go to his rescue."

Will did not remain with his friend for long after the shaken Crofts had embarked on what promised to be a marathon of paper-signing, but he stayed long enough to extract a promise from Julian not to go jauntering off to London, however urgent his affairs might be.

"Nattering again, Will?" Julian raised his brows. He had begun to look less white about the mouth.

"Yes. And what's more I'll keep you to your word."

"I've no intention of going to London." Julian held out his hand.

Will clasped it. "Your hand on that?"

Julian smiled. "I can't very well leave until after my first try at godfathering."

Both men, having come to a tolerable understanding, rightly ignored the dismayed bleat with which Crofts greeted their pact.

Shortly thereafter, Will found his wife in that condition not un-common to ninth-month-pregnant ladies. Impatient.

"You took a great while to deliver the pork jelly." Her voice, normally soft, rang rather shrill.

Unfortunately, the remark set Will off, and it was some few minutes before he recovered himself sufficiently to relate to her the story of his

13

afternoon. She was so dumbfounded that she forgot to question his laughter, and after listening open-mouthed to his narrative, subsided into half-phrases. "Dear me. Only fancy. Poor Julian, but my goodness. Bless me, what a surprise," and so on.

Margaret was, however, the kindest of women, and she soon overcame her astonishment sufficiently to grow very distressed for their friend, so that Will had to explain to her what he knew of the late Lord Meriden's character as a parent. At that she grew indignant, for she had vaguely imagined Julian to be orphaned and felt that such a neglectful family deserved nothing better at the hands of Providence.

"Well," Will said cautiously, "Providence may have had a hand in it, but from what I gathered of that snerp, Crofts, Ju may find his elevation something less than providential. I believe he has, in addition to a barony of the first creation, succeeded to a load of debts and the guardianship of seven brats he's never laid eyes on. It don't bear thinking on."

"What a very odd family they must be, to be sure," said Peggy rather faintly.

3

DIRECTLY JANE, HER father, and Miss Goodnight set out for Dorset it commenced to rain. The journey, which should have taken no more than five days by easy stages, dragged to a week as one of the horses lamed itself on the heavy roads and then to ten days when the rear axle splintered. Mr. Ash, never cheerful out of sight of his chalky acres, grew gloomier as the miles dragged on. He was sure the potatoes he was trying on as an experiment would rot in the ground and the mown hay would mould.

Jane thought his absence would do her elder brother, Tom, a deal of good, for he seldom had a free hand. She did not say so, however. Although she was far too occupied ministering to Miss Goodnight, a poor traveller, to soothe her father as she ought to, she could at least contrive not to set him fresh anxieties. She forbore to mention Tom.

By the time they reached Dorchester, all three were too cross to admire that handsome county-town. They passed through Whitchurch and up into the rolling hills in which Meriden Place lay, but Jane should not have had the time to admire the pleasant prospects their elevation must have allowed them, even if she had been able to see through the murk of rain. Miss Goodnight cast up her accounts. As for Mr. Ash, he announced his intention of repairing to Lyme Regis or Bridport forthwith.

"Perhaps," he said plaintively, averting his eyes from Miss Goodnight; "there will be some vessel there to take me home. James may return the carriage, for you know, my dear, he is most reliable, and I must see to the potatoes myself."

"But Aunt Louisa—"

"I shall speak with your aunt." He drew a sheaf of closely written papers from his coat. "I took the precaution last night of writing down such advice as I think will be of use to her."

Jane made no reply.

Her father added, rather defensively, "I am sure Meriden's man of business has dealt honourably with her. Perhaps I can return when this stepson of hers comes to take up his residence."

"If he stays away until after the last harvest...." Jane murmured.

"Eh?"

"Nothing. Only look, sir, surely that is a gatehouse or lodge of some sort."

"It seems familiar," Mr. Ash said doubtfully. He had once or twice visited his sister at Meriden. Jane had not, her sojourn with her aunt having been spent entirely in London. She began at last to feel some anticipatory interest. She would be staying here several months, perhaps even until Christmas. She hoped the grounds would not prove insipid.

No one at the gatehouse showing a disposition to bar the way, they continued up a curved avenue set between plantations of rhododendrons which were just now drooping in a melancholy fashion, their dark leaves hanging down like soggy dusters. An admirable sight in early summer, no doubt. Jane would have preferred beeches. However, the drive was rising and presently they came into open ground and could at last perceive Meriden Place itself, set on a knoll of some natural prominence and surrounded by handsome stone terracing.

The house itself was built in the same grey Dorset stone as the terraces and was not above seventy-five years old, so there was nothing in the lofty windows and severe façade to give one a disgust of its proportions, but it did not look precisely cheerful. As they bowled up the carriageway, Jane could see that a large black crêpe bow had been appended to the main door and that it, like the rhododendrons, drooped with damp. About the exterior of the house, small jarring signs of neglect betrayed an indifferent master. The privet wanted trimming.

They were ushered into the mansion by an aged butler who looked as though his feet hurt him. Addressed by Mr. Ash as Turvey, this worthy unbent sufficiently to tell them that her ladyship was not yet down but would be informed of their arrival forthwith. He took their wraps—Jane's pelisse and Mr. Ash's greatcoat, for Miss Goodnight confessed to a chill—then shuffled off in a dispirited manner, leaving them to their thoughts. The large salon into which he had shown them loomed grimly. Drapes of a sombre hue shut out the watery daylight, and a small fire of seacoal did little to take the chill off the air.

Jane gazed about her in some surprise, for her memories of her aunt's London house called up a blaze of wax candles and glittering crystal. The dank gloom of the salon could scarcely have contrasted more sharply. She opened her lips to make some such comment to her father, who was rubbing his hands and looking about him with an air of forced cheer, when there was a rustle at the door, a mutter from the dispirited butler, and Lady Meriden entered.

The dowager, then in her fortieth year, was a tall woman of gaunt, rather dramatic good looks much marred by years of childbearing. Swathed in yards of becoming crêpe, she tottered into the room on the arm of her eldest daughter, Maria, and, raising her great sunken eyes to Mr. Ash—no mean feat considering he was just her height—she exclaimed, "Oh, John, best of my friends, my dear, dear brother, how I have needed your wise counsel!"

Jane saw appreciatively that Lady Meriden had caused one of the footmen to hold a branch of lit candles so that the soft light haloed her head and deepened the shadows on her ravaged features. Jane scarcely had time to school her expression, however, for her aunt turned to her at once and swept her into a rose-scented embrace.

"Dear Jane. So comforting, my dear." The soft powdered cheek brushed Jane's damp brown curls. "Now we shall learn again to be cheerful!" And, on a little sob, "If ever we may smile again in this doomed family. Ah, John, John, whatever shall I do? My poor wee bairns...."

Jane and her father tried simultaneously to pat Lady Meriden's quivering shoulders. Bairns, Jane thought, embarrassed and unwillingly amused. Lady Meriden came of good Sussex stock and had never in her life been closer to Scotland than Harrogate.

"Mama!" Maria exclaimed at last. "Please don't! You'll make yourself ill again. Please!"

Her mother essayed a final sob and allowed herself to be ensconced in the deepest chair, with her own maid, a young footman, and Maria hovering near with screens and shawls. Miss Goodnight, reviving magically under the stimulus of another's distress, fluttered about the chair making noises like the cooing of many doves.

Jane and her father exchanged glances. Aunt Louisa was entitled to a scene—a grand tableau, even—but not an entire folio. Jane could see her father's determination to fly to Lyme Regis harden. For herself, she merely felt sorry for Maria. The child had always gone in awe of her mother's many ills, but the supreme tragedy Lady Meriden now enacted clearly terrified her. Indeed, I am unfair, Jane thought. Aunt has great sensibility, and her sufferings are always real. If only she did not enjoy them so much.

Jane took a deep breath and without scruple cast her father and Miss Goodnight to the wolves. "Dear Aunt," she pronounced, "you will wish to tell Papa all. *I* shall ask my cousin to show me to my room. And if it is not too much trouble," she added, softened by her father's harassed grimace, "Papa will be needing a light nuncheon. The day is really most inclement, and he must be fortified if he is to go on to Lyme Regis."

Mr. Ash breathed his relief. Lady Meriden reproached Jane with a mournful glance, but her unrepentant niece merely gave her a quick kiss and slipped from the salon with Maria firmly in tow.

In the room assigned her, Jane was relieved to find a cosy fire and the light streaming wetly in undraped windows. Her trunks, unfortunately, had not yet been brought up.

She poured steaming water into a generous porcelain bowl. "Now, Maria, tell me everything, my love."

Maria burst into tears.

Jane allowed her cousin time for a healthy cry and meantime washed her own face and smoothed her unruly curls into order. When she was as satisfied with her hair as she could be in damp weather, she settled a handsome Norfolk shawl about her shoulders and pulled the girl down beside her on a French sopha that fronted the hearth.

"I am very sorry for you, Maria," she said firmly, "but indeed more crying will not help, besides blotching your very nice complexion."

Maria gave a startled sniff and wiped her eyes, which were grey and long-lashed and by far her best feature.

"Now, tell me how things are left and why Aunt Louisa is so overwrought. Lord Mer—that is, your papa has surely left you all well provided for. I cannot think otherwise."

When Maria's face clouded again, Jane said with asperity, "Maria, you must not turn yourself into a watering pot for at least ten years."

Maria gave a damp chuckle.

"That's better. Now, I collect your brother ... what is his name?"

"J-Julian."

"Yes. Your brother Julian.... Why is it I keep wanting to call him Vincent? Oh, that is the *next* brother. Up at Oxford when I last saw you, was he not? He must be nearly one-and-twenty now." She gathered her thoughts. "Very well, then, Julian has succeeded to his father's honours."

"He is the greatest b-beast in nature," Maria stammered. "Such a cold letter as he has sent Mama, and he is to have *everything*. Vincent and the younger boys are cut out entirely. Mama is at her wits' end."

Jane stared, taken quite aback. "But surely your papa—"

"Papa," said Maria bitterly, "did not make a new will upon Harry's death, so all the provisions he directed Harry to implement—by name, was ever anything so foolish?—are quite overset, and the eldest surviving son must take all. Except Mama's portion, of course. That was settled on her daughters. Drusilla and I shall be well enough, but the poor boys! And Vincent! He is mad as fire and means to—do something dreadful. Mama is so worried, cousin. What are we to do?"

Jane swallowed. A pretty coil. "But surely," she essayed, "Lord Meriden cannot be without proper feeling for his brothers."

"Ah, but he can!" Maria burst out. "When Mama married my father, she felt she could not undertake to raise three stepsons. She was only nineteen, after all, and not strong. Vincent was a sickly infant, and Harry and Julian were so … so lively. I believe they set fire to the nursery drapes. Harry was heir, and, of course, was obliged to stay at Meriden, so Mama asked that Julian be sent to his mother's family—Lord Carteret, you know—and he was. Julian has never come to Meriden since. Indeed he does not know us at all. How can he care for brothers he has never seen? And Mama! How he must hate Mama!"

She paused, much agitated. "Depend upon it, his grandfather will have set him against her, for Carteret, you know, was used to think my papa had dealt ill with his daughter, the first Lady Meriden. Truly, Jane, Mama is sometimes inclined to … to exaggerate, but in this instance she must be said to have cause for her fears."

"Have you met Lord Meriden?" Jane asked after a moment.

"No. I saw him once. In London. He paid a courtesy call on Papa, and I caught a glimpse of him as he left, but all I remember is a peculiar green jacket and the b-back of his head. His hair is mouse-brown like mine, but straight."

Jane smiled slightly at the inconsequentiality of this intelligence.

"Vincent met him in London," Maria went on. "He said Julian is a … damned dull dog. Not up to the rig."

Jane repressed a grin. A direct quotation, no doubt. Reprehensible Vincent to use such language in his sister's presence. He sounded a delightful tulip. From what Jane recalled of Vincent, he had been at eighteen as sporting mad as his brother Harry and in a fair way to inheriting his father's ill luck at cards. Very much in the Stretton style. His strictures, of course, meant exactly nothing, but it was unfortunate that the two brothers had not hit it off.

She settled the shawl again about her shoulders—really, it was the

19

draughtiest house—and gave Maria's hand a comforting pat. "It all sounds most irregular, but I'm sure something will be worked out when the beastly baron arrives. Let us go down to Papa and my aunt. They must have said everything three times by now, and I shall see that Papa takes nuncheon. Otherwise he, too, will be wholly overset, and that, I assure you, is a far greater trial than my aunt's megrims."

Apparently her matter-of-fact tone helped, for Maria went down with her in tolerably good spirits and even ventured to ask for the pattern to Jane's travelling dress.

Privately Jane thought that what had promised to be a brief visit was going to extend further than she wished or intended, for either Aunt Louisa was right in her imaginings and *someone* would have to make Lord Meriden see to his obligations, or Aunt Louisa was the victim of a heat-oppressed brain, in which case her children must surely need help.

Jane's consolation was that Edward Wincanton, balked of his prey, would surely fix his attentions on some more nautically minded female in her protracted absence.

4

WHEN MARGARET TARRANT's child, a daughter, came at last, Will's brothers' plump wives descended on the Tarrants in a storm of cackle that drove Will out of the house and off to Whitethorn.

He was soon soothed with a glass of claret and one of the black cheroots Margaret would not allow him to puff in the house.

"I say, Ju, this is the life."

"I like it. Indeed, I'll be sorry to leave it."

Will choked. "You're not marrying?"

Julian looked blank. "Leave the house," he said, after a moment, "not my wild bachelor existence. What an ass you are, Will."

Will was not to be trifled with. "What is this? I collect you must go off to London and Devon."

"Dorset."

"Wherever," Will snapped with a Yorkshireman's fine disregard for lesser counties. "These other properties must be visited, of course, but surely you may live where you choose."

Julian shook his head. "I wish I could."

"What's to prevent you? Or don't you choose to stay here? I suppose your great Dorset manor is much finer than Whitethorn," he added in a hurt tone, "but you'll not find a tidier piece of land than this in England."

"No, nor better company."

Mollified, Will took a last luxuriant puff and threw the seegar butt inaccurately at the fender. "Well, then...."

"The truth is, Whitethorn is the only property I own that is in shape to be left without my supervision," Julian said rather crossly. "If I can rely on what Horrocks says—" He broke off, frowning, then shrugged. "I'll have to go to Meriden."

"You can't," Will muttered.

"Certainly not before my goddaughter's christening. One of each now. Very discerning of you—and Peggy, of course. What are you going to call her?"

Will regarded his friend over the rim of his glass. "Julia."

"Good God—horrible. Like a parrot-nosed Roman matron. Julia Augusta Claudia Victoria, I suppose. You didn't throw in Alexandra and Cleopatra, too?"

"Julia Margaret Sarah," Will said sternly, then relented. "It does seem rather Spartan. No offence, old man. We'll christen her Julia and call her Margot."

"Very pretty."

Will waxed paternal. "She's got black hair and great long lashes. Pretty as she can stare, Ju, or will be when she's not so red in the face."

"A diamond of the first water," Julian said gravely.

Will grinned. "Takes after Peggy, thank God. Imagine a gel with my chin. Don't have to imagine. Only have to look at m'sister, Sarah." He sat up. "Damn your eyes, you've pushed me off the subject again. You wasn't set on removing to Meriden last week. Why the change? And don't feed me rot about overseeing estates, you landless nobody. The only estate you ever supervised was this one. Much better hire a good agent."

"So you don't think I can put the screws on my tenants in the manner born?" Julian smiled.

"No, I don't. Never knew a softer touch. Sneck up, friend. What is it? The damned family, I suppose."

Julian was silent.

"They've no claim on you," Will said explosively.

"That's just the trouble."

"What do you mean?"

"My father made no provision for my brothers at all—and there are five of them."

Will described the late Lord Meriden in profane detail.

"Just so," Julian agreed. "An abominable old windsucker. But it wasn't entirely his fault. You see, because of the entail, Harry's pre-deceasing him has thrown everything into confusion. It's not quite as terrible as if my father'd died intestate, but it puts everything off onto me. I bagged the lot, and the lot includes my brothers." He added wryly, "You're not the only one suffering an attack of parenthood."

"D'you mean you'll have to see to their upbringing?"

Julian rubbed his forehead. "Vincent, I fancy, is down from Oxford, but he seems not to have any fixed object in life. The others except the youngest are mere schoolboys. Or should be. From what I gather, they're being educated at home."

"Then direct your man of business to ship 'em off to school."

"Sight unseen? Would you do that, Will?"

"No," Will said glumly. He brightened. "What of Lady Meriden? Her brats, ain't they?"

"Vincent isn't. I *was* inclined to leave matters in her hands," Julian said slowly, "but that was before I had corresponded with her. I wish you will read this letter, Will, and tell me what you think."

He got up clumsily and riffled through a pile of papers. Finally he handed his friend a black-bordered screed that reeked of otto of roses.

Will squinted. "Sorry. Can't make it out."

"Try."

Will persevered. At last he laid the letter down. "Touched in the upper story," he said simply. "See what you mean. Plain fustian."

"That was *after* I wrote to reassure her. Her first was even stranger."

Will shook his head, depressed.

The christening went smoothly. Julian had graduated to a walking stick. Peggy kept hovering near him during the ceremony on the theory that if he lost his balance and fell she must be at hand to catch the baby, but, as Will told her afterwards, the godfather showed the greatest aplomb, even holding young Margot right-side up, so that no one would ever have imagined him the raw recruit he was. This was said in Julian's presence, after the guests and kinsfolk had taken themselves off.

Peggy bridled. "I thought you did very well, Julian, and we're much obliged to you." She looked so much like an indignant pigeon that both men smiled at her.

"Your daughter drooled on my sleeve," Julian murmured. "I took it as a sign of affection."

"Toad-eater." Will made an idiot face at his complacent child and tickled one pink foot, which had somehow emerged from the yards of white embroidered lawn.

Peggy scowled at him. "Don't set her off. She cried for half an hour when your sister insisted on jiggling her about, and I've only just got her quietened."

Will desisted, and the baby yawned hugely and went to sleep.

"What a blessing she's not colicky like Willie." Peggy settled back in her chair and smiled at their guest. "Well, Julian, very lordly, I must say. I've not had a chance to felicitate you."

Julian grimaced. "Don't, please." He reached into a pocket and drew forth a neatly done-up box wrapped in silver paper. "I must leave in a moment, but I've brought my goddaughter a gift."

Peggy took the packet, smiling. "Did you send poor Mrs. Bradford into York to buy this? It's very kind in you, Julian, but I hope it's not another silver cup. She has half a dozen."

"No." He looked rather wary. "Not a cup."

Peggy pulled the paper loose and sat speechless, staring at the exquisite object in her hand. A tiny casket, jewel-studded and wrought, so far as her dazzled eyes could tell, in gold, lay on her palm.

"What is it?" she whispered.

Julian reached over and pressed one long brown finger against a minute catch. He lifted the lid, and there, in a black velvet foil designed to set off some priceless Renaissance jewel, lay a quite ordinary string of coral beads. He said in a dry tone, "Unexceptionable, I think. I'm told they're for teething."

"Oh, it's too lovely. But surely this casket is an heirloom?"

"No." He smiled. "That is, I had it from my grandmother, but I believe she was given it by one of her cicisbei. An Italian gentleman of advanced years with clocks on his stockings and padded calves. He conceived a hopeless passion for *Grand-mère* in his youth and, in her behalf, fought a duel with my grandfather when they were both young and silly. He and my grandmother became excellent friends in later years and spent hours together prosing over the more boring Roman philosophers." His eyes danced. "*Grand-mère*, you know, was a French woman and a great belle in her day. She must have driven the old *marchese* wild."

Peggy's brown eyes shone. "How romantical. I don't know how you can bear to part with it."

He shrugged. "What use should I put it to? It's a lady's bauble, my dear. I could pop my tiepins in it—"

"Or sell it for a king's ransom," Will interrupted grimly. He had been staring at the box with a lowering expression for some moments and now reached down and took it from his wife. Peggy squeaked in alarm.

"I won't have it, Julian," he snapped.

"How very fortunate, then, that I'm not giving it to you."

"I've seen that sort of thing. King Joseph's train after Vitoria. The Prado. It's Cellini, I collect."

"It may be," Julian said coldly. "I don't know. I do know I had it as a gift from a lady who did not go about putting price tickets on her gifts or anyone else's. I'm free to give it where I choose, and if I choose to give it your daughter, that's my affair."

Will set the casket down with deliberation. He had flushed scarlet as Julian spoke, but he was now white as his neckcloth. "My daughter is very much obliged to you, Lord Meriden. Or is it Lord Bountiful?" He turned on his heel and stalked from the room.

Peggy watched him leave, her lips compressed in a severe line. "Oh, don't look so stricken, Julian," she said after a moment. "Windy Will." He managed a rather twisted smile. "I'm sorry."

"Well, so am I."

He got up, leaning heavily on the stick. "You might tell Will from me that giving goes two ways and that I'm not the only Lord Bountiful hereabouts."

"I know," she said gently. "But he needed to help you. He feels so guilty."

He stared. "What about?"

"About selling out before Waterloo."

"Why the devil should he? Does he suppose another corpse would make the world more wonderful? Or another cripple?" he added, bitter.

"I don't wish to seem coldhearted, but I must say I agree with you completely."

He looked so startled that she smiled. "There, I've sunk myself beneath reproach, and since I'm being tactless I'll compliment you on how well you're getting about."

Abruptly Julian smiled, too. "Peggy, what a pity it is that you're so thoroughly married. We'd deal famously together."

"So we would," she said with affection. "Perhaps I'll murder Will. You'd best go home now and leave me to deal with my stiff-necked husband. Don't worry. He knows he's behaved very ill. And *I* thank you for my daughter's gift—or should I say *cadeau*?"

He grinned.

"It must be as lovely in its way as the lady who gave it you."

"It is," he said gratefully. "She was very beautiful and very kind. It reminds me of her."

Peggy blinked hard. "Then I value it, and someday my daughter will value it as she ought. Just now, however, I think she'll prefer the coral."

"So do I."

She went with him to the door and kissed him lightly on the cheek. "Don't worry about Will."

But it was nearly two weeks before Will came round and then only because he chanced on Thorpe who mentioned, in passing, that Julian had fallen again.

"Bust his damn leg," Thorpe grumbled.

"Good God, when?"

"Round about t'end of t'week."

Will forgot his dignity and rode off to Whitethorn without further ado.

"I don't know that he'll see you, sir," Mrs. Bradford said doubtfully. "He's cross as crabs."

"Just show me in."

She disappeared into the bedchamber and after a moment beckoned to him. Julian was propped up in bed and surrounded by ink-stained papers. When Will entered, his mouth tightened.

"If you've come to jaw at me over that damned box, you can turn round and march back out."

"Well, I haven't," Will said mildly. "Thorpe said you've broken your leg."

"No. I tore something."

"How?"

"I thought I was ready to ride. I was wrong."

Will curbed his exasperation. "I'm glad you've not broken it."

"I nearly told the damned sawbones to chop it off and be done with it," Julian said in the same flat voice.

"You'll be laid up here for a time?"

"It means starting over again with the walking." He summoned a smile that went nowhere near his eyes. "You're stuck with my presence until the New Year, I'm afraid."

"Excellent," Will said gruffly. "Care for a game of chess?"

Julian opened his eyes wide, and Will flushed, grinning a little. Julian always beat him.

"How generous," the man in the bed said drily. "Lord Bountiful, in fact."

"Oh, God, Ju. I'm sorry."

"So you should be. I'll give you a pawn. And, Will," he added as his friend rummaged in a cabinet for the chess set, "if you ever use my...that title to my face I'll imitate my lamented brother and call you out."

"Yes, my lord," Will said meekly.

5

Toward the end of October, it became apparent that the new baron was in no great rush to take possession of his lands and dignities. Lady Meriden received a brusque note to the effect that his lordship regretted he would be unable to leave Yorkshire before the New Year and that she was to apply to Leak and Horrocks as usual if she found herself in any difficulty. He trusted that all was well with the family and remained her ob't. servant, Meriden. No explanation, no apology. In fact, very lordly.

Unfortunately he added a *post scriptum* which threw her ladyship into fresh megrims, for in it he indicated his intent to close the London house forthwith and desired her to remove any thing that might serve her convenience before his agents acted. Abrupt. Lady Meriden had had no intention of appearing in London in mourning, but she was indignant nonetheless at the want of consideration.

Jane had seen the infamous reply Lord Meriden had made to her aunt's first communication with him—the letter to which Maria had so feelingly referred on Jane's first day at Meriden—and had not been able to discern ill intent in it. It had been merely a polite message of condolence, unrevealing of its author's nature. That it contained no effusions of grief seemed to Jane reasonable in the circumstances, even perhaps evidence of good taste, but her aunt felt far otherwise.

The fact that Lord Meriden had not inquired after any of his brothers and sisters by name was taken in proof that he must be an indifferent and unfeeling monster. Jane could not agree. She was ready to suppose him as ignorant of his family as they were of him.

They knew remarkably little. Lady Meriden guessed his age to be some six- or seven-and-twenty years, but she could not remember precisely. He was either taller or shorter than Vincent and may or may not have been schooled at Harrow, or was it Winchester? Maria thought that he had served in one of the line regiments but did not know which—only that Harry had stigmatised it as unfashionable. She re-

27

membered the green uniform jacket because she had been expecting scarlet. How long his lordship had served in the army and where and what his current rank might be they had no notion. More important considerations of character and interest remained a blank. Lady Meriden did not even recall whether Julian or Harry had set fire to the drapes in the nursery which, if laid to the infant Meriden's door, might at least have shown a tendency to pyromania. Alas, even that clew led Jane nowhere in her cautious inquiries.

When she pointed out to Maria that to reproach his lordship *in absentia* for indifference and want of family feeling must be absurd, as it was clear that his family had shown no interest at all in him, Maria bridled.

"Why should we have? We had no notion Harry would die young."

"Nor had Meriden," Jane said drily. She did not press the point, however, for she assumed his absent lordship must soon appear and dispel the unseemly mystery surrounding his character. The October letter indicated otherwise. Jane resigned herself to several more months of her cousins' fretful imaginings.

His lordship's plan of closing the London house drove Lady Meriden, when she had recovered herself sufficiently to speak, to utter a flurry of contradictory orders and to send at once for Vincent. Why it was Vincent was not clear except that her ladyship felt, vaguely, that she required a Man's advice.

Everything in the house called up affecting recollections. She could not bear to be parted from the portrait of Lady Sarah in the large withdrawing room. The Hepplewhite breakfront! The red lacquer screen in the bookroom! Those charming china figurines! Torn between emptying the house of its contents and nobly refusing to touch so much as a stick of That Man's possessions, Lady Meriden soon exhausted herself and everyone around her. Finally Jane ventured to suggest that she herself go up to London with Vincent and select for her aunt whatever should be clearly indispensable.

Her aunt brightened. "Would you dislike it, Jane? Such a wearing task. Heartbreaking. I could not bear it, of course, but you know my tastes so exactly...."

"Indeed I should enjoy a visit to Town of all things," Jane said with fervour. "I'll take Maria and Drusilla with me, for you know, Aunt, Maria will be needing all manner of new gowns for spring."

At that, Lady Meriden wept a little. "My poor child, to be wearing black gloves on her eighteenth birthday."

"Her come-out must certainly be postponed," Jane murmured, "but she cannot go about dressed like a schoolgirl after she has put up her hair."

Jane had every intention of seeing that the girls put off their black at the first decent moment—February at the latest. She was heartily glad not to be forced to wear black herself, for she looked very ill in mourning.

"I do not think the girls should be frolicking off to London—" Lady Meriden commenced.

"Not *frolicking*," Jane said in shocked tones. "Nothing of the sort, Aunt. We shall visit museums and perhaps an exhibition of paintings. Unexceptionable, I think. We'll buy up a few gown lengths and make our sad selections in the London house and take care, of course, that they are bestowed safely. Then I believe I shall take my cousins to see how my father does...."

"You will return, Jane!"

"Certainly." Jane patted her aunt's hand. "Only my father, you know, is most importunate that I come to Sussex. Do you not think that if I explain to him myself why you require me he is more likely to allow me to remain at Meriden?"

Much struck, Lady Meriden at last agreed to the scheme.

At one-and-twenty Vincent Stretton bade fair to rival the late Harry in good looks and dash. His eyes were brilliantly blue. His hair, so dark a brown as to be almost black, tumbled fashionably over his creamy brow. His figure was solid and well muscled, and he moved with the grace of a born athlete. Already an excellent whip, he wore even the absurd rig of the F.H.C. with an air, and contrived in more conventional dress to look so very much like a young girl's dream of manhood that it was no wonder his sisters hung upon his lips.

He was inclined to indulge them, for he was kindhearted as well as beautiful and ready enough to give his sisters his escort, so long as they should not seriously interfere with his pleasures. At present, he alternated between his usual high spirits and the gloom occasioned by his grief over his brother Harry's demise and by his own uncertain circumstances. He seemed to Jane, accustomed to her own beloved but woefully unfashionable brothers, to be destined for great things in the *haut ton*. It was a pity he had not come into a handsome fortune, for, if ever a young man deserved the privilege of running through ten thousand a year, it was Vincent Stretton.

He arrived at Meriden as Jane laid the last preparations for the journey. She had decided to leave Miss Goodnight to keep her aunt in spirits, and when she saw how taken her companion was with Vincent, she did not repent her decision. To listen forever to Miss Goodnight's raptures over yet another handsome young man was what Jane least desired. Miss Goodnight, fortunately, had made herself indispensable to the household in many small ways, in chief, as *confidante* and reader to the next Stretton son, Felix.

Felix was blind. He had lost his sight some eight years previously in a terrible illness and, though otherwise recovered, had never regained his vision. Tall for fourteen and rather plump, he had been so much petted by everyone and so much pitied by his mama that he had grown into something of a despot, and Jane could have disliked him heartily had he not, now and then, shown signs of rather more intelligence than anyone else in the family.

Musical and, unfortunately, gifted with perfect pitch, Felix bore very ill the less than perfect efforts of others to sing or play at the pianoforte. Miss Goodnight, however, had great patience. She listened for hours to Felix's playing, helped him with his lessons, and was content to read to him until her voice failed. Felix should not be deprived of Miss Goodnight, as even Miss Goodnight perceived, though she could not like Jane's gallivanting about Town without her stout self as chaperon. Jane overcame her objections by promising to stay with her maternal Aunt Hervey, though she said teasing, "I am four-and-twenty now, Goody. Not a green girl."

Miss Goodnight sniffed.

Jane considered what dispositions could be made for the rest of the children. Young Thomas at two presented no difficulties, for he was entirely in the charge of his nurse. There remained the twins, Horatio and Arthur.

Horatio and Arthur—Jane was not yet perfectly sure which was which, although she thought Arthur talked more—figured as imps of Satan, hell-born brats, and other, less genteel, epithets bestowed upon them by tormented servants and by Felix when he discovered they had put frogs in his boots. Jane did not think the twins hardened in sin but they were, at eleven, entirely beyond control.

Lady Meriden doted on them on the rare occasions when, scrubbed and angelic, they were brought before her by their suffering governess, Miss Winchell, and, as her ladyship never saw them in their natural savage state, all representations that they must soon be broken to bridle fell on deaf ears.

Horatio had been named for Lord Nelson—in anticipation of Trafalgar, as it were, for the twins were born in 1804—but the choice of Arthur for his twin was a fortuitous bit of bad taste, His Grace of Wellington's Christian name not then being upon everyone's lips. Jane thought the twins should be packed off to school or, when their antics drove her to despair, packed off as cabin boys in some ship bound for Botany Bay. As neither course would find favour with her aunt, she merely charged Miss Winchell to watch them narrowly and hoped that the removal of Felix, Drusilla, and Maria from the governess's charge might allow that unfortunate woman sufficient time to deal with the heavenly twins as they deserved.

As for Lady Meriden, she made the departure of the London-bound party the occasion of high drama, but she did not wish to be deprived of her London gewgaws. Jane was not surprised to find that her aunt so far moderated the last farewells as to allow the girls and Jane's Abigail to leave in tolerably good spirits and not above an hour late.

Vincent posted along good-naturedly beside the carriage. Once out of sight of the melancholic rhododendron drive, the two sisters in Jane's charge began to chatter excitedly about the sights they would see in London and the treats they would enjoy, and Jane listened to them and made no attempt to dampen their ardours.

She listened and smiled, but her thoughts kept wandering back to Meriden Place. It was odd how in a few short weeks she had become so entwined, or possibly the *mot juste* was "entangled," in the fears and wishes and anxieties of her aunt's young family. Jane felt almost as if she were responsible for their well-being. Nonsense, of course, but so many of the disorders they suffered under were remediable.

What ills she could remedy, she had. Thus she found herself become, insensibly, a figure of authority not only to the children but also to the servants. It was so much easier to settle a minor dispute herself or make a small decision about the household than to explain the matter to her aunt and coax her ladyship into exerting her authority.

Jane had not been used to think of herself as a managing sort of female, but her sojourn at Meriden had taught her to reflect upon her own character and to recognise that, even in her father's house, she had been inclined to take up the reins. A lowering reflection. She could only hope that her hand lay easy and that the horse would not bolt.

She had also come to recognise that her Aunt Louisa had changed sadly in the years since that memorable London season in which her ladyship had figured as Jane's fairy godmother. Now Lady Meriden would or could not have summoned the energy to perform so arduous and disinterested an office. It was problematical that she would bestir herself to present her own daughters to the *ton*, for she had turned inward to a kind of private phantasy which fed on her real and imagined ills and which did not require her to exert herself very much. Her children she reduced in her mind to cliché figures and created fictional needs for them while ignoring their real requirements of counsel and constant affection.

Jane could not condemn her aunt. To have borne with so selfish a husband as Lord Meriden, so indifferent a father to her children, for so many years must turn all but the most resolute intellect to self-indulgent phantasy, and Aunt Louisa's understanding had never been more than moderate.

Briefly Jane indulged the hope that the new Lord Meriden would remedy his family's ills, but his projected further delay in coming argued a displeasing indifference. The carriage jolted and righted itself. Drusilla and Maria chattered on. Jane drifted.

That evening as they supped in the private dining room of a pleasant inn, Maria made some comment which set Vincent to talking of his elder brother. As Vincent, however unreliable a judge, had at least met and spoken with his lordship, Jane listened with interest.

It transpired that the fateful first meeting had occurred in Hyde Park early in the Easter holidays of the previous year. Vincent and a friend, down from Oxford, were sauntering through the park—hoping to be taken for pinks of the *ton*, Jane thought, amused—when they had bumped into the friend's elder brother, a military man, in a knot of officers discussing Bonaparte's remarkable progress through France. The older men had good-naturedly allowed the two sprigs in on the conversation. In the course of the obligatory introductions, Vincent had found himself being made known to his brother, Julian.

"It was dashed embarrassing, I can tell you," Vincent said feelingly. "Other chaps don't have to be introduced to their brothers."

Drusilla snickered.

"Well, it was. Pipe down, Dru."

"Did he wear a green jacket?" Maria asked, her own brief glimpse of the prodigal recalled to mind.

"Of course not. Buff pantaloons. Hessians. Blue coat. It was outdated—wrong in the lapels. He puffed a great black seegar and

32

laughed at me and said I must be his little brother. Little brother," Vincent repeated in repellent accents. "I can tell you I was ready to sink."

"How reprehensible," said Jane, directing a quelling glance at Drusilla.

"And what's more," Vincent went on in an aggrieved tone, "when I did the civil and offered to show him some lively gaming at one of the houses Ned was taking me to that evening he just said it was above his touch, thank you, and that he was off in the morning anyway."

Gaming hells, Jane thought. Oh, Vincent.

"Was he off to Belgium?" Maria asked breathlessly.

"No, daff-head. Kent."

"Oh."

"Is that all?" Drusilla demanded.

"Well, nearly. They were all prosing on about what this regiment or that colonel would do and who was posted where and had they seen so-and-so. It was devilish dull, so Ned and I took ourselves off as soon as we decently could."

His sisters expressed their disappointment in unflattering terms. Jane intervened.

"It was merely a chance meeting. Vincent cannot have foreseen how much you would wish to know, and besides I daresay he observed a great deal."

"No, I didn't," Vincent said crossly. "Too dashed embarrassed."

There was a pause. Drusilla giggled.

"Did you ascertain which regiment your brother serves in?" Jane asked.

"Not then. Asked m'brother ... that is, Harry." His brow darkened as it always did when he thought of Harry, for Vincent, more than any of them, had idolised the heir. However, he sighed and went on, "Harry said he didn't perfectly remember, though he knew it wasn't one of the crack cavalry regiments. Not the Life Guards. I daresay it couldn't be the Highlanders either."

"Why?" Clearly Maria was disappointed. She had a passion for Mr. Scott's novels.

"No kilt," Vincent said simply. "I must say that relieved my mind, for I didn't half fancy a brother of mine going about with his knees hanging out like a dashed *sans-culotte*." Apparently there was in Vincent's mind some dim connexion between Jacobites and Jacobins.

Maria animadverted at indignant length in defence of the plaid.

33

"That will do, Maria," Jane interposed and caught herself. How very like a governess she sounded.

Vincent helped himself to an apple and began to pare it carefully so that the peel came off in a perfect spiral. He admired his handiwork and took an enormous bite. "Mmench."

"What?"

"Beg pardon. Harry said Julian was in Portugal. Thought he was with the Fifty-ninth or Sixty-fifth or some such outfit." He took another bite.

"I collect your brother Julian must be a junior officer," Jane said when she thought he might again articulate. "He is not very old."

"I don't know. Ned's brother was a light colonel. Must've been about the same age as Julian. *Aide-de-camp* to the Irish viceroy."

"That argues influence."

"Well, it must. Dashed stupid fellow, Ned's brother." He took thought. "Harry said my grandfather—Carteret, you know—bought Julian a pair of colours when he was seventeen—Julian, not my grandfather. Then, after Carteret died, my father procured advancement for Julian. Harry said something about just in time for the Denmark campaign, but I thought he couldn't have had it right. Wasn't fighting the Danes, was we?"

"After the Battle of Friedland," Jane said patiently.

Vincent looked blank.

"I daresay you were in short coats, so it may just have escaped your notice."

Vincent frowned. "Can't have been that far back." His brow cleared. "Eight or nine years ago when Carteret stuck his spoon in the wall. Must've been after that." He laughed indulgently. "No head for figures, females. Why I daresay I must've been at Eton by that time! Short coats indeed."

Jane preserved her countenance. It surprised her very much to hear that her uncle had exerted himself in his son's behalf.

"Lieutenant's commission," Vincent said suddenly. "Harry said it must've cost the old man the earth, but Carteret cut him such a wheedle before he died that my father felt obliged to. Shouldn't have thought m'father would've known how to go about it. Not his sort of thing."

"Perhaps he directed his man of business to buy the commission," Jane managed.

"Now what's sent you into stitches?"

Jane shook her head. She did not in general approve the army practice of buying promotions, for it seemed to her probable that such a system must place men of few natural gifts in positions of gravity. The navy—Edward Wincanton notwithstanding—was much better ordered. However, the picture of her indolent uncle deftly pulling political strings and dropping judicious bribes in judicious places struck her as comic in the extreme, and it was some time before she composed herself.

"Very handsome of my father," Vincent said, hurt.

"Yes, indeed. I beg your pardon, Vincent."

He eyed her warily. "So Julian must be at least a lieutenant."

"Very likely a captain after so many years, if he exerted himself."

"I don't know about that Weedy sort of chap. No address."

He did sound unprepossessing. Anyone foolish enough to call a young man of twenty "little brother" must want for common sense. And to laugh about it. He cannot be kind, Jane reflected. Poor Vincent.

The conversation then proceeded to matters of greater moment, such as whether Vincent could be prevailed upon to take Drusilla to Astley's Amphitheatre and was that establishment open year round, and whether Mama would approve a lilac gown for Maria.

"I could wear black ribbons on it, you know, cousin."

"Lilac will do very well," Jane said. "And let us hear no more about black ribbons."

6

LONDON PROVED A thorough success. The Stretton house, indeed, gave Jane a pang. To see it shrouded in holland and echoingly empty could not be cheerful. But Jane's Aunt Hervey caught the party up in a swirl of schoolgirl treats that suited Drusilla and Maria very well. As that good-natured lady had fired off the last of her own daughters several years before, she was perfectly happy to have young people about again and, without offending against the forms of bereavement, gave the girls an excellent time. Jane could only rejoice—and trust that Aunt Louisa would not examine the girls too closely when they returned home.

Mornings were spent shopping at the cloth warehouses to which Jane gave her patronage where, as Maria naively remarked, there was a deal more *variety* to be found than in Dorchester. Lady Meriden had been generous. There was no stinting or making do, and even Drusilla, who in general thought fashions a great bore and was in any case far too young to wear the feathers and taffeties that did catch her fancy, was persuaded to choose some becoming swatches.

For herself Jane ordered up fabric for a walking dress which she chose partly because green became her and partly because the luxurious material would make up into a dashing rig. Convinced that the longer she lived in her aunt's household the more sober and sensible she would, in self-defence, grow, she decided to forestall a sartorial descent to brown stuff and merino.

I may show the mentality of a housekeeper or governess, she reflected, recklessly buying a handful of silver ribbon and frogs dyed to match her fabric, but I refuse to look like one.

When the girls gave signs of feeling guilty for enjoying themselves, Jane directed them to buy gifts for the twins. A small *crise* ensued, but Drusilla was in time dissuaded from selecting a working model of the guillotine for her brothers. Although Jane privately thought nothing would suit the boys' tastes more than to institute a miniature Reign of

Terror, she did not wish to encourage them in blood-thirstiness or, indeed, Jacobinism. Leaden soldiers were substituted as unexceptionable.

Jane took it on herself to select Felix's gifts. He must have music, of course, sheets and sheets of music. The trick was to find compositions which would suit his severe tastes and still lie within Miss Winchell's capacity to play for him. This proved a knotty problem. Finally Jane chose several Haydn sonatas she thought Felix would like and left their execution in the lap of the gods.

She contemplated a musical box and rejected it as beneath Felix's contempt, and purchased instead a small wooden flutelike instrument called a recorder, which she had once heard played at a concert of ancient music. It seemed perhaps too simple a thing for Felix, but the tone must please.

She then bethought herself of the coming holiday season. Lady Meriden must not be allowed to render Christmas hideous with excesses of grief. Although her own funds had by now fallen rather low, Jane spent what was left on books and games and puzzles and jars of boiled sweets. These purchases she concealed from everyone. As a sop to her conscience she bought two remarkably mournful black mantillas for her aunt and a box of the finest camphor pastilles.

"I have quite outrun the cobbler, Papa," she confessed to her bemused father later, when the party had reached Sussex. "So I know you will not object to advancing me monies for the winter. I'll repay you on quarter day."

Jane's income—she had inherited a competence from her mother—usually proved more than sufficient to her needs, and she did not care to be running to her papa for pinmoney. However, he had a dislike of too much independence in females, and her request flattered his vanity, as she had known it must. He wrote her a handsome draught on his bank.

"But to be gone from home at Christmas!" he exclaimed, returning her kiss with a hearty smack. "I do not like it, Jane."

"Dear Papa, nor do I. But you have Jack and Tom and Joanna and young Tomkin to comfort you."

"Roast pork!" her father murmured. "Parsnips!"

Jane laughed. "Joanna will soon learn to study your tastes. And only consider, Papa, if I were to marry a Scotsman or an Irishman, I would not be able to come to you on every holiday."

"What Scotsman?"

"I said, 'if,' Papa."

Her father grumbled something about encroaching foreigners, but the mention of marriage caught his attention. "Young Wincanton will wish to call on you." He glanced at her from the corner of his eye. "He has bought Studleigh, you know."

"Oh, no! Papa, is Edward still hanging about?"

"Yes, poor fellow. He holds you in greatest esteem, my dear, and you might do worse."

"No, I might not." Jane bit her lip. She had near forgot Edward Wincanton.

"Well, I shan't teaze you." Her father sighed. "You are not growing younger, you know, but there, I shall say no more on that head for it is not the least use."

"No, indeed," Jane said cordially.

"Did you execute your aunt's charge?"

"Oh, yes. I sent a note to his lordship's man of business, and when he called on me I presented him with Aunt Louisa's authorisation. There was no difficulty. I am persuaded she might have removed anything at all, for it is clear that Lord Meriden has not yet troubled to visit the house."

"An indolent young man."

"It would seem so. It doesn't augur well for the future. I did not question Mr. Horrocks about his lordship's affairs, for it wasn't my place to do so, but I confess to curiosity. You see, neither my aunt nor my cousins know anything about the new baron."

"It was an ill-managed business," Mr. Ash said shortly. "I told Louisa no good would come of it at the time."

Jane's face must have shown her puzzlement, for he went on in a constrained tone, "There was bad blood between Meriden and his first father-in-law. Carteret undertook to raise the boy on the understanding that Meriden would have no say in the upbringing. It seemed dashed irregular to me. Louisa should have done her duty by the lad, but my father could not be persuaded to interfere—he never threw the least rub in Louisa's way—and Meriden was so incensed by Carteret's strictures that I scarcely liked to bring the matter up. After a few years, of course, Louisa grew too much occupied with her own nursery to be looking after schoolboys."

"In short, my aunt and uncle forgot him."

"You've a sharp tongue, my dear. Take care it don't lead you to unbecoming ways."

"I beg your pardon, sir," Jane said meekly, but she had spoken too warmly. Her father would not pursue the subject further.

It was a delight to Jane to show her cousins the beauties of Walden Ash and, for herself, to ride Fairy again about her father's lands.

Even the mangel-wurzels pleased her. Indeed so taken was she with her home that she might have succumbed to her father's entreaties to remain, had she not endured another declaration from Captain Wincanton.

This interview took place the second evening of her return. She had wandered out to the orchard and was revelling in the solitude and the crisp October air when the snap of a twig below her broke her mood.

"Miss Ash!"

"Oh, dear. How do you do, Edward?" She infused a moderate warmth into her tone. After all, he must rank as a friend.

"Dear Miss Jane, how we have missed you. What joy it is to find you at home once more."

"Thank you. I believe I must congratulate you on having acquired a very handsome property."

He had stopped puffing from the exertions of his climb and replied with some complacency. "Yes. I flatter myself that I have come into port at last. Hrmphm. But a house, you know, does not take on the character of a home—"

"Edward, how is your dear mother?"

"Very well," he barked, adding in softened tones, "I trust you have come back to stay, my wandering star."

"No," she said crossly. "I have not come home to stay. I shall be off again to Dorset within the week. And it is most improper in you to be calling me such a name."

"Miss Ash! Jane!" He flung himself on his knees. "Does my constancy mean nothing to you?"

"Indeed, I am very sensible of the honour you do me," Jane said in a colourless voice. Down, Rover.

He grasped her hand in his own rather moist palm. "Damme, Miss Jane, I would offer you the moon, the stars...."

"Edward, you *must* not. Indeed we should not suit. I beg you, get up!" Jane took a breath and went on in a less agitated manner, "You will ruin your handsome breeches in the mulch."

He rose like a shot and brushed off his knees.

"Edward, I have changed a great deal from the girl you first knew."
"Not a jot," he roared. "Lovelier than ever."
"What a bouncer! And I was speaking not of my looks but of my tastes, my interests, my ... my sentiments. You have persuaded yourself that you love me, but you do not know me as I am now."
"I can't know you if you're never here," he replied, so like a sensible man that she almost wavered, but he went on, "I shall worship you forever."
"I am very sorry for you then, for, Edward, we *should not suit*." She began walking down the small slope in a determined way, and presently he followed.

Her brothers were inclined to teaze her about her nautical lover, but, as she had long ago perfected the art of ignoring them, they soon left off and she found herself again in charity with them.

On her last morning at Walden Ash, she rode with her younger brother, Jack, through the wood above the home farm to visit the wife of her father's chief tenant. On their return, Jack enlivened the way with anecdotes—here he had run a badger to earth, and there he had had a clear shot at a goshawk, truly Jane, and what a fine spot this was, Jane; there was not such fine sport to be had in France.

That put Jane in mind of her brother's brief service as a volunteer in the Belgian campaign, which had transformed him from plain Jack Ash, a lad his friends were altogether too quick to stigmatise as old Jack Ass, to something of a local hero.

Though Jack had not himself seen action at Waterloo, that did not prevent him speaking in a Crispin Crispian manner of the glorious battle and of the subsequent pursuit—which he *had* taken part in—of the broken Grande Armée. He bored his family very much. The dashing tales went down well with the wide-eyed damsels of the neighbourhood, however. Jane, though she found his stories quite as tedious as the rest of the family did, felt a deal of sympathy for Jack. He had been with the Duke in France. Nothing in his young life could equal that fact.

"Jack," she ventured, "how well do you know the army?"
He stiffened. "I say. What a question to ask."
"I'm sorry. I only meant *I* know very little...."
"Know more about the navy, eh?"
She reproved him with a glance. "I'd like to find out for Aunt Louisa something of her stepson's service, for she knows almost nothing about him, and he will be coming soon."
"Don't want to make too many howlers." Jack nodded sagely.

"Just so. Only you'll have to fill in rather a lot of blanks." She gave him what information she remembered.

He did not seem hopeful and told her, mincing no words and at some length, what he thought of the family's having such ignorance about their own relation. "Something above a lieutenant. Might be a sepoy general for all you know. Pouf!"

Jane agreed meekly that it was scandalous.

"Well, I shall do my possible for you, Jane."

"Thank you, dear Jack, best of my brothers."

He eyed her uneasily. "Dash it, Jane, my Aunt Louisa's a bad influence on you. You was never used to be sickening. By the by, where is our demi-beau?"

"No, that is too bad of you, Jack. Vincent is snap up to the rig, a regular out-and-outer."

He snorted. "Much you know." He was rather jealous of Vincent's polish, and knew she knew it.

"Vincent has tooled off to Brighton for the day, though of course it's sadly flat at this time of year. He is visiting his friend, Ned."

"Ned Coldfield. Rackety fellow."

"I daresay," Jane murmured, "but do not, I beg you, say so to Vincent."

Jack grinned. "Not such a cawker."

The return journey to Dorchester dragged out tediously. Vincent grudged them his escort, for he had some scheme afoot with his rackety friend, and Drusilla developed the toothache. At last, however, they reached Meriden, dispensed their gifts, were kissed, shouted at (by the twins), wept over (by Lady Meriden), and sank back into the bosom of the family.

Everyone had survived their absence. Indeed, life thereafter went on without major disaster through the holidays. The New Year, however, began with an unusually severe snowstorm. Everyone—except the twins who built forts and pelted the grooms with water-soaked snowballs—grew edgy and short-tempered. Lady Meriden announced that Maria and Drusilla might not put off their blacks until a year had passed from their father's death, and Jane spent nearly a week coaxing her ladyship to a more reasonable frame of mind. Maria wept a great deal. Felix threw a tantrum so spectacular that he broke a clock, a vase, and two figurines. Drusilla renewed the toothache.

As January drew to an end, Jane gave up hope of his lordship's coming and, rather draggled, set about civilising everyone again.

Fortunately the snow thawed. She bore Drusilla off to the tooth drawer by main force. That battle won, she coaxed Felix, who had sulked in his tent for a week, to try for her some airs on the recorder, and set Maria to trimming spring bonnets. She could think of nothing to improve the twins and rather gave them up.

February saw a diminished order restored, but Jane began to feel more than a little weary. She had not even had time to stitch up her dashing green gown. Every fortnight brought an indignant letter from her father threatening to fetch her forthwith. She almost wished he would, but it was nearly time for him to oversee the spring ploughing, and she knew that only the prospect of her death or seduction would have dragged him from Walden Ash at such a time. Vincent, who might have enlivened the party, remained in London.

7

It HAD BECOME Jane's habit to rise early and, whatever the weather, walk in the small garden, returning for breakfast before the others came down. To be alone was luxury.

March showed its mixed mind in the extravagant yellows of forsythia and daffodil and the bleak roiling grey of the sky. Blustery. She inspected the unkempt beds where the crocuses had blown and the green fuses of newfangled tulips now pushed their tips through the loam, and felt the damp wind on her cheeks and wished for some sort of resolution.

To be an oak round which her cousins twined could not, she decided, be good for her character, and to encourage them in dependence on her must certainly strike any right-minded person as wrong. Yet she could not bring herself to go. Apart from the family's needs, she liked Meriden Place. At home, Edward Wincanton lurked, ready to spring. It was all very troublesome.

She entered the breakfast room frowning and did not immediately perceive that she was no longer alone.

"Which of my sisters are you?"

Jane started and stared at the man who had risen politely from his meal upon her entrance. He smiled and raised a quizzical eyebrow.

"I fear you mistake me, sir," she said when she had at last gathered her wits. "I collect you must be Lord Meriden. I am Jane Ash, your stepmama's niece."

"How d'you do, Miss Ash, and I beg your pardon." His smile turned to a grin. "Shocking, isn't it? I don't believe I've laid eyes on either of my sisters in my life."

"But you must know that Maria, the elder, is not yet come out," Jane said, rather severely, for she was flustered. "They are both much younger than I."

"No, are they? Infants? I can't have mistaken the matter by so much."

"I believe you are bamming me, my lord, and I must tell you that I am not at all witty before breakfast. You have me at an unfair advantage."

"Then by all means let us see you fed," he replied composedly. "Shall I serve you?"

"Thank you, no. That would give Turvey—your butler, you know—a very poor notion of your consequence, and besides I'm persuaded you cannot wish your buttered eggs to congeal. Pray be seated."

She busied herself with the chafing dishes and at last sat down, eating for a time in silence, for she was aware that she felt a quite unbecoming degree of curiosity. So this was the unfeeling monster. She kept her eyes on her plate for as long as she could bear it, then stole a glance at him.

"Marmalade?"

She felt herself flush. "No, thank you. You must have arrived very early, sir. I have walked in the small garden this past hour, and I heard no one."

"I came last night. Late."

"Disarming."

"Yes. I breached the walls and took the keep without a struggle. Very tame."

"Did you anticipate opposition?"

"A skirmish perhaps," he said lightly. "My brother Vincent at the barricades, at least. Where is Vincent, by the way?"

"Will you know him when you see him?"

"Oh, yes." His voice was bland. "F.H.C. rig, Byronic curls, slight pout. Vincent and I have encountered each other."

In Hyde Park, Jane thought, where you, sir, were a damned dull dog. "Vincent is in Town, I believe."

He made no reply to that, but sat silent a moment staring into his coffee cup and frowning a little. Jane had leisure to look at him unobserved.

He was a thin man, rather taller than Vincent so far as she could discern. Although he had the high-bridged Stretton nose, his features were less splendidly regular than Vincent's and more definite. His colouring was unremarkable. On his nose a small patch of skin was peeling. Jane wondered where he had found the sun to be burnt.

"Vincent can't have known you were coming." She found herself defending the absent brother. "No one knew."

"Very true. Er, who *is* in residence? It's remarkably quiet."

"The younger children, of course, will have breakfasted in the school-room. The others are not early risers. I expect Drusilla to be down presently and Felix, if he has had a good night."

"Why should he not?"

"He is subject to migraine," she said shortly and wondered if he knew of Felix's blindness. His lordship, as she had predicted, was ignorant. Whether he was also indifferent she could not tell. Certainly he was wary.

"I have a great deal to learn," he said quietly as if reading her thoughts.

"Yes." She reached a decision. "I am afraid, my lord, that you may meet with ... I will not call it hostility ... coolness. Yes. And apprehension. They fear you."

He stared at her. His eyes, like Maria's, were grey, and very direct.

Her own dropped before them, and she found herself adding apologetically, "I believe, nay, I know them to have been very much shocked by last summer's tragedy. My aunt is inclined to, er, anticipate ills and, what with the closing of the London house and your long delay in coming ... ."

"Yes, I see. Thank you for warning me." He poured another cup of coffee for himself. "I beg your pardon. Coffee?"

"Thank you. With milk, please." She saw with some revulsion that he drank his quite black and sugarless. Horrible.

Catching her repelled gaze, he smiled slightly. "Force of habit."

"Do you generally read thoughts?"

"No, but yours is a singularly expressive face." He took a sip. "Quite tolerable, you know. The coffee."

She flushed again. Her confusion was broken by the unmistakable sound of Felix bumping down the hall. There was time to warn Meriden of his brother's disability, but, rather maliciously, she said nothing except, "That will be Felix."

"Jane? Is it true that the beastly baron has come? Jane?" The boy groped for a chair.

"I'm right here," she said, resigned, "and so is Lord Meriden."

"Oh."

"Welcome to Cyprus. Goats and monkeys," said Meriden. "What will you have? Ham?"

After a chagrined moment, Felix gave a whoop. "*Othello*! I make Goody read the plays to me for hours. She didn't like that one."

"Not in the female taste, perhaps."

"I thought it was splendid." Felix made a hideous sound in his throat. "Especially when he strangles her. Urrk."

"Yes. Very affecting," his brother said. "Ham?"

"Ham and toast and comb honey. And ale." Felix essayed the last

45

rather defiantly. When he had been served without comment and had wolfed down a large slice of ham which, under Meriden's fascinated gaze, he tore with his fingers, he lifted the tankard of ale and gulped, choking a little. "Phew! I say, do you mean to turn us out into the streets to beg our bread?"

Aunt Louisa. Jane closed her eyes.

"Not yet. How old are you, Felix? Sixteen?"

Felix preened. "Fourteen. I'm tall for my age. Don't you know anything about us?"

"Not much. If you're fourteen, why are you slopping your food about like a baby?"

There was a moment of awful stillness in which Jane held her breath and Felix turned purple.

"I'm blind, you stupid beast! Can't *you* see?" Felix picked up his plate like a discus, scattering toast. As he had been known to throw an entire china service on the floor in one of his furies, Jane cringed.

"No. That won't do." Meriden had risen unhurriedly and now grasped the boy's wrist and set the other vulnerable pieces deftly out of range. "Come, I asked you a civil question, and you gave me a foolish answer. You have had time, I believe, to accustom yourself to your loss of sight."

Felix wriggled, snarling.

"And," Meriden went on, in no way relaxing his grip, "as your hands and intelligence are not impaired, I don't consider you have answered me."

"You don't know how it is!" Felix's face crumpled.

Meriden was watching him intently, long brown fingers still circling the boy's wrist. He said in a calm voice, "No, that's true, I don't. I can guess, however, how it is with you. A friend of mine was blinded in the assault on Ciudad Rodrigo."

"I suppose he was noble and selfless and allowed everyone to bully him," Felix sneered.

"No. Quite the contrary. He became an insufferable bully himself, a domestic tyrant. Because his family allowed him to."

"I suppose you mean I'm a ... a domestic tyrant."

"No, merely childish."

Felix sniffed.

"I should judge you to be dextrous." Meriden turned the boy's hand which, though rather plump, was shapely and well muscled. "Forks and knives and spoons should present no insuperable problem."

Jane let out her breath in a small sigh.

"Oh, all right," Felix muttered ungraciously.

"Good." Meriden stared at his young brother for a moment, considering. "Do you play a musical instrument?"

"The pianoforte."

"Bach?"

"Yes." Something flickered in Felix's face, though his tone remained sullen. "And Haydn and Scarlatti and whatever anyone will play for me. But they all play so badly."

"That will have to be remedied."

"How?" Caution and hope mingled in Felix's expression.

"By bringing a master to you who can play well. I'm surprised your tutor didn't think of that."

"There's only the governess, and she don't care for anything but stupid minuets and waltzes. Dancing music," said Felix with contempt.

"Not everyone understands the art," Jane interposed. "Miss Winchell is perhaps deficient in musical training but otherwise, I believe, a very good kind of woman."

"She taps her feet and hums!" Felix said, indignant.

Meriden smiled. "Intolerable."

"Are you musical, sir?"

"My name is Julian."

"Very well." Felix flushed. "Are you?"

"I'm afraid I've not had much opportunity—"

"I thought so!" Felix interrupted. "You're trying to cut a wheedle."

"My occupation prevented me from indulging my taste for music as I could have wished," his brother said rather coldly. "I'm thought to perform tolerably on the Spanish *guitarra.*"

Felix digested that. "Vincent says music ain't a gentleman's pursuit."

"How very provincial of Vincent." Lord Meriden flashed Jane an amused look. "I have heard that the elector of Holz-Hanau plays the viol very creditably."

"Oh, foreigners."

"How very provincial of *you.*"

Felix smiled at that. "Would you care to hear me play?" he asked shyly after a moment.

"Of course."

"When?"

Oh, dear, Jane thought.

"Now, if you like."

"Really?"

"Well, perhaps you should finish your meal first."

Felix contrived to look pathetic. "With knife and fork?"

"Certainly." Meriden set the plate back in front of Felix. "The forks are generally laid on the left."

"I *know.*" Felix took up the necessary utensils and by dint of much grimacing and poking completed his breakfast.

When the two brothers left a few minutes later, conversing amiably about the rival merits of organ and pianoforte, with Felix in the lead—And why shouldn't he be? Jane thought, rather dazed; he's lived here fourteen years—Jane did not immediately rise from the table. She felt rather as if she had witnessed the Iron Duke on manoeuvres.

"The first skirmish is not the war, my lord," she muttered to herself and wondered wryly which side of the affray she would find herself on.

8

THAT DAY MERIDEN spent above an hour with Felix, made himself
known to Miss Goodnight and Miss Winchell in an unexceptionable
way, then disappeared. One report had him in the stables, another
closeted with Peavey, the estate agent. His lordship did not appear at
Cook's excellent nuncheon, disappointing his brothers and sisters and
seriously offending Cook. Jane wondered if he had fled. At three o'clock,
however, a footman appeared in Lady Meriden's boudoir, where Jane had
been calming her aunt's uncertain nerves, with a polite request from his
lordship for an interview in an hour.

Lady Meriden gave a faint shriek which the footman heard with
widened eyes. Jane directed him to wait in the hallway. When he had
gone she said bracingly, "Come, dear Aunt, this is excellent. A brief
word with his lordship and the worst is over."

At length, she screwed her aunt's courage to the sticking point and
sent an appropriate reply. In no time at all, it seemed, the same footman
scratched at the door and announced, "Lord Meriden, my lady."

Aunt Louisa moaned but had no time for further action, for Meriden
was bowing over her hand.

"How do you do, ma'am?"

"Very ill, I assure you, M-Meriden." She gasped over the title and
wept a little into a scented black-bordered handkerchief.

Jane watched for Meriden's reaction with anticipatory pleasure. Aunt
Louisa at her most daunting—and without a deal of preparation, either.
True, her ladyship had burnt—or, rather, caused Jane to burn—a
pastille of camphor so that the very air seemed melancholic. All the
drapes were drawn. Very few preparations had been required, for the
shrouded boudoir was, after all, Aunt Louisa's setting.

Meriden looked pale, and his mouth was set, but he waited without
comment for his stepmother to compose herself.

"I trust they have put you in … *his* apartments?" Lady Meriden uttered at last.

"Yes. Thank you." The corners of Meriden's mouth relaxed in an unwilling smile. Jane had seen the suffocating splendours of the late baron's rooms several times and almost betrayed herself into an answering grin. Fortunately Aunt Louisa was busy wiping her eyes and did not observe either of them.

"And my children … you have met them?"

"Not all of them."

"Jane! Call Whisset! I shall bring them before you at once."

"No! That is, I shall be very glad to see them, ma'am, but not just at this present. I have met Felix."

"Ah, my poor Felix. So tragically helpless in a cruel world!" She continued in that vein for some time.

Meriden's lips compressed, but he made no untoward remarks, saying merely that he believed Felix's gift for music was exceptional.

"You must hear my poor love perform some evening, sir, upon the pianoforte."

"I *have* heard him," Meriden replied.

"Oh."

His lordship took refuge at that point in further polite comments and withdrew shortly thereafter, only asking the favour of another audience the following afternoon when, he trusted, she might feel ready to discuss matters of some weight to them both.

Lady Meriden acquiesced with a mournful nod. Apparently she felt she had taken the honours of the field, for when he had gone she proposed to go down to dinner—she had kept to her rooms for a week—announcing that she did not wish to appear backward in these small attentions to form.

Jane looked for great things from dinner, but the meal proved anticlimactic. Perhaps Lord Meriden had been awed by his stepmother, or it might be that he felt unequal to the challenge of five female adversaries, for Miss Goodnight always dined with the family. Felix had eaten in his room—practising, Jane collected, with the cutlery. In any case, his lordship appeared somewhat abstracted and did not enter into their constrained small talk except to reply courteously to direct questions. These were few. Drusilla and Maria were too much afraid of him to speak, and Jane found herself from time to time covering the silences with polite inanities.

"Does Meriden Place please you, sir?" she ventured over the fish.

"A handsome prospect."

She had not meant to ask his views of the scenery and suspected he knew it, but the remark supplied Lady Meriden with stimulus for a gentle dissertation upon the beauties of the countryside. Because she rarely ventured from her apartments, her comments were naturally rather general. As she waxed eloquent, she began to sound very much like Minchinhampton's *Guide to West Dorset*. Jane wondered if her aunt had swotted up for the ordeal. It seemed unlikely. Aunt Louisa was not given to reading.

A very dull dinner—and very long, also, for Cook outdid herself in the lavish style that had appealed to Jane's corpulent uncle. Remove after remove, with every course; side dish after side dish.

Meriden made no adverse comment, but Jane observed that he declined most of the proffered delicacies with a polite shake of his head. He indicated that they should be offered to the ladies—at least his manners were not faulty—and tranquilly ate a meal Jane's father should have stigmatised a trifling snack. Jane might have been amused had not the prospect of soothing Cook's twice-wounded feelings loomed before her.

Who had given orders for a feast? Jane had not. It was possible that Lady Meriden had, although it seemed more likely that the housekeeper had acted in the absence of direction. But Lord A, it seemed, was not Lord B. Jane resolved to oversee future menus and helped herself to some of the excellent cheese. Drusilla had eaten some of everything and would probably be ill.

Next day Jane soothed Cook for the better part of an hour and listened to the housekeeper's apprehensions, collecting in the course of her staff work a rumour that the agent, Peavey, had been sent packing along with several of his cohorts more nearly concerned with the household. Thus she went in to her cousins rather troubled. They, at least, seemed calm.

True, Felix, his head swelled by a second musical session with his brother that morning, had made the music room forbidden territory to his sisters, the twins, Miss Goodnight, and especially Miss Winchell, and was heard to be practising furiously. The girls were used to Felix's fits, however, and merely took their sewing to Jane's room where their chatter soon drove her out.

She had wished for a little privacy, a little leisure to think before the second dread descent of his lordship upon her aunt. However, it was not to be, and she went in to her aunt rather earlier than she desired and once again set the scene at her ladyship's direction.

Meriden entered the chamber with less ceremony than he had used the previous day, although he again went through the courtesies. He looked surprised to find Jane in attendance.

Jane said cautiously, "Aunt, I believe his lordship would prefer to speak with you alone," and made to withdraw.

Meriden cast her a grateful smile, but her aunt would have none of it.

"Sir! You would not deprive me of my prop, my dear niece, my best friend!"

"Certainly not permanently, ma'am. I had intended, however, to discuss matters concerning the family...."

Jane took a cautious step towards the door.

"No! Do not!" her aunt wailed. "Jane *is* family, sir. I can have no secrets from my dear Jane."

Meriden gave Jane a searching look. She wished herself in Sussex—not for the first time—and coloured to the roots of her hair.

"Very well," Meriden said shortly. He went over to the nearest window. "Would you object to a little light?" He did not wait for her ladyship's negative shriek, but opened the heavy hangings with a jerk. The watery sunlight did little to brighten Lady Meriden's calculated gloom, but it did enable Jane—and Meriden—to see.

"I beg your pardon," his lordship said. "Did you speak, ma'am?"

"No. My poor eyes...."

"Have you the headache? I find fresh air very helpful." He unlatched the window and pushed it gently outward. "There. Better?"

Jane was hard put not to laugh. Her aunt had fallen back on the chaise longue uttering feeble protests. Her rooms were always kept closed against the perils of unwholesome air.

"Now," Meriden said briskly, "I'll come to the point, for you'll not want me to keep you forever, ma'am. Why are Horatio and Arthur not in a preparatory school?"

Lady Meriden sat upright. "My babies!"

"No, no, not the baby. The twins. What are they, twelve?"

"Eleven," Lady Meriden said with a good deal more energy, "and far too young to be sent from their home into a cold world."

Since Aunt Louisa had caused her stepson to be sent away at a younger age, Jane could not help thinking her aunt had made a tactical blunder. A gleam of amusement in Meriden's eyes made her wonder if he had not been thinking the same thing, but he said nothing.

Flustered, Lady Meriden fiddled with her vinaigrette. "I need my children about me."

"You have your daughters, Felix, and the infant—what's its name?"

"Thomas," Jane supplied drily.

"Thank you. Thomas. If I thought two more children material to your comfort, ma'am, I should not suggest removing the twins. I cannot think, however, that they are other than a grave worry to you, for they seem to me to be outside your control—or anyone else's."

Lady Meriden gaped.

Meriden went on imperturbably, "I have spoken with Miss Winchell. It appears that she is a satisfactory governess for Drusilla and Maria and, at least now, for Felix, but she confessed to me that Horatio and Arthur have not been seen in the schoolroom for a week and that they have made almost no progress."

"A week! Good God, sir, where are they?" Lady Meriden made to rise.

"In the stables." Meriden smiled slightly. "My groom has them in charge."

"Upon my word, your groom!" Lady Meriden's fine eyes flashed. "Your own brothers in the charge of a groom! I suppose I may infer from that your feelings for them."

"I have very little feeling at all for them," Meriden said reasonably. "How should I? I have seen them twice and at a considerable distance. However, you may set your mind at rest. Thorpe is reliable and far more likely to influence them to behave civilly than I."

"How will he do that, I wonder?" Jane murmured.

"He has a glass eye," his lordship replied gravely, "and promised to take it out if they help him groom my horses."

"I see. Unexceptionable."

He smiled.

"Jane! Have *you* no proper feeling? How can you? Grooming his horses!" Lady Meriden buried her face in her hands.

Meriden raised his brows. Jane gave a small shrug and bent to pat her aunt gently on the shoulder. "Come, Aunt Louisa. Be calm, my dear. He does not plan to leave the twins in Thorpe's care forever. And at least we shall know where they are."

Her aunt made an inarticulate sound.

"What?"

"No doubt you will 'prentice them to a b-blacksmith," she wailed.

Meriden walked across the room—rather stiffly—and stood for some moments by the open window. When Lady Meriden had again composed herself, he turned back to her.

"Will you tell me, ma'am, what course you would have me take? I propose to send them to a respectable school in Lyme Regis. Next week, in fact. They must be prepared to enter Eton or Harrow next year and probably not together. In any case I cannot allow my wards to grow up as ignorant as a pair of savages."

"You will not separate them!"

"Not directly. Next year."

It seemed as if Aunt Louisa must fly into further exercises of passion, so Jane, for the first time, spoke straitly. "They will not like it, Aunt, but his lordship is charged with their upbringing."

Aunt Louisa moaned.

"And they must someday live apart," Jane coaxed. "How much harder at eighteen or one-and-twenty than at twelve. Come, Aunt, *that* event is some time removed. Now they must merely go together an easy two hours' drive from us, and their holidays will bring them home."

Jane grimaced at his lordship, willing him to leave, but he did not take the hint and remained standing obdurately in the middle of the room like a cactus in a bed of hyacinths.

Presently Lady Meriden so far regained control of herself as to speak. She uttered a number of remarks, the sum of which was that she supposed she must resign herself to further instances of cruel change, every feeling offended, every comfortable habit overset. Fate, she announced, had never been her friend.

"Fortune was ever a fickle goddess," Meriden replied gently. "However, the twins will soon learn to bear their adversities with fortitude if they are guided in that virtue by their mother's example."

Lady Meriden looked thoughtful. Clearly she fancied herself in the rôle.

Meriden then spoilt everything by adding that he thought he must just mention that the fickle goddess had also been less than generous to his late father and brother.

"I'm sure I know nothing of that," his stepmama replied with a sniff.

"No, indeed. How should you? Unhappily their ill luck at faro and deep basset must soon have forced them to a much plainer style of living."

"What do you mean?"

"Retrenchment, ma'am. A course I also am required to follow."

"You've closed the London house."

"Yes," Meriden said baldly. "I propose to close half of this house, also, and to make a number of— No, my lady, pray do not succumb to the vapours until you have heard the whole." He did not raise his voice, but her ladyship, eyes dilated, sat up.

"The whole?"

"Yes. I have dismissed Peavey. He was found to be milking the estate. Indeed I believe he has done so for some years. Fortunately he has taken a number of his accomplices with him, so you need not go through the unpleasant process of reducing your household staff much further. If you will direct your housekeeper to close off the state apartments and the long gallery, I think we may go on tolerably well. I have taken steps to reduce the stables and the outdoor staff. Also," he added, descending to a less general plateau of discourse, "I trust that dinners at Meriden will not always take on the proportions of a royal banquet...."

"I required Cook to serve a dinner, sir, in keeping with your consequence. If you do not know what is owing to your state, *I* do. Your dear father...."

"My appetite is not so large as my consequence," Meriden said drily. "Thank you for your efforts, ma'am, but a plain style would suit me better."

Lady Meriden burst into offended tears and was heard to compare his lordship unflatteringly with his father and to speak of shabby gentility and cheeseparing ways.

His lordship merely looked satirical. When his stepmama's tirade at last drew to an end he said, without much evidence of remorse, "Well, ma'am, I am sorry my tastes accord so ill with my state, but if I were a famous gourmand, there must still be greater economy in your kitchens." He added thoughtfully, "I believe the change will fall hardest on my sister, Drusilla."

"Would you have us eat husks?" Lady Meriden demanded in thrilling accents, her eyes flashing. Jane could not help thinking her aunt looked magnificent.

"I have never tasted husks," Lord Meriden said at last with awful politeness. "My man, Thorpe, has a method of roasting green acorns, however, which I *can* recommend from experience. Shall I direct him to give your cook his receipt?"

Jane flung herself into the breach. Directing a quelling frown at his lordship, she murmured, "Dear Aunt, those of us who *know* you realise, as Lord Meriden unfortunately cannot, that your mind is above these mundane matters. Will you not allow me to take this housekeeping burden from you? Temporarily, of course," she added, for she saw at once that Lady Meriden was about to make a noble and self-sacrificing refusal of help. As this act of denial would inevitably be couched in terms so dramatic as to draw further ill-advised satire from Meriden, Jane felt she must settle the matter with despatch.

"Dear Jane...."

Jane patted her aunt's fluttering hand. "I am sure his lordship would not wish you to exhaust yourself in his behalf." She darted another quelling glance at him, for his lordship's mouth had quirked in a way that suggested he was near laughter. "And you know, Aunt Louisa, Mrs. Pruitt and I deal famously together."

"As you wish," said Lady Meriden in fading accents. "As his lordship wishes...."

Jane raised her brows at Meriden. Somewhat to her surprise, he did not smile but regarded her with a troubled look in his eyes. She shook her head.

He took a breath. "That's very handsome of you, Lady Meriden. And of Miss Ash. I'm sorry I resemble my father so little in my tastes, but I fear I'm past reform."

Aunt Louisa sniffed.

"There must be changes, you know," he went on. "If you will ready the boys for school, I shall try to trouble you as little as possible."

She turned her face away.

For a moment, Meriden stared at her, his mouth set in a rather stern line so that Jane feared he might begin again. At last, however, he merely shrugged and took his leave of her ladyship's purple-shrouded back.

"Has he gone?"

Jane started. "Oh ... yes, of course."

"Jane, Jane, whatever shall I do?"

"Compose yourself and try another strategy," Jane said drily. "I think his lordship does not respond well to weeping women."

Lady Meriden raised her hands to her breast. "If he is not moved by a mother's tears...."

"No, dear Aunt, he is not, and I must say he is right about the twins. They have got utterly beyond Miss Winchell's control. Do not fight him on that head."

"I shall have to give in to him in all things?"

Jane plucked up her courage. "My dear Aunt, no. You possess a handsome competence and may set up your own household whenever you choose."

"But not here," Lady Meriden wailed.

"No, not here," Jane said steadily. "I don't doubt that it is unfair, for his lordship cannot think of Meriden Place as you do, with affection that comes of living in it. If fortune had been kinder, you need never have seen a stranger in possession."

"Ha!" her aunt sniffed. "For all his prosing about debts and retrenchment, he is glad enough to have been so unjustly elevated."

Jane controlled her impatience. "Lord Meriden's loss is certainly not so great as yours, Aunt Louisa, but I beg of you, do not deal ill with him. He had no hand in either death, you know."

"I did not say so!" Aunt Louisa sat bolt upright.

"Then you must stop reproaching him for existing. He exists. He is here. Wishing will not make it otherwise, and to be constantly setting yourself against his will and, indeed, his needs, must turn him from a man who is minded to serve you and your children into the sort of ogre your worst fears make you imagine."

"Perhaps not," Jane said drily, "but he can serve Vincent and Felix and Horatio and Arty and little Tom."

"Very well, I shall humble myself...."

"No, dear Aunt, that is *not* in his lordship's style."

"Style! He has no style. And styles himself Lord Meriden—pshaw!"

This metaphysical flight of wit not surprisingly gave Jane the headache. She said carefully, "Aunt Louisa, he is not like my uncle. Do you wish him to be?"

Lady Meriden stared at her with dilated eyes.

Jane rose and left without ceremony, a thing she had never done. She had said what must seem unforgivable, however true, and because she felt a real affection for her aunt, she also felt some remorse. Even so, she did not turn back to apologise.

In the sanctuary of her own room she wept a little, laughed at herself, and, taking out a sheet of foolscap, set about making a list of directions for the housekeeper to implement. How fortunate that Mrs. Pruitt was both honest and competent. If she, like Peavey, had been sent packing, Jane's task would have been much more difficult.

A scratching at the door interrupted her thoughts.

"Come."

Turvey entered, looking crosser than ever. "His lordship's compliments, miss. When you can spare a moment, he is desirous of speaking with you."

"Very well. In the library?"

Turvey cleared his throat. "I apprehend his lordship has established himself in what was Peavey's office."

"Down the hallway?"

"Aye—that is, yes, miss." Turvey, it seemed, was upset. Perhaps he liked change as little as his mistress.

Jane did not feel up to soothing him, so she said merely, "You may inform Lord Meriden I shall be with him directly."

"Very good, miss." Turvey hesitated. "I beg your pardon, miss. This has come for you. Somehow young James mislaid it." He handed her a letter directed in her brother Jack's unformed hand.

A little late, Jack dear, she thought, and laid it aside to be read at leisure.

She sat still for a moment feeling rather uncertain as to her course of action. She was aware of the impropriety of her offer to take up the reins of household management from her aunt. No doubt his lordship wished to impart a rebuke. Poor man, he must be sorely puzzled by the melodramatic reception he had met with. She decided to comport herself meek and civil as a nun's hen.

Nevertheless she entered the former estate office with some uneasiness.

Meriden rose from behind an ugly desk and indicated a chair. Jane had learnt to read amusement in his features, but he was not now amused. His thin face presented no emotion she could decipher. She decided to play a waiting game and sat without saying anything.

He remained standing a moment looking down at her, then smiled slightly. "Miss Ash, I find myself at a loss. I did not go to Lady Meriden's salon intending to provoke a battle. Indeed I'm not perfectly sure how it happened, but I do beg your pardon."

Disarmed, Jane could think of no reply.

He went on cautiously, "It may be that I made an error of procedure. I had thought it courtesy to inform her of these changes, for I supposed that she must want time to give her orders...."

"Lord Meriden?"

"Yes."

"My aunt has left the management of the household to Mrs. Pruitt for some years now."

He frowned and sat on the desk. "Is that usual?"

"No, sir, it is not, and in general it is an unwise practice. I daresay you may have noticed some small inefficiencies."

"A few," he said drily.

Jane looked down at her clasped hands. "My aunt has been unwell since the twins' birth, but I believe she maintained some control of the household until Thomas was born two years ago. Since that time she has kept largely to her rooms."

"I see."

"I think you do not," Jane snapped. "Five stillbirths in ten years...." She bit her lip, angry with him for being his father's son and with herself for transgressing the bounds of delicacy. "I beg your pardon. She is unequal to any great exertion, and though she may play off the airs of an invalid to perfection, I assure you, sir, she is not shamming ill health."

"Miss Ash—"

"It is most unfair of you." She blinked back angry tears.

"Please do *not*."

Jane stiffened.

"I believe I haven't suggested that Lady Meriden is in the bloom of good health."

"Oh."

"I meant to ask you to clarify for me how best to deal with her, for you seem to have her confidence."

"It would be unbecoming in me to instruct you, my lord."

He rubbed a hand across his forehead as if he, too, had the headache. "Could we begin again?"

Jane drew out her list. "I had started to sort out what must be done."

"No." He reached out and took the paper from her. "It was kind in you to offer to take on the task, but I cannot be obliged to you to that extent."

She felt her cheeks burn. "If there is obligation, it is my aunt's."

"You're a guest," he said mildly. "Does it not seem odd to you—"

"It seemed odd at first," Jane said through her teeth, "but *someone* had to see to this family's well-being. You, sir, or your agent, must be the proper one to put things in order. I would remind you, however, that your father died last summer and that it is now March. If I have been encroaching, if I have from time to time given your servants direction or seen to Drusilla's abscessed tooth or ... or ... "

"You misunderstand me. I am very grateful to you."

Jane sniffed.

"Did Drusilla indeed suffer from the toothache?"

"Yes, and she was a great baby about having it drawn. Oh, dear." She gave a damp chuckle. "I meant to be on my dignity."

"So you were. Very frightening. My poor child, what a time you have had."

Jane considered informing his lordship that she was not above three years his junior and no child, but she forbore, saying merely, "It was rather daunting at times. They're all so helpless."

"So I perceive."

"May I have my list back?"

He frowned, the same troubled look in his eyes she had seen earlier.

"*You* cannot deal with Mrs. Pruitt," she said, "and my aunt will not."

"Therefore you must? I don't agree, Miss Ash." The flicker of a grin crossed his face. "Besides, you know, I have a way with housekeepers."

"Not with housekeepers who have been used to contend with your late father."

"A formidable woman?"

"She hates men," Jane said frankly.

There was a disconcerted pause.

"I suspect you are embarrassed to find me thrust into your concerns," Jane ventured, "but it's too late to prevent my knowing how things stand."

"Miss Ash, this entire chain of events has been a great embarrassment to me from the beginning. Physically, financially, and socially. Pray do not regard your rôle in it as singular."

Jane smiled. "The list, sir."

He handed it back reluctantly.

"I shall faithfully execute your wishes," she assured him.

"Thank you. But Lady Meriden—"

"My lord, surely you must see that it is not these particular changes she objects to, but change in general. Only contrive not to disturb her small world unduly, and you may make what alterations you will elsewhere."

"I see. That is sensible advice, and don't, I beg you, say anything foolish about encroaching, for I shall take it in very ill part."

Jane flushed.

"The twins must go to school and the state wing be closed, but I shall try to avoid other major catastrophes for the time being."

"You're very quick, sir."

"Thank you." He grinned. "If I am hit on the head with a fact I can generally recognise it. Now tell me, does Felix play chess?"

Jane blinked.

"He needs diversion. I thought to have a game with him."

"I believe he knows very few games."

"Then I'll teach him the game of kings directly. My grandfather was always used to say that chess is your great teacher of craft and patience."

"Felix would no doubt benefit from both qualities."

"Oh, I was thinking of myself," he said in a bland voice. "I am sorely short of both."

Jane chuckled. "I think not.... My lord?"

"Yes?"

"*Green* acorns?"

He began to laugh. "That was shamefully ill done. I'm sorry, but you must allow I was goaded."

"I believe you invented the entire idea from whole cloth."

"No. After Burgos, you know, on the retreat to Portugal, we lost the supply waggons—or rather they lost us. Thorpe was not pleased. The acorns are a sore point, in fact, so I don't as a rule mention them. He was usually more resourceful."

"A man of many parts."

"Yes. My bâtman. In his younger days he was a famous poacher—which is how he came to be in the army."

"Very reliable."

Meriden smiled. "I've always found him so."

Upon later reflection Jane decided that Lady Meriden should be spared the groom's history, at least as long as the twins were in his charge.

Somewhat surprisingly, Lord Meriden's history also came into clearer focus through the medium of her brother Jack's letter. Jane had given up on Jack, unjustly it seemed.

> *Dear Sister,*
>
> *How do you in the West? I have got sport shooting crowes but its Devlish muddy. So I come early in to Write you these news. Old Keighley {Jack's captain, Jane recalled} writ me a J. Stretton was in the 95th—the Rifles, you know. Light Bobs. Daresay that explanes the green jacket. Keighley says Stretton was in Port {Portland? No, Portugal, Jane surmised.} as lt. and capt., wounded at Toulusse. Brvt. maj. Invalided out after Water-loo.*
>
> *Will that do? Keighley sd. at first he thot. Maj. Stretton had got himself kilt but when I sd. no he lookt into it. By the by Joanna has a Girl. Has my cuz. Vincent come a cropper yet? Shdn't be surprised.*

Yr. Bro. Jack

Post Scriptum. Love from Father and when do you come home?
PPS. Don't my Aunt read? There was casuality lists pub'd. after
W-loo.

"Is something amiss, dear Jane?" Miss Goodnight asked, peering at her
over the spectacles she wore for sewing, for Maria and Miss Goodnight
were engaged in stitching shirts for the twins.

Jane schooled her features hastily. "No. Not at all. Joanna has a
daughter, Jack writes, but he does not give me any particulars."

"How like a man," Maria said in an elderly manner so reminiscent of
Mrs. Pruitt that Jane longed to box her ears.

"It's a little thoughtless in Jack," Miss Goodnight murmured. "You
must write directly, Jane. Joanna will be missing your help. How you
must wish to be with her!"

In general Jane could have wished nothing less heartily than to be with
Joanna, but now she could willingly have been whisked away to Walden
Ash, even if three sisters-in-law were there encouched. What in the
world should she do with Jack's intelligence?

She listened to Miss Goodnight's account of Joanna's many ills with
half an ear and tried to think. It did not occur to her to doubt Jack's
report, however ill-spelt and elliptic. Too many small items that had
puzzled her fell into place, and at least one major puzzle.

Clearly Meriden's long delay in coming must be laid rather to injuries
than to malice or indifference. Why he had not explained his absence
exercised her for no little time. At last it struck her, with some horror,
that he must suppose Lady Meriden, indeed all of them, to know of his
wounds. Jack's *post scriptum* was well taken; there had been nothing secret
about the Waterloo casualty lists.

She did not care to imagine what his lordship must be thinking of
them, and although several lines of defence passed through her mind, she
determined to offer no excuses even to herself. His lordship's father must
certainly have been informed. It was hard to envision why even a man as
indolent and self-occupied as the late baron should not have mentioned
the matter to someone in the family. Probably, she thought crossly, he
directed his man of business to despatch a basket of fruit and forgot about
it.

She must make the news known. At the thought of her aunt's probable
reaction, however, her courage failed her, and she tucked the letter into
her reticule. She would await the right time. When in doubt, do
nothing.

9

LORD MERIDEN MADE a strategic withdrawal next day, apparently at some distance, for he took the gig and an undergroom with him, and apparently on an errand of some urgency, for he fled very early. Jane suspected her aunt had stunned Meriden as severely as Meriden's proposed changes had stunned her aunt.

Lady Meriden had retired, *hors de combat*, to her bed, which did not surprise Jane. What did surprise her was that his lordship's disappearance affected her cousins. Felix sulked and practised and practised and sulked. Maria wept sporadically. Drusilla asked a great many loud unanswerable questions.

No one had the temerity to warn Horatio and Arthur of their impending doom, however, so the twins, troubled neither by their brother's presence nor by his absence, went on doing whatever they had been doing in the stables and for once troubled nobody. Except possibly Thorpe.

Jane waited a full day before making her way down to the stables. She went not so much from a wish to see the twins as from vulgar curiosity about his lordship's domesticated poacher.

She found Thorpe rubbing down a sturdy bay hack and directing gruff remarks from time to time at her cousins. Horatio and Arthur were perched in the loft and appeared intent on a difficult task.

Jane cleared her throat. The twins looked up.

"Oh. Just Jane," said Arthur. Horatio grunted. They were engaged in polishing brasses, Jane observed in some astonishment, and bent back to their work without further comment.

"Mr. Thorpe?"

A lined brown face appeared over the bay's rump. One brilliant blue eye twinkled at her, and the other canted vaguely off to the left. An auspicious and a drooping eye. Jane wondered what she should say to this apparition.

"I came to see how the boys do," she ventured at last. "I'm Jane Ash, their cousin."

"Ah, now, miss. Yon's a hard question. Thur none so quick wi' they brasses as a man'd wish, think on." Two straw-coloured heads poked up momently from the loft, then bent again over the tackle. Thorpe scratched his chin and favoured Jane with a twitch of his scarred eyelid. "But they do show some promise, miss. Some promise." The boys began rubbing with supernal energy.

"I'm relieved to hear it." Jane smiled. In fact she *was* relieved—and mystified. Hers not to question Providence, however, even in the guise of a one-eyed groom. She found it hard to place the man's speech—a hybrid with northern overtones—but ventured a reasonable guess. "Are you a Yorkshireman, Thorpe?"

"Aye, Huddersfield way. Born in Yorkshire, bred in t'army, as they say."

"You're far from home, then, on both counts."

"That's so, miss." He gave the horse a final brisk rub and regarded her amiably from his good eye. She thought he was amused.

"Er, have you served his lordship long?"

"Matter of seven years."

"From Portugal to Waterloo, I collect?"

His eyes—or eye—narrowed. "And in Yorkshire after. Bâtman I was after Talavera. Trooper afore that. Lost me eye."

"I'm sorry to hear it."

"Ah."

Jane gave up. "I hope you're settling in comfortably at Meriden Place."

"Tolerable, thank you, miss. It's none so snug as Whitethorn. Yon's t'major's place in t'East Riding," he added in affable explanation. "A sight smaller nor this billet, but reet comfortable, think on."

"I'm sure it is," Jane murmured. Meriden Place reduced to the status of a mere billet, and not a snug one. How very fortunate Aunt Louisa never visited the stables.

Jane suspected Thorpe of bamming her, but as she didn't know how to respond in the proper spirit, she made as graceful an exit as she could manage and went blinking out into the daylight.

"His lordship's just off to Dorchester," Thorpe said blandly from the stableyard. "In case they was wondering, up t'house."

Jane fled.

The afternoon was enlivened by Vincent's arrival in a dashing phaeton drawn by a pair of matched greys. Strangely he seemed in high spirits. As he had left them after Christmas sunk in gloom and muttering animadversions upon his still absent brother, Jane did not quite know what to make of this alteration, but she saw to his room, which lay uncomfortably near his lordship's, failed to prevent him from closeting himself with his stepmama where he would be regaled with his brother's latest atrocities, gave up, and decided to wait on events. She anticipated another scene without pleasure.

Julian had not, in fact, intended to leave Meriden in enemy hands after so brief an engagement. However, the same post that had brought Jack's letter to Jane had summoned Julian to Dorchester to a meeting with Horrocks, his man of business.

He was not unmoved by Lady Meriden's performance. To have stigmatised her as a mere purveyor of Cheltenham tragedy would have been unjust, for she had clearly suffered a grave ordeal, and, in any case, Julian did not wish to think unkindly of her ladyship. It was some relief to him to find her relatively coherent, for her letters had left him in some doubt of her sanity, but he was sorely puzzled by her attitude towards him. Resentment he could understand. Underneath the bravado, the excessive language, however, he had detected real apprehension. He knew he was not the most soothing of mortals, but he did not suppose himself such an object as to strike terror into a mother's bosom.

He had only the dimmest recollection of her ladyship from his childhood and, contrary to her imaginings, bore her not the least ill will for sending him off to his mother's family. From what he had briefly observed of the family at Meriden Place, he was inclined to think she had done him a favour.

In Lord Carteret's huge household he had found cousins his age to play with, an indulgent, elegant *grand-mère*, and a severe but devoted grandfather. And, more immediately, a new pony upon which he could roam freely across acres of Devonshire moor. It was true that he had sometimes in the first months wished for his brother Harry and more than once dreamt of his own mother, but she was dead, in any case, and beyond wishing for. If Lady Meriden had openly accused Julian of bearing her a grudge, he would have been very much startled, for he remembered his childhood with pleasure.

His stepmother aroused in him an uncomfortable mixture of compassion and irritated bafflement. It can be no easy thing to find oneself and one's children in the hands of a total stranger, but that must, after all, be laid to his father's door. Why Lady Meriden assumed—a belief she had apparently transmitted to her children—that he meant to deal unjustly with them Julian could not imagine. The estates were grossly encumbered, but he had every intention of seeing that his brothers did not suffer unduly from his father's folly.

The trouble was that they had already suffered some injury from his father's indifference. How to repair the damage without bringing on further of her ladyship's megrims exercised Julian's imagination all the way to Dorchester. There, however, he found other matters to bedevil him, for Horrocks presented him with news. More of Harry's debts had come to light and must be discharged directly. His dead brother had borrowed heavily on the expectation of his inheritance, and from friends at that.

Horrocks disliked every place but London and indeed every part of London that was not properly the City. Dorchester pleased him not at all. Thus he was in no very cheerful temper when he laid Lord Meriden's tangled affairs before him. Nevertheless, he regarded the silent young man across the table from him with curiosity and some sympathy.

"Why the devil did Harry need such sums?" Meriden looked sick.

"Your brother, my lord, was a leading member of the *ton*. Which you'll never be from the look of you. He was used to attend all the race meetings, of course, and must hunt with the Melton men. I believe he also frequented the more exclusive gaming houses. Faro, you know. The allowance your father made him proved, er, unequal to the charge."

"So I should imagine," Meriden said glumly. "Well, Horrocks, what do you suggest?"

"There is the London house. A valuable property."

"Encumbered?"

"No."

"Entailed?"

"No."

"Then sell it."

Horrocks cleared his throat. Although he had dealt with his lordship at some length in London that winter, he still found such despatch alarming. His noble clients were generally far more inclined to curse him and delay action until matters had become desperate than to cooperate. His lordship's father had, indeed, been among the more maddening, considering his creditors honoured by his patronage and debt the only gentlemanly condition. The Honourable Harry had been cut from the same cloth. Horrocks was torn between admiring his present lordship's

66

determination to clear the estates and thinking him somehow not quite the gentleman.

"Well, what is it?" Julian asked.

"That should account for about half the sum."

Meriden swore.

Horrocks straightened the loose papers on the table and set the standish carefully beside them.

"I beg your pardon, sir," Meriden said, after a moment's pause. "Not your fault."

Startled by this unwonted courtesy, for his lordship's father had been known to throw things at him in moments of strong emotion, Horrocks hesitated.

Meriden ventured a suggestion. "I suppose a second mortgage...."

"No. Unwise, I think. I would suggest ... your Yorkshire property."

"No! I won't sell that, by God! That's *mine*."

"Indeed, my lord, I had not intended so drastic a measure. I believe, er, Whitethorn is clear of debt?"

"Yes."

"A loan on the next year's income would realise a respectable sum. The price of wool...."

"Oh." Meriden's face set in bleak lines, but he did not reject the notion.

"Er, if you could contrive a reduction in the expenses of running Meriden Place—beyond what we spoke of."

"Horrocks," Meriden said gently, "have you made Lady Meriden's acquaintance?"

Horrocks blinked. "Why, no. I have corresponded with her. I thought perhaps her ladyship might be persuaded to remove with her daughters to Bath. She, after all, has an excellent portion."

"Meriden is her home."

"Yes, it has been, sir, but if, for an instance, you were to marry, she must then set up her own establishment."

Meriden gave a short laugh. "Unlikely—unless you mean to sell me to an heiress."

Horrocks made no reply.

Meriden stared at him. "My good man...."

"No, no, my lord. No such thing. An instance, merely. As I was saying, if her ladyship were to remove to some congenial watering place, then you would be able to close the house and yourself remove with your brothers to one of your other properties."

Meriden smiled slightly. "Take myself back to Yorkshire. No, it won't do. I must say I'm strongly tempted, but if I'm to be Lord Meriden, and God knows at this moment I wish I weren't, I shall have to spend the greater part of my time in Dorset. The properties here are not in good repair, and the tenants have long-standing grievances. My father spent little time on their concerns, and his agent, I don't scruple to say, was little better than a thief. I've sent him packing."

Horrocks stared. "Er ... surely your lordship means to replace the man directly."

"Of course...." Meriden's eyes narrowed. "No," he said softly. "Why should I?"

"My lord—"

"Do you think I should make a muddle of it? Perhaps, but I could scarcely mismanage things worse than Peavey, and at least I'd have my own interests at heart."

After a long, considering pause, Horrocks nodded. "Your experience in Yorkshire would stand you in good stead. It might do. You'll keep on the bailiffs at Fern Hall and Rosehaugh?"

"If they're competent." Meriden leaned back, smiling a little. "As to closing Meriden Place, if ever I decide to cast Lady Meriden from her hearth, Horrocks, I shall require *you* to explain the matter to her. Only consider how narrowly you have escaped this time."

Horrocks covered an alarmed titter with his dry cough. Really, a most unnerving young man.

"I take it that we have once more steered a clear course out of the River Tick."

"Er ... just so, my lord."

Horrocks left Dorchester next morning, having won his major points but feeling most unreasonably as if he had been outflanked, out-manœuvred, in a word, *rompéd*.

Horrocks's feelings would have dumbfounded Julian, for he perceived no victory. He had what he knew to be irrational protective impulses about Whitethorn. Anything that touched it touched him to the quick. Thus he went, not home, but back to Meriden, blue-devilled and edgy and possessed of an unreasonable notion that he had forgot some vital piece of business. To make matters worse, he smashed his bad left knee climbing into the gig. Instead of merely aching, it burned and stabbed at every jolt in the way, and he convinced himself he would be hobbling about of no use to anyone for weeks.

In his misery he snarled at the timorous undergroom he had brought with him, and the boy lapsed into terrified silence which remained unbroken until they drew up before the stables.

"Eee zur," he blurted. "'Tes Master Vincent's rig."

Julian very nearly turned the gig about and headed for the nearest inn. However, his sense of duty prevailed. Leaving the boy to haul his traps up, he steeled himself and entered the stables. Vincent was not in sight. Thorpe was—stolid and solid as ever.

"How did you go on with my brothers?"

"Yon niffy-naffy sprig?"

"Vincent? No. I meant the twins."

Thorpe grunted. "A fine pair of *bandidos*, me lord. Kept me to me word." He laid a thick finger on his scarred eyelid.

"Did they? You must've worked 'em hard." Julian sat, with what grace he could muster, on an upturned keg.

Thorpe grinned. "That I did. Like as a pair of ferrets and twice as knacky, ain't they? Full of t'old Nick."

"Hell-born brats." Julian stretched his leg cautiously and drew an involuntary breath. After a moment he went on, "They won't take kindly to being parted."

"No, they won't, then. School 'em together."

"You sound like her ladyship."

"Ah." Thorpe gave him a shrewd look. "It was in me mind they'd be fair frighted without each other."

"Frighted?"

"Noan but lads, me lord. Never been apart."

"Small for their age, are they not?"

"Aye."

Julian frowned. "Well, it won't be for some months. I hope that school Horrocks suggested in Lyme Regis will suit them, and God help the masters. D'you think the boys are quick to learn?"

Thorpe scratched his chin reflectively. "Young Arthur, now, he's got a quick tongue. T'other don't say much, but to my mind yon's the one for the plotting and planning. Fair see un think."

Julian was silent, turning Thorpe's observation over in his mind.

"Twins is reet odd that road."

"I know. That's why I thought to separate them ... but you think they'll be frightened? I'd not have said so."

"Thur none so bold and brassy as they'd have tha think, me lord."

Julian stared at his hands, which had clenched involuntarily. "What if I guess badly? My God, what business have *I* to be rearing children?"

69

"Nay, then, let's run off to the Indies." Thorpe took up the leathers he had been braiding into a quirt and resumed his task.

"There's the other boy, too. Felix."

"Blinded?"

"Yes. And vile-tempered and spoilt and bright as the lot of 'em lumped together."

Thorpe clucked his tongue.

"They've made a great baby of him." Julian drummed his fingers on the rim of the keg, torn by a vast impatience. The notion of himself in the rôle of parent might have seemed amusing or at least ironic from the safe distance of Whitethorn. Close to, the prospect was little short of nightmarish. He lurched to his feet and grabbed for Thorpe's shoulder without thinking.

Thorpe steadied him. "Crocked tha leg again. Thought so. Stiffened oop yet?"

"No, but it will." Julian's temper snapped. "Mind your business, damn your eyes."

"Tha may damn un all tha likes," Thorpe rejoined, lapsing with acid dignity into broad Yorkshire, as he always did when he was strongly moved. "Thur sharp enow for all tha damning. Sneck oop and use tha stick. Me lord," he added as a palpable afterthought.

Julian smiled reluctantly. "I'm in the hell of a temper, Thorpe. Sorry."

Thorpe grunted, unmollified.

"That's all it needs, you know. A stick, a melancholic complexion, perhaps the least suggestion of a fevered brow—I'd find her ladyship drooping all over my waistcoat."

"Thought tha meant t'make peace with un."

Julian shivered. "Not on those terms."

"A watering pot, eh?" Thorpe's normal speech reasserted itself. If he took umbrage often, he rarely held a grudge.

"Tragedy Jill," Julian agreed. He took a few steps, keeping his grip on Thorpe's shoulder, and discovered that at least the leg held. "I don't know how it is, Jem, but you always bring out the worst in me. Her ladyship has undergone great trials."

Thorpe chuckled. "They two rapscallions among un, I'll lay odds. And yon twig of deviltry wi' the flash rig."

"Vincent—oh, God. I'd best go on up to the house, and do not," he added grimly, "mention the word *stick*."

Thorpe forbore, but recommended bed and a particularly vile-smelling liniment which had, he asserted, done wonders for Dancer's right foreleg. These and other well-meaning prescriptions followed Julian out into the yard.

He made his way to the house. It seemed a very long way, every five yards barred by some hideous obstacle such as a flight of terrace steps or a patch of loose gravel, and he gained the door of his rooms in no very pleasant state of mind. His hand was on the ornate latch when Vincent erupted from a near chamber, slamming the door with thunderous violence.

"Oh, I say, I'm glad you're back. Devilish late, ain't you? M'sisters expected you before noon."

Julian resisted the impulse to plant his brother a facer. "How are you, Vincent?"

"Merry as a grig. I say, Meriden, I must talk with you."

"*Now?*"

Vincent stiffened. "When it's perfectly convenient, of course."

"Very well," Julian said as civilly as he could through the door, leaving Vincent staring after him, open-mouthed.

He went down to dinner late, feeling unenthusiastic and not one whit guilty about keeping everyone waiting. He stood outside the small salon a moment, mentally holding his breath, then pushed the door open.

"...and it's my belief he was foxed. At four o'clock in the afternoon," Vincent was saying in ringing tones.

"Oh, it's you, Meriden," his stepmother murmured. Plump Drusilla peered at him around her sister, hoping, no doubt, that he would fall drunk at their feet; Maria uttered a tiny shriek; and Vincent flushed to the roots of his hair.

It was Jane Ash who rescued everyone from the horrors of imminent melodrama. She rose with her customary composure and, tidying her aunt's shawl into neat folds, said calmly, "If you are quite ready, Aunt Louisa, perhaps you will take Lord Meriden's arm. Cook's temper has been most uneven of late, and if we do not go in now I am persuaded the soup will be spoilt."

After that, events proceeded with excruciating stateliness. It seemed to Julian, who had no appetite at all, as if the nauseating parade of courses and removes would never end. He was, moreover, conscious of behaving badly. He ought to have dispelled their embarrassment with some light remark, but his mind had gone quite blank. In consequence, everyone chattered uneasily about nothing and kept asking him meaningless questions, to which he made monosyllabic replies.

He pushed a portion of greyish mutton about on his plate and found Miss Ash's eyes on him. Catching his glance, she looked down quickly at her own plate as if she were ashamed of something, and he began mentally composing excuses and explanations. At the foot of the table Lady Meriden droned on in a plaintive contralto. Drusilla waxed shrill.

At last, however, the ladies withdrew. The servants removed the cloth, brought in the heavy decanters and, in their turn, withdrew, leaving Julian alone with Vincent.

"Brandy or port?"

"Brandy."

Julian poured a measure into the glasses, and because his hand was not quite steady spilt a little on the table.

"I say, that'll cause a mark...." Vincent's voice trailed off.

Julian mopped up the liqueur and pushed the glass towards his brother without speaking.

"I'm sorry I said that," Vincent blurted.

"Said what?"

"About being foxed."

"Poor timing," Julian said nastily.

Vincent turned scarlet.

"What did you want to talk with me about?"

Vincent looked as if he would have liked to throw his drink across the table, but he took a stiff swallow instead and choked.

Julian regarded him without sympathy and sipped at his own brandy, which was excellent. He toyed with the idea of drinking himself into a stupor to satisfy everyone's expectations but, somewhat reluctantly, rejected the notion. Very good brandy. Cognac. Probably run, he reflected sourly, but the spirits worked their mellow way, and he felt the muscles at the base of his neck begin to unknot. He glanced at Vincent and said in what he hoped was a more civil tone, "You might as well open your budget. It must be a matter of some weight to send you posting out here at the height of the Season."

"No, dash it. Meant to wait on m'stepmother. In mourning, y'know."

Julian's mouth twitched. Cawker.

Vincent eyed him uneasily. "Sorry. Cork-brained thing to say. Of course you know."

"Yes."

"The thing is, Meriden, I must talk with you about my allowance."

72

Julian's brows snapped together. "What about it? I directed Horrocks to continue it, didn't I?"

"Oh, yes." A constrained silence fell; then Vincent burst out, "The thing is, it ain't enough."

Julian stared.

"I suppose you're going to throw it up at me that m'father never made *you* an allowance," Vincent said sulkily.

"No, why should I? I had my pay." He added thoughtfully, "Of course it amounted to less in a year than you run through in a quarter and was usually months in arrears. I trust Horrocks is more punctual than the peer's paymaster."

Vincent flushed. "I knew how it would be."

Julian began to feel rather ashamed of himself. A priggish thing to have said. "I'm sorry. That was unnecessary. You know I mean to establish you, Vincent, but I can't see my way to it yet. Bear with me."

"I can't live on it."

"You mean you won't, I collect." Julian caught at his flying temper.

"Do you give me the lie?" Vincent's hand clenched on the table.

"Oh, God, Vincent, stop talking fustian."

"*Do* you?"

"I suppose you intend to call me out," Julian said unforgivably, his temper flown beyond any curb. "Pistols at dawn, just like dear Harry. Grow up, Vincent."

Vincent had gone perfectly white. After a moment he rose and left the room without speaking, whereupon Julian had leisure to recall that Vincent had worshipped Harry. He cursed himself softly and comprehensively.

Several hours later, Jane set out in search of Meriden and found him hiding in the library. She was not insensitive to atmosphere, but she had reached the end of her patience with Stretton melodrama, for Vincent had Created a Scene.

He had flung into the withdrawing room and taken his farewell of his stepmama in such extravagant terms as to entirely discompose her ladyship. Jane had had to call for hartshorn. Whether Vincent meant to put a period to his existence, or to his brother's, or merely to spend the night at an inn was far from clear, but he had flung out of the house in the best Kemble style, leaving Jane to cope with his female relations.

As usual in a crisis, Maria wept and Drusilla asked embarrassing questions in a voice that must carry to the farthest reaches of the servants' hall. Lady Meriden moaned antiphonally. In the midst of this pandemonium, Felix entered and announced his intent to remind Meriden forthwith of the promised music master. Jane suggested that he wait until morning, and that set Felix off in his worst mood of whining self-pity so that she found herself promising to beard his lordship if only Felix would calm himself and go to bed.

Indeed, by the time she had calmed everyone, the hour was advanced, and Jane had hopes that Meriden would already have retired. However, it was not to be.

When she entered the library, he did not look up but said, in repellent tones, "Go away, Turvey."

"Pray do not trouble to rise," Jane snapped. "I wish to speak to you, sir."

He sank back as she took the wing-backed chair opposite him. "I beg your pardon, Miss Ash."

"For mistaking me for Turvey? Well, I think you might. I fancy I am somewhat lighter on my feet. He suffers from corns."

"Does he? How very well you know my household."

Jane let that pass. "Are you ill, my lord?"

"No! And not foxed either."

"Then I am persuaded you have injured yourself."

"I hit. My knee. On the footboard."

"That explains all," Jane said cordially. "You have every excuse for driving Vincent wild, oversetting my aunt, and causing Cook to comfort herself with the kitchen sherry. I believe you refused every side dish."

He stared at her and presently his mouth relaxed. "No ... have I driven Cook to drink?"

"Yes. It is ill done in you, though perhaps not irremediable. But she is the only one, you see, who knows how to prepare my aunt's gruel."

"A terrible coil."

"I don't know how it is," Jane reflected, "but gentlemen do not regard these small domestic consequences to their acts. So it is when my father is in a rage. I squander a deal of time comforting offended servants, for, you know, people cannot work well when they feel themselves to be held in small esteem."

He raised his hand in the fencer's salute. "*Touché*. I shall amend my ways. Do you customarily lecture in Domestic Economy, Miss Ash?"

"Only to those who obviously require instruction," Jane said warmly. "Indeed, sir, you have been remarkably maladroit. Cow-handed."

His mouth set again. "I know. Has Vincent left?"

"This hour past."

"I suppose he is putting up at the Rose and Crown. I'd best go fetch him back." He made to rise.

"What a practical notion, to be sure," Jane cried, exasperated. "Vincent will suffer no harm. He has been looking for a setdown these three years at least, and you, I am persuaded, would wind up on crutches. How long do you propose to continue this foolishness?"

"What foolishness?" He looked blank.

Jane regarded him warily. "You *are* the Major Stretton who was recently invalided out of the Ninety-fifth, are you not? Wounded, I collect, at Waterloo?"

"Yes, of course," he said impatiently. "These are scarcely news. It has been nearly ten months since the battle."

"My lord, surely you realise they do not know you were injured."

He shrugged. "How should they not? They must have known the Rifles were engaged. My God, we were at the centre—La Haye Sainte. We took the brunt of Ney's assaults alongside the KGL. I am tolerably sure my colonel informed Lord Meriden."

Jane was silent. It was not her place to point out to his lordship how very indifferent his late parent had been to his welfare.

Meriden's eyes narrowed. "My father!" he exclaimed and began to laugh immoderately.

Unsmiling, Jane waited until he had regained his composure. "In general I do not care for sweeping judgements of character, but I must own I consider my uncle-in-law to have been a most reprehensible parent."

"I feel sure you are right. As usual." He grinned. "What am I to do, Miss Ash?"

"Your long delay in coming...."

"I was learning to walk."

Jane's throat tightened, but she said in what she hoped was a matter-of-fact voice, "You must inform them."

Meriden shook his head and began to laugh again. "What a famous joke. I *thought* they were all being unnaturally tactful. Especially her ladyship."

Jane essayed a smile. "I had nearly resolved to tell them, but when I considered the probable reaction, my heart sank and I could not." She paused, frowning in thought. "I abhor deceit of all things. However, in this instance, I believe I was justified. Only consider, sir, how my aunt would carry on. Fallen warriors! Saviours of Britain! Our brave heroes in scarlet!"

"Green, Miss Ash," he interposed in a shocked tone.

75

She smiled. "I know, but you may be sure that such a consideration would not weigh with my aunt."

"Verisimilitude?"

She shook her head. "I fear you do not understand her."

"Oh, I think I read her tolerably well. She goes in for sweeping effects. Mere details may go hang." There was a pause. "You know," he added thoughtfully, "I believe I'll take the coward's way out, at least for the time being, and tell no one. Though I should think it very obvious...."

"It is not noticeable except as a certain stiffness of carriage," Jane interposed in her driest tone. "I daresay if they had known you well...." She let her voice trail.

"I see." He was frowning a little, in surprise, she thought, but he did not pursue her remark further, saying merely, "If you do not object to joining me in deceit, I think I shall leave well enough alone. My stepmother's possible ardours seem more terrible to me than her present loathing."

Jane agreed in an absent tone and sat for a moment abstracted.

"What is it?" he asked gently. "I'm afraid you must be very tired of my family's quirks and megrims."

She met his eyes. "In general I find them diverting. If I did not I should harden my heart and abandon Aunt Louisa to your evil designs. My father writes in the most affecting terms of his need for me."

He frowned and started to speak, but she held up her hand.

"My brother's wife fed him roast pork, which he abominates. Indeed I feel very sorry for Papa, but Joanna must take up the reins of the housekeeping at some point, for I do not propose to be at their beck and call forever. And besides," she added without thinking, "there is Edward Wincanton."

He sat up, eyes agleam.

Jane sighed and flushed a little. "A naval officer, sir. I developed a *tendre* for him when I was very green."

"Ages ago."

"Nearly seven years."

"Do I take it—?"

"My sentiments did not endure, though it was melancholic at the time. When Captain Wincanton was a mere ensign and a younger son, my father forbade the match. I was, er, quite cast down. Oh, for months. Aunt Louisa entered into my feelings most exactly."

Lord Meriden grinned.

Jane gave him her best governess-look, reproving. "She was very kind, and the next year exerted herself so far as to present me to the *ton*. So I feel a sincere obligation to her, sir."

"No doubt, but you are not, surely, going to leave me in suspense, Miss Ash. It is too unkind. What of your nautical friend? I say, Wincanton … it's not old Shivers?"

"I couldn't say, sir. Edward Wincanton."

"Florid complexion, gooseb … er, rather prominent eyes, carrying voice…."

"Yes. He barks. I don't know why that should send you into the whoops," she added crossly.

"I beg your pardon."

"Indeed he was very well looking when I first saw him."

"Oh, an estimable man," he agreed. "An excellent officer. Bound to rise."

"He did," Jane said firmly. "I am sure any young lady must consider his attentions flattering. So I have told him. Repeatedly."

"But he won't listen."

"No," she said in something like despair. "He is *devoted* to me, sir, and I find I cannot return his sentiments however I may try."

Meriden's eyes glinted. "It is too bad in you, Miss Ash."

"I think I must be quite heartless. A lowering reflection. Unfortunately my father now no longer objects to Edward's suit, so, you see, I am not at all eager to return to Sussex."

"Certainly not."

He looked as if he were enjoying a private joke, and she wished she could share it, but she thought it time to return to more material matters, for he also looked very tired.

"I am sure you must think me a thrusting sort of female, and indeed perhaps I have been, but you know, sir, though I may have come to Dorchester partly to put myself beyond Edward Wincanton's importunities, I did find your family in a very sorry state."

"And that surprised you?" he asked with unexpected shrewdness.

Jane regarded him thoughtfully. "I confess I should not have thought my aunt inconsolable, and your father, of course, did nothing to gain his children's affections…." At that, Meriden showed signs of lapsing again into unseemly mirth, so she went on quickly, "If you had been able to come at once and reassure my aunt, all must have been well."

"You overrate my powers of persuasion, I'm afraid."

"Perhaps. Certainly you handled Vincent very ill. There is no vice in him, you know."

"I'm relieved to hear it."

She ignored the wry comment. "Only he is a little addicted to gaming. Not faro so much as those absurd wagers boys of his age must always be laying one another."

"Vincent is not a boy. He is one-and-twenty and down from Oxford."

"I must say he seems a boy to me. Do you not think, sir, that 'varsity life often prolongs childishness, especially in young men who are not bookish?"

"I must yield to your superior knowledge."

"I had thought you must have taken Vincent's measure at once," she said candidly, "for you have dealt famously with Felix."

"Felix!"

"I meant to remind you of your promise to engage a music master for him. Indeed that is why I sought you out tonight."

He looked conscience-stricken. "I knew I'd forgot something important. Good God, Miss Ash, what am I to do? Is he very angry?"

"No, merely impatient." She looked at him curiously. "Is the matter so urgent?"

His brows drew together. "Of course. I promised him."

"Well, he will certainly kick up a dust...."

"And so he should. His gift is remarkable. I'm astonished that he has borne with inferior instruction for so long. How criminally stupid in me."

Jane was somewhat taken aback by his vehemence and said after a thoughtful moment, "Perhaps the Calverts might be persuaded to share Mr. Thomas."

He looked puzzled.

"Rosehaugh. Mr. Calvert is your tenant—the MP."

"Yes, I know that."

"They have engaged Mr. Thomas of Lyme Regis to instruct their daughters. He is a superior performer, although I believe the girls are terrified of him. They are neither of them musical, and he *will* tear his hair and rap their knuckles with his bâton."

"Is he competent?"

"I believe so, Lord Meriden, but my judgement is not precise. I enjoy dancing music, you see, which sinks me beneath Felix's reproach."

"What a rude cub he is, to be sure."

"Oh, yes. I begin to see some justice in his tantrums, however. No one has troubled to encourage his gifts in a serious way. He has been coddled and cossetted, of course."

Meriden scowled.

"And his disability confines him so," Jane added. "It is no wonder he frets."

"Why is that?"

"I beg your pardon?"

"Confines, you said. He's nearly fourteen and well grown. Healthy, I believe."

"Oh, yes, very."

"You speak of him as if he were an invalid."

Jane stared. "How true. Oh, dear, what a fool I've been."

"Not you. My estimable stepmother." He met the reproof in Jane's gaze, and his mouth relaxed. "Well, I shall have to see about this Mr. Thomas. Has Felix heard him play?"

"Once, at Christmas. He enjoyed the performance, I believe. At least he made no derogatory remarks."

"Encouraging. Thank you, Miss Ash." He hesitated, then said rather gruffly, "Should you object to driving with me to Rosehaugh tomorrow? I'm not well acquainted with Calvert and know his family not at all."

It was on the tip of her tongue to blurt out that he had far better stay in bed on the morrow with a poultice on his knee than to gallivant about the countryside, but she caught herself in time. A fatal slip to have made.

Apparently he misread her silence for maidenly reserve, for he added in colourless tones, "Perhaps my sisters could be prevailed upon to join us."

"I should be very glad to come." Jane rose to go, being careful not to notice his clumsiness as he rose, too. "Good evening, sir, and pray do not refine too much upon Vincent's behaviour. He'll come about." She held out her hand.

He took it. "Good night, Miss Ash."

"Someday you must tell me how Edward Wincanton came by the peculiar nickname you used—Shivers?"

His eyes gleamed. "Oh, no, I must not."

Jane laughed. "Very well. How abominable in you to pique my curiosity. You had much better not have mentioned it, for now I shall be imagining all sorts of things."

He smiled and shook his head. "My lips are sealed."

Mr. Thomas was next afternoon seen, heard, and approved. The Calverts, surprised but flattered by his lordship's unannounced visit, soon agreed to share the music master. Thomas, an intense Welshman, must also be persuaded. At first he seemed disinclined to take on a blind pupil. Meriden explained that Felix already played tolerably well, that what was chiefly required was a competent pianist to play for him and criticise his techniques. Thomas relented.

Jane thought Thomas too astringent, but when she saw in the ensuing weeks how pleased and excited Felix was and how quickly his temper as well as his performance mended, she was glad to have remembered the musician's existence.

Vincent did not return. However, a stiff note came for her ladyship, indicating that he was bound for Brighton to console himself at the races. If Jane had not supposed him desperate, her aunt had. The news that Vincent, instead of laying a pistol to his head, meant to lay his blunt on a nag he knew to be a sure thing, restored Lady Meriden to some semblance of good cheer, although she did not forgive Meriden.

Meriden himself did not mention Vincent, nor did he trouble his stepmother with any further visitations. It appeared that he was far too busy. Having deposed Peavey, his lordship apparently took on the agent's duties as well as his office. Jane questioned the wisdom of such a course, for Meriden must necessarily be inexperienced in the management of large estates, but she did not consider it either prudent or, indeed, proper to remonstrate with him. Instead she breakfasted with him.

Previous to his lordship's coming, Jane had been the only early riser in the family. Now she found herself companioned with fair frequency over the buttered eggs and ham. At first she was inclined to resent the intrusion of another person upon her solitude, but gradually she came to rely upon his lordship's presence.

She had now a great many more household decisions to make. Some required Meriden's consent, and more required the kind of discussion he seemed willing to enter. It was convenient to have such a time—free from fear of interruption—available. Besides, Jane found him a pleasant table partner and had begun to form a good opinion of his judgement. When he loaded the twins and their traps into the gig and carried them off to Lyme Regis at such an early hour that Lady Meriden, dragged down to bid them farewell, was too sleepy to create a scene, Jane silently applauded. First-rate tactics.

She noticed with amusement that he took Thorpe along as heavy reinforcements—but the twins, like March, went out like lambs. It occurred to Jane that perhaps they *wanted* to leave, a reflection that made her feel uncomfortable—but not so uncomfortable as to wish for their speedy return.

She considered the family to be shaping well, much better than she had hoped, for his lordship—though by no means a paragon, especially in regard to Vincent—showed both a general and a particular sense of his brothers' and sisters' needs and seemed inclined to do more than the letter of his duty towards them. After several weeks she felt herself to be tolerably well acquainted with him and ready to form a few tentative judgements.

He was odd, at least in the context of Meriden Place. His habit of living seemed unnecessarily austere and his thirst for activity drove him to work like a Puritan on estate matters, so that she might have thought him a sort of Malvolio and felt very sorry for Vincent, whose style was more that of one of the caterpillars of the Commonwealth, had his lordship's austere ways not dissolved so often into comedy.

True, his disposition to be amused took the form of satire more often than Jane quite liked, and his irreverence towards her aunt sometimes bordered on disrespect, but he kept within the line of what was tolerable, and his manners had nothing of the rustic or the boor, nothing to disgust. Jane thought he might Do.

Almost she wrote as much to her father. However, she found she was even less inclined to return to Edward Wincanton's courtship than before, and considered with only a small twinge of guilt that what her father did not know couldn't injure him. With that unfilial resolve, she entered happily into the new regime at Meriden.

10

IN THE EVENINGS after dinner his lordship formed the habit of listening to Felix play. Sometimes the press of affairs kept him from the small first-storey salon in which the pianoforte and the children's game table had been set up, but he was remarkably faithful. Afterwards, when he could spare the time, he contested Felix at chess.

At first the girls, intimidated by Meriden's presence, took themselves off, but when he showed no disposition to be rid of them, his sisters began, rather shyly, to stay and listen. Felix played well. The old Felix must have driven his sisters off with howls of rage, but when he indicated resentment of their presence his brother merely pointed out that all good musicians require an audience, and the new Felix, after visible cogitation, agreed.

Jane found the manoeuvre amusing. It put Maria and Drusilla on their best manners and forced Felix to behave as if he were civilised. After the music, the girls read or sewed or drew Jane and Miss Goodnight into a card game while Felix and Meriden played chess.

Jane would have found Felix's game maddening. At first Meriden had to wait while his young brother *felt* where every piece was. The problem of distinguishing whose men belonged to whom was solved by using pieces from two sets of different weights and carved in dissimilar style.

Play was constantly interrupted by Meriden saying, "No, no. Only consider, Felix, if you move your pawn there what an advantage you give me," or "What courses are open to you? I have moved that bishop a pace to the right. Your king is in check."

And Felix would scowl and touch the men and sometimes knock them over. Gradually, however, the boy gained confidence. He memorised the board, and since it soon grew impossible to complete an entire game in an hour or so, Meriden always set him the task of recalling where each piece lay when they quit for the evening.

Jane marvelled at Meriden's patience and even more at Felix's, and grew greatly to respect Felix's intellect. It was not many weeks before he was devising strategies and even winning a game or two. She perceived that, as Felix grew in skill, Meriden was gradually reverting to a more ordinary style of play and in the process teaching Felix the manners of the game.

She remarked on the fact one morning at breakfast.

Meriden looked up from a slice of cold beef. "What a noticing female you are. He will be wanting other partners soon, and the less eccentric his style the easier it must be to find him a match. When I discover a tutor for him, I'll have to look first into the man's capacities as a chess master."

"Shall you take Felix from Miss Winchell?"

"Yes. I'd like to see Felix at one of the universities. He will require a companion, of course." He cocked an eyebrow at her. "I think he'd benefit from a good classical education rather more than Vincent has, don't you?"

Jane laughed, but it seemed to her so elegant a solution to the complex problem that was Felix Stretton that she wondered why no one had thought of such a plan before. "Shall you tell Felix now?"

"Not yet. He has some distance to go with Greek, and besides there may be an impediment I can't foresee. I shouldn't like to disappoint him." He frowned. "Do you know whether Felix has ever been away from Meriden Place?"

"I believe only once since his loss of sight."

The frown deepened. "He'll be frightened, then. Has no one ever taken him to Dorchester or Lyme Regis?"

"No." Jane read censure in Meriden's expression and added defensively, "He was used to kick up such a dust over the least change...."

"Rather like his mother."

Jane sighed. "I don't know how it is, my lord, but just when I am most in charity with you, you contrive to spoil everything with some such satiric comment."

"It's very bad in me, to be sure. But come, I'm in earnest. Felix must learn to go about in the world. Will you help me?"

"Of course."

"Thank you. I'll not be free before Thursday, but I could drive him into Whitchurch then. It's a small enough place; I think it wouldn't frighten him overmuch. Help me think of a reason to give him for going."

"If you asked him, sir, he would probably go without reasons."

He looked startled. "Why should he?"

Jane regarded Meriden in some amusement. "You must have observed that he is in a fair way to idolising you."

"Good God!"

"You object to being toad-eaten?"

His eyes lit. "I should enjoy it of all things, but I think you must be mistaken, Miss Ash. Only last evening Felix flung a pawn and two rooks at my head. Come, you were a witness...."

"He hangs upon your lips," Jane said firmly. "It is 'Meriden says this' and 'My brother would not like that' with him all day until we are heartily sick of it."

"If that is true, I must pick a quarrel with him directly."

He did not, however.

On Thursday Felix was borne off, bolt upright and white as linen, to Whitchurch. He returned in high gig several hours later wearing a deplorable spotted neckerchief which he had, he announced, chosen himself. He had also apparently examined the famous brasses in the church and tried out the organ.

As Jane and Miss Goodnight had been lurking in the garden in some apprehension over the outcome of Felix's excursion, Meriden delivered the boy into their charge.

"Thank you for your opinion of the organ," he said to Felix gravely. "I'm sure the vicar will be gratified to know of the defective reed."

"Well, it made a devilish racket," Felix replied. "I'm surprised the organist can bear to play with it howling away. Oh, is it you, Goody? I suppose Thomas is waiting for me. My musical lesson, you know, sir."

"Of course. Give Mr. Thomas my compliments, and tell him I am sorry to have delayed you."

"Oh, stuff," Felix said scornfully. "He don't care."

"Nevertheless, startle him with your suave good manners."

Felix grinned, and Miss Goodnight bore him off, chattering, to the house.

"Felix's adventure seems to have gone off well." Jane raised her brows. "The kerchief...."

Meriden smiled. "Some of the Spanish *guerrilleros* wore that style of thing, and I made the mistake of saying so. How fortunate he's too young to grow *mostachos*."

"It doesn't bear thinking of. Was he very frightened?"

"Apprehensive, perhaps, at first. I explained what the noises that startled him were, and he soon began to enjoy himself. The vicar will recover in time."

"Unfortunate man. Shall you organise further expeditions?"

He was silent a moment, then said slowly, "It must be followed up but I've a deal of work in these weeks...."

"Lord Meriden?"

"Yes."

"I had planned to take the girls to Lyme Regis to fetch Arthur and Horatio home for the holidays. Perhaps Felix could be persuaded to accompany us."

Meriden frowned.

"It might prove confusing to him," she admitted, "but I should be very careful."

"I'm sure of it." He hesitated. "Do you think the twins could be kept from teazing him? He has gained some confidence, but what must still seem to him a voyage of great peril must seem very small beer to them. They're not necessarily tactful."

"Oh, dear, no."

He smiled. "Don't look so downcast, Miss Ash. The holidays are some time off, and perhaps we may contrive something."

The musical evenings continued, and the chess. It amused Jane to see how quickly Maria and Drusilla came to require his lordship's attention also. Drusilla must show him her sketches, Maria the latest bonnet she had trimmed. When her ladyship did not dine with them—she seldom appeared above once or twice in the week—the conversation, like the food, was lighter. On those evenings, the party, for Felix now dined *en famille*, moved naturally from the small dining room to the music room for Felix's performance. When his lordship must occasionally be absent, Jane found herself almost as blue-devilled as Felix.

She came to realise what a task she had taken on that winter. Before Meriden's arrival, the burden of civility had fallen solely on her shoulders. She had been forced to plan every evening like a general taking the field. Now everything was ease and good temper—except, of course, when Felix roared at his sisters for whispering while he played or, frustrated in some strategy, overturned the chessboard. These reminders of the old savage in the new Felix grew rarer, however, for when he did overturn the board, Meriden required him to replace all the pieces as they had been and quit the room himself. Annihilating.

The worst hurdle to general family harmony was that Felix did not wish to allow anyone else accomplishments. Unfortunately he was so far superior at the pianoforte to either of his sisters that Jane had not the heart to request them to show themselves up.

One evening, however, when Felix had played for them the first movement of a sonata he had not completely mastered, instead of requesting another more polished piece for encore, Jane ventured that Drusilla had a very pretty voice and his lordship might sometime care to listen to one of her airs. Drusilla the Bold blushed and sat rooted to her chair.

"I won't play for her," Felix said flatly, "and I don't care to listen to niminy-piminy ballads."

"No, why should you? I'm sure it's nearly your bedtime," Jane said. "Jane! My *bedtime?*"

Meriden listened to this interchange with a bemused expression. He made some civil remark to soothe Drusilla who clearly did not wish to sing under the circumstances and later left off the chess game after a few moves. Felix stalked from the room and knocked over a whatnot table, a thing he generally did not do accidentally. Meriden excused himself and left, too.

"Jane, how could you?" Drusilla wailed.

"You do have a pretty voice," Jane said coolly. "You were taken unawares, and I'm sorry for that but, Drusilla, surely you are not shy?" For Drusilla, if anything, tended to put herself forward unbecomingly.

"I don't care to sing for my brother," she said sullenly.

"You mean Meriden, I collect. Why not? I fancy he has heard girls sing before."

"But Felix—"

"Oh, don't let Felix's distempered freaks overset you. If he does not care for ballads, it is only because he is at the wrong age to understand the words."

Maria giggled. "Only fancy what Felix will be like when he turns romantical."

But Drusilla refused to be diverted and burst into tears. "You have spoilt the whole evening, Jane."

It occurred to Jane that such dependence on Meriden's good opinion could not be well for any of them and would probably give him a swelled head when he came to know of it. She went off to her room rather depressed. Even Miss Goodnight had looked at her censoriously.

However, a scheme presented itself to her in the middle of the night in the form of a dream—or nightmare. In this vision Felix, who bore a much more marked resemblance to Lord Meriden than was the case, wore the infamous spotted scarf and chewed a flaming black seegar. As he chewed, he played a martial air over and over on some twanging instrument. He kept shouting at his sisters to be still.

In the dream, however, Maria and Drusilla were not present. Instead Jane herself talked on and on in a raucous yet governesslike voice, all the while tromping up and down the music room in spite of the fact that the music Felix played changed midway to a saccharine ballad and she did not keep the time.

Waking, she sat bolt upright in bed, and several minutes passed before she could laugh at herself and several more before her inspiration occurred.

The Spanish *guitarra*. Of course. Felix had been playing upon that instrument in her dream. Half asleep, Jane resolved to ferret out Meriden's guitar, if he had brought it from Yorkshire. He had claimed expertise, after all, the first morning she had met him. She should require *him* to accompany Drusilla. Unexceptionable—and calculated to spike Felix's guns.

The project did not seem so brilliant by light of day. In fact, to be rummaging among his lordship's belongings must strike any genteel lady as improper in the extreme.

He doubtless kept it in his chambers, Jane reflected, and of course it would not do for her to intrude there, but surely no one would object if she happened on it in the lumber room. No harm to look.

Nevertheless she caused the housekeeper to open the lumber room on a specious excuse. She discovered her own bandboxes and trunks, and dusted them, remarked the quantity of chairs and tables in every style and period that jumbled the attic, and fortuitously stumbled upon Meriden's gear. These consisted of a battered portmanteau and a sea trunk that looked the worse for a saltwater dunking, and beside them a squidgy cloth-wrapped parcel which must be her quarry.

"What is this, Mrs. Pruitt?"

"I'm sure I don't know, miss," Mrs. Pruitt said repressively.

Jane arranged her features to express surprise. "Why, it's a musical instrument of some sort! His lordship's, I collect."

"No doubt." Mrs. Pruitt drew her lips into a severe line.

"What can you be thinking of to allow a fine instrument to lie in the dust? It must be cared for properly." She eyed the housekeeper warily, for the "fine instrument," when she drew it from its wrappings, proved to be battered and scratched and adorned with a knot of disreputable faded ribbons, and altogether something that seemed to have strayed into the house from a Gypsy waggon. "Not the sort of thing I'm accustomed to, miss." If Jane had heard that refrain once from Mrs. Pruitt since Meriden's arrival, she had heard it fifty times.

Now, however, Mrs. Pruitt merely sniffed.

"I shall remove it at once to the music room," Jane announced. "I hope his lordship will not be angry at this instance of carelessness."

Mrs. Pruitt was heard to murmur that his lordship had only himself to blame for the niffy-naffy way his belongings was knocked about, being as how he had caused That Person—Jane took her to mean Thorpe—to drag the traps up here.

Jane rather fancied herself as a burglar. She was conscious of having behaved ill, however, and was so pensive at dinner that Miss Goodnight asked her if she were sickening for something.

Jane started. Finding Meriden's ironic grey gaze upon her, she flushed scarlet.

"No, I'm perfectly well. Fit as, er, a fiddle."

"I am relieved to hear you say so, dear Jane," Miss Goodnight said earnestly, "for I have thought you was looking hagged lately. It will not do to have you pulled about." She continued in that vein, prosing on about all the trifling illnesses Jane had endured in the previous five years until she put Jane wholly out of countenance. The other members of the party regarded Jane with some surprise.

Meriden carved several slices from the roast of beef which had been placed before him. "Perhaps Miss Ash is suffering a surfeit of Strettons. Meat, Miss Ash?"

Jane nodded and wished she might sink through the floor.

"You shan't leave us, shall you, Jane?" Maria, on a note of anxiety.

"No, of course not," Jane snapped. "Oh, dear."

"Good gracious," Meriden murmured. "Bless my soul."

Jane said warmly, "You are insufferable, sir. Oh, dear." She surrendered to laughter. "To tell the truth, I'm suffering from embarrassment."

His eyes glinted, but he said nothing.

"I have done a sadly encroaching thing," Jane confessed.

"I cannot credit it." He placed a large pink slice on Felix's plate.

"Oh, be still. You are spoiling my confession. Felix, you have dipped your wristband in the sauce."

"Ill timed, Felix," Meriden murmured.

Jane said with dignity, "I, er, happened to find myself in the lumber room this afternoon, and as I was dusting my trunk—"

"You *are* going to leave us."

"Sir!"

He smiled.

Jane stared at the tablecloth. "As I was rummaging about I discovered your ... the Spanish guitar. And I beg your pardon, sir, for meddling with your belongings, but really the instrument must not be allowed to moulder!"

"Indeed not," he said, much struck. "What have you done with it? Given it to the vicar of Whitchurch?"

"Sir! I have placed it in the music room."

"Ah."

"And it seemed to me, since it is there—"

"That you might as well learn to play it."

Jane cleared her throat. "I have very little aptitude for the art."

"Her ear's not exact," Felix said helpfully.

"How fortunate that you warned me, Felix. I had very nearly volunteered to teach Miss Ash to play."

"Oh, *do*, Meriden," Drusilla burst in. "What a famous thing! Will you rap her across the knuckles for her errors?"

"No," Meriden said promptly. "But I'd tear my hair."

Jane glared. "I wish you may snatch yourself bald, my lord."

Meriden, resuming his interrupted task, passed Miss Goodnight her portion of beef, and smiled at Jane. "I had not thought your ear *that* deficient. Shall we dine? I fear to lower myself further in Cook's esteem by allowing her roast to turn icy."

Jane sawed furiously at her meat, but a footman had entered with other dishes and she forbore to respond as Meriden deserved. Everyone commenced eating. When the servant left, Jane favoured his lordship with a sweet smile.

"If you truly wish to win Cook's favour, sir, may I suggest that you occasionally try one of her excellent side dishes," for, as was his wont, he had declined those exquisite viands without glancing at them.

"It would not do to appear to *curry* favour."

Jane choked.

Miss Goodnight had been following these exchanges with the vaguely bewildered look that was her response to the satiric.

"Well, we are all very merry tonight," she ventured. "My lord, it occurs to me that, if you should not dislike it, you might accompany Drusilla in an air or two yourself, for I believe the Spanish instrument blends pleasantly with the human voice."

Jane felt her jaw drop. To be rescued by Goody! She composed herself. "Pray do, sir."

Meriden did not demur, although he shot her another satirical look that suggested he knew himself to be the victim of a plot.

He showed a disappointing tendency to pedagogy, however, when the time finally came to perform. Felix must examine the *guitarra* knob by knob, string by string, trying out under his brother's critical eye all the possible noises the instrument could produce. Jane soon had her fill of disconnected twanging.

"I believe the guitar is chiefly employed in accompaniment?" she ventured.

"In this country." Meriden reached an arm over Felix's shoulder. "No, Felix, if you wish to form a full chord across the neck, you must place your left thumb here."

Felix complied. "I say, it's surely not in tune?"

"I believe you're right. Our auditors grow impatient, Felix. Strike E for me on the pianoforte so I can put it to rights."

There followed a tedious interval in which the method of tuning a *guitarra* to itself was demonstrated to Felix's satisfaction. Drusilla began to lour. Jane wondered what the penalty was for throttling barons.

"Will that do?" Meriden asked at last.

"I think so," Felix grudged.

"Thank you. Now, Miss Goodnight, the choice is yours. What shall it be?"

Miss Goodnight beamed rosily. "Whatever your lordship wishes."

He bowed. "Then we'll leave selection to Drusilla since my repertoire is no doubt *passé*. Ah, but first—the mode of the performance. Shall it be standing, Miss Goodnight, as beneath the auditor's balcony? On one knee? ... No, I think not." He shot Jane a satirical glance. "Sitting, in fact. I require a chair. No, Maria, *mi vida*, entirely too low and enveloping. One requires the freedom of the elbow."

His sisters by this time were giggling in an unbecoming way, for his accent became progressively more Latin as he spoke. Felix looked puzzled. At last Drusilla pulled forward a plain chair.

"Yes—I mean, *sí, bueno.* Now, *alma de mi corazón*, what shall it be?" He seated himself and regarded Drusilla blandly.

" 'Go, Lovely Rose'?" Drusilla suggested. Now that the moment had come, she had turned rather pale and tentative.

"Ah, Waller. Unexceptionable. So impeccably *a la inglesa*." He saw that his manner flustered her and added with less affectation, "I don't perfectly recall the air. Perhaps if you sang a few bars...."

Drusilla planted her feet and swallowed hard. "Go, lovely rose," she warbled, opening her throat, "tell her that wastes her time and me when I resemble her to thee how sweet and fair she seemstobe...."

Meriden nodded. "Yes, very well. Rather slower, however. Have mercy on my stiff fingers."

Presently they twined the voice and the guitar-strum into a pleasant sound. Drusilla sang some half-dozen airs in the pretty, clear voice that was so much at odds with her rather boisterous character, and the *guitarra*, as Jane had suspected it must, did service in the accompaniment in an unexceptionable way. Drusilla's voice predominated. Even Felix was brought to admit that the combination fell pleasantly on the ear. Jane was very well pleased with her scheme and, when Drusilla would not be persuaded to sing another song, murmured, "I liked that very well, sir. It is most obliging in you."

"*A sus órdenes, señorita.*"

She flushed. "I do not have Spanish, sir."

"No? A pity. I'm persuaded it should suit your style."

She did not know what to reply but thought he must mean she had behaved in a rather autocratic fashion. She was satisfied that her meddling ways had produced an harmonious evening, however, so she merely smiled.

Meriden smiled back. "Do you dance well, Miss Ash?"

"Tolerably."

"Jane dances to perfection," Miss Goodnight said helpfully.

"Splendid. I'm delighted to hear it." He picked out a mournful little catch. "There is one quality of this instrument"—thrum—"which is very little understood outside Iberia. Perhaps you should not object, Miss Ash"—thrum—"to aiding me in a small demonstration." He ruffled his right hand across the strings in such a way as to produce a rapid, rather loud tattoo.

Jane started. "I—that is, what can you mean, sir?"

"Have you never heard this style of thing?" He began to play, and abruptly there was nothing inobtrusive about the *guitarra*. He started slowly, but the force of the music—she could not call it a song, yet it was music—drove faster and faster, interrupted or augmented at intervals by the peculiar four-finger ruffle. He bent his head over the guitar, for such intricate sound must demand concentration, and continued for some minutes the furious, dramatic noise, his long fingers flashing, finishing at last in a resounding thump.

Jane blinked.

Meriden looked up and smiled at her again with the bland expression she had learnt to mistrust.

"I say, what was that?" Felix asked in hushed tones.

To Jane's bemusement, Miss Goodnight leaned forward. "It is the *fandango*, sir, is it not?" Her unremarkable middle-aged face was flushed with delight.

"The ... oh, *no!*" Jane exclaimed. "Indeed, sir, I could *not*. I *would* not."

"Then perhaps my sister Maria might be persuaded...."

"Sir, you must know it is most improper."

"Is it? Then what shall I do, for you cannot properly appreciate the dance without the dancer."

Jane felt her cheeks burn in mortification.

Rather daringly, Maria rose to her feet and expressed a willingness to be instructed. Meriden rose, too, and set the guitar carefully on the chair.

"Ah, Maria, *hermana mía*, so *you're* ready to defy convention, are you?" Maria smiled timidly, and he said in a milder voice, "There will be a deal of stomping and hand-clapping. Perhaps you should set down the reticule."

Maria complied.

"Very good. Now, a rose over one ear would be altogether fitting."

"Lord Meriden."

He turned in his rather stiff way and smiled at Miss Goodnight apologetically. "I'm sorry, ma'am. Shall you dislike it so much?"

Miss Goodnight had risen, and now she came forward. "Indeed not. How it does take me back! San Sebastián, Jane. Dear Lady Wilbraham!"

Meriden and Jane stared.

"I believe you do not remember my mentioning Lady Wilbraham after all, Jane," Miss Goodnight said, rather hurt. "I was some time in her employ, and she, you know, was used to travel widely. Quite five-and-twenty years ago. No, thirty. Before your time, sir."

Meriden snapped his fingers. "The Rose of the Pyrenees! Famous! You said San Sebastián...."

"Yes, for we visited with the consul general there some months, and if

I have seen the *fandango* danced once, I daresay I have seen it a hundred times. So splendid a sight. Egyptians, you know, Jane."

"Gypsies?" Jane murmured feebly.

"*Gitanos*," Meriden amended.

"If you should not object, sir, *I* shall be very happy to show Maria something of the manner of the dance."

"I should like it of all things," Meriden said formally. His eyes gleamed.

"Very well. Do you sit then, sir, and Maria you must stand very tall. So."

Meriden resumed his chair and took up the instrument. Jane closed her eyes.

Later that evening Miss Goodnight came to Jane's room. Wilkins, the abigail, had been brushing Jane's hair, but when Jane saw Miss Goodnight's expression, she sent her maid off directly.

Miss Goodnight sat down on the French sopha.

"Goody dear, whatever is the matter?"

"I was sure you must be angry with me," her companion wailed. "Oh Jane, I had forgot it is a house in mourning. Dear Lady Meriden...." She looked as if she might burst into tears.

Jane went to her and gave her a swift hug. "Indeed, Goody, we all forgot. Don't refine too much upon it."

"But your aunt...."

"As it is my fault for resurrecting that wretched instrument, I shall explain the matter to her myself. But not," she added hastily, "unless Aunt Louisa requires an explanation. I daresay she may never find out."

"Oh, Jane ... too good."

"Nonsense," Jane said ruefully. "It's the least I can do, for I don't know when I have been so diverted. Goody, you were marvellous."

Miss Goodnight blushed. "I must have presented a comic spectacle."

Jane took her hand. "No, you did not, and I wish I might have seen you as a girl, for I suspect you took the shine out of all the other belles. Such a very fine sense of tempo, such a quickness."

"Oh, I was never anything out of the ordinary." Miss Goodnight still blushed, but she no longer writhed with guilt. "How it took me back, Jane. And his lordship—so very kind."

Jane's eyes kindled. "His lordship is entirely without principle."

"No, Jane, how can you say so? He was perhaps a trifle angry with you, or I daresay he would not have put you to the blush, but you must own you provoked him."

Jane set her jaw.

93

"After you and the children retired, he talked with me quite half an hour about Spain," Miss Goodnight said shyly.

"*I* see how it is," Jane murmured. "You have developed a *tendre* for Meriden."

Miss Goodnight looked thoughtful. "No. He is not a romantical figure, I'm afraid, but I *like* him very well, for he has been excessively kind to Felix, and now—such distinguishing attentions! Portugal! Spain! I am quite in charity with him."

Jane laughed.

"And I should not have put myself forward this evening so unbecomingly had I not been convinced that he meant to show Maria the steps of the dance himself," Miss Goodnight added with dignity. "Such stamping and twisting about could not have been good for him. I daresay you may not have noticed, Jane, but his lordship is a trifle lame."

Jane stared.

"I have not mentioned it," her companion murmured, oblivious, "for, unlike your dear papa when the gout is troubling him, I believe his lordship does not care to be cossetted."

"Very true," Jane said weakly.

"If I did not believe Lady Meriden must know of such a mischance, I should hazard he had been injured in the Belgian fighting, for that would explain his prolonged absence in an unexceptionable way."

Jane began once more to laugh.

"It is not a happy possibility." Miss Goodnight frowned her reproof.

"No, and you are quite correct in your surmise. Meriden was wounded at Waterloo. The thing is—"

"Lady Meriden. I see. Now why are you laughing, Jane? Indeed it is too bad in you."

Jane gave Miss Goodnight another hug. "It is only that you notice so much more than one supposes."

"My dear, I hope I am *discreet*."

At that Jane called up the picture of her discreet companion footing it featly in the *fandango* and laughed so hard that Miss Goodnight was genuinely offended. Jane had to soothe her with explanations and apologies until the ruffled lady left the room in her usual cheerful spirits. When Jane slipped into bed at last, however, she was still chuckling.

Fortunately no officious soul saw fit to report the incident to lady Meriden. Jane did not forgive his lordship at once, but she felt some responsibility and resolved not to allow a word of reproach to fall from her lips. Dignity—not too much reserve, of course, for that would drive

Meriden to further satire—must be her watchword. She would be grave and civil and distant. So.

The days passed civilly. It was almost Easter, time to fetch Arthur and Horatio from their school in Lyme Regis. Jane had not forgot the plan to take Felix, but as nothing further had been said, she supposed the matter had slipped Meriden's mind. His lordship had been much occupied—some urgent matter had called him to Fern Hall for several days—so Jane was very much startled on the morning of the expedition when Meriden appeared at breakfast to announce that he and Felix meant to join the ladies in their outing. If there were no objections.

As Felix and Drusilla were in the room, Jane acquiesced civilly.

"Are *you* coming, Felix?" Drusilla's tone expressed surprise and small enthusiasm.

Felix bridled. "I intend to walk upon the Cobb. I have never done so. Meriden says it is unique and historical."

"Monmouth's rebellion," Jane murmured and scowled at Drusilla. "I daresay you will want to explore the strand, too, Felix."

Felix nodded. He looked white with apprehension, but determined.

"We mean to call on Mr. Thomas," Meriden interposed. "You've sent for the carriage at ten?"

"Yes."

"Then you'll have to make ready, Felix. It's nearly nine."

"Good heavens, Maria has not yet broken her fast!" Jane exclaimed. "I am persuaded she will be ill in the carriage if she doesn't take something. Drusilla, run up to your sister and bid her make haste."

Drusilla stuffed a piece of bread into her mouth and jumped up, mumbling to Felix to hurry. She grasped his elbow and led him off.

"I hope we have not overset your plans," Meriden asked. Civilly.

"There is the small problem of fitting seven people into the carriage on the way back."

"Oh, I'll ride. I could never abide closed carriages. You can stick Horatio and Arthur on top with Thorpe."

"They'll rattle the tin all the way to Whitchurch."

"Yes. A diverting sensation for Felix. He'll be quite ready for Dorchester, or even London." Meriden raised his brows. "I thought you agreed that Felix should go about more."

Jane swallowed her vexation. "I do. I'm sure it will turn out well enough. If you will excuse me, my lord, I shall just tell Cook there will be two more to partake of her pic-nick."

"Good God, don't do that. If her little light nuncheons are anything like her plain dinners, there will be more than enough for all of us."

In spite of herself Jane smiled. "Well, it is too bad in you, sir. If you'd warned me sooner ... last evening...."

"Last evening I spent persuading Felix to come."

"I thought you had still been at Fern Hall."

"So I was. I returned later than I meant to, but I caught Felix on his way to bed."

"I see." Wondering what cajolery he had used to persuade Felix to take on the world, she went off to the kitchen to warn Cook.

The party reached Lyme Regis without incident, stopping first at Mr. Thomas's modest house, where Felix was persuaded to play for the musician's pupils, and then at the boys' school from which the twins shot like arrows from a drawn bow.

Jane was heartened to see that the masters of the school had not, as her aunt had prophesied, beaten and starved the twins into decorum, but as the morning progressed she began to wonder if a little beating and starvation might not be called for. Given the princely sum of a shilling apiece to spend as they willed, the two made shambles of shop after sweet shop through the steep streets of the town.

She and Meriden and Felix caught up with the twins finally at an establishment which purveyed licorice whips. Arthur stood inside in earnest conference with the proprietor, but they found his brother, disconsolate, on the step.

"How, now, Horatio?" Jane said in rallying tones.

He looked up and, catching sight of Meriden, brightened. "I say, sir, could I have tuppence? They make the most splendid whips."

Meriden regarded him sadly. "Pockets to let already?"

The boy nodded.

"Thrift, thrift, Horatio," said Jane and Meriden in one breath.

Felix gave a crow of startled laughter. "*I* know that one. It's from—"

"Very good," Meriden interrupted, "but this is a grave matter, Felix. Do not be laughing at your brother's plight. Now, Horatio, consider. Arty has tuppence to squander on whips. You don't. What have you that your brother has not?"

Horatio fumbled in his pockets and drew forth a number of grubby objects which he told over with great earnestness. "This and this ... and this. No, we both ... oh!" His face lit, and he pulled a deadly looking sling from the recesses of his chocolate-besmeared jacket. "Isn't it famous, sir?"

"Worth at least a dozen licorice whips," Meriden agreed gravely.

Horatio looked wistful. "Oh, well, I daresay Arty will give me a chew. I say, sir, there are terrific cliffs with swallows and seagull nests." Arthur came out with a fistful of plunder and added his raptures to his twin's.

"Yes, I know," Meriden replied. "Just now, however, we are bound for the Anchor. Thorpe is waiting there for us with the carriage and a small hamper...."

No further words were needed. The twins dashed off shouting, "Thorpe! Thorpe!" and left their elders to follow at a more sedate pace.

Drusilla and Maria being discovered at the circulating library, nothing remained but to find a pleasant spot for the nuncheon. A green knob of field near the famous cliffs and overlooking the strand was pronounced suitable, and the cloth no sooner spread for Cook's basket than the twins fell on the roast chicken and boiled eggs and pasties and cakes and apples as if they had never seen a sweet shop.

"Can they truly be starved at their school?" Jane surveyed the broken remains ruefully.

Meriden laughed. "I'll warrant they think they are. All schoolboys do. Felix, the lemonade is perched by your left elbow. Don't move."

He rescued the sticky vessel and set it up at a safe distance. "Here, you two!" he called to the twins, who were pelting each other with fistfuls of pebbles. "Take something to Thorpe. He can't follow you up the cliff if he's faint with hunger."

The guilt-stricken twins gathered up a cloth full of sustaining viands and darted off to their idol who was standing by the equipage smoking a pipe.

Thereafter peace reigned. The girls drifted off to look for pretty stones. Felix and Meriden talked, or rather Felix, his face alert to every breeze, asked countless questions and Meriden answered equably as he helped Jane tidy the food away. Some half an hour later, however, the twins roared back with Thorpe following at a leisured pace that suggested they were rather more eager to climb the cliffs than he was.

"Sir! He says we may not scramble down for eggs."

"May we, sir?"

"By no means. You are to obey Thorpe in all things. The edges of the cliffs sometimes crumble."

Their faces fell. "Thorpe says we may see as far as Portland, but I daresay it is all a fudge." This from Arty.

Horatio punched him. "Stupid. Probably we shall see as far as France."

"With a glass you may see the ships in the Channel," Meriden interposed, "and the Chesil Bank and possibly Portland Bill. Here." He pulled a small spyglass from his pocket.

"Famous!" The boys rushed to the edge of the strand and began testing out the device's capabilities.

"You've left a boy with the horses?" Meriden cocked an eyebrow at his resigned groom.

Thorpe grunted. "T'lad'll walk un." He belched. "Beggin' your pardon, miss."

Jane smiled. "Cook surpassed herself, did she not? It is kind in you, Thorpe, to be chasing after my cousins."

"No trouble." He looked rather dour. Meriden grinned heartlessly.

"Well, I'm sure they'll obey you sooner than anyone," Jane said warmly, indignant at his lordship's callousness.

Thorpe's scarred eyelid twitched. "Knacky lads, ain't they? Never tha mind, miss. Us'll see they hellions down safe as houses."

Arthur and Horatio dashed back.

"It's splendid, sir. I saw old Davorel chasing his dog on the Cobb!"

"Did you, Arty? I take it Davorel is a school mate. See that you keep that glass clean."

Arthur began rubbing the lens vigorously with his shirt frill.

"Thank you for the glass," said Horatio, remembering his manners belatedly. "I wish you will come, too, sir."

"Oh, yes! Famous!" Arthur piped. "I daresay you could show us everything. Do come, sir."

Meriden laughed. "No. Run along. I believe Thorpe is sufficiently recovered to join you."

"*Please*, sir."

"No. Thorpe knows far more than I do about ships of all kinds, including runners. And besides I've promised Felix a game of chess."

The twins groaned but were finally persuaded that their elder brother was set on this altogether tame pursuit. They scampered off, and Thorpe followed stolidly.

"If you'd liefer climb the cliff, sir, I can wait for my game," Felix said, rather white-faced.

Jane stared at Felix. It was probably the first unselfish remark of his life.

"No," Meriden said after a moment. He, too, was looking at his brother, a slight frown between his brows. "Thank you. I prefer chess. Shall I set up the board now?"

"Really, Ju ... Julian, it must be a splendid view."

Meriden took a breath. He did not look at Jane. "Felix," he said gently, "I *could* not climb the cliffs, even if I wished to, which I don't."

"What do you mean?"

"Do you recall the battle that was fought in Belgium last summer?"

"Waterloo? Of course."

"I was wounded. In both legs. I walk and ride tolerably, but I don't caper up mountains like a goat. In fact, I found the streets of Lyme Regis rather steep going. If I tried to scramble up that precipice, I'd be brought down on a hurdle."

"Oh." Felix digested that. "Does my mother know?"

"No, and I'll thank you not to go blabbing to her," Meriden snapped, incautious.

"Why not? She don't like you above half, but I daresay if she knew it'd bring her round in a trice."

Meriden was silent.

Jane wondered how he would extricate himself. Felix had been using his mama's easy pity to advantage for years. She could think of no escape and would not, in any case, have intervened for the world, for Felix had forgot her presence entirely. That Meriden had not she knew very well. She gazed hard at the cliff. The twins were mere specks.

Meriden said slowly, "Your mother is a good sort of woman, and I should like to be on easy terms with her. However, she is a little inclined to make a fuss. I believe you understand me."

Felix pondered.

"I don't know how it is," Meriden added, "but I find excesses of sympathy rather more tiresome than honest dislike."

"Oh."

Deft, my lord, very deft, Jane thought. She began to be a little amused. Felix was not by any means stupid, and he took Meriden's judgements very much to heart. She wondered if in the next days, they would be edified by the spectacle of a new, stoical Felix.

His lordship did not pursue the matter. "Shall I fetch the board?"

"What? Oh, yes. I say, I'm sorry you was hurt, Julian," Felix said shyly.

Meriden let out his breath in a whoosh. "So am I, but it can't be helped. I'll be back directly." He got up, indeed rather stiffly, and went to fetch the chess set from the carriage.

When the twins finally pelted down the cliff, full of thrilling descriptions of the perilous ascent and the nesting seagulls which had screeched at them, and the hundreds of swallows they had bagged with

Horatio's sling, and the hundreds of smugglers and ships of war they had seen, Felix listened with fair humour to their chatter. Tiring of it at last, he announced in a world-weary tone that Julian had trounced him again and that he meant to go for a walk on the Cobb with his brother.

"Tame," Arthur snorted.

"Oh, who cares about a lot of dashed seagulls?"

Unfortunately a gull at that moment flapped by quite close to Felix's head and he started wildly. "What was that?"

The twins convulsed in mirth. Jane gave them a repelling stare. "Where have you put the glass?"

"Thorpe has it," Horatio said carelessly. "Come on, Arty. Let's go hunt shells." They raced off again.

"Shall we go, Felix?" Meriden pulled the boy to his feet. "There's a tolerably smooth path here, and if you'll just lend me your arm...." He threw Jane an apologetic grin. She smiled back and shook her head. She would not have intruded for any consideration.

Felix went off, flushed with pleasure and importance, to examine the historical seawall.

When Thorpe draggled down and sat on a nearby tuft, Jane regarded him with deep sympathy. He looked as she felt—exhausted.

"Should you care for this bottle of hock, Thorpe? It's quite untouched, and I daresay you are worn to bits."

"Thank you, miss. I'm that thirsty."

Jane began, softly, to laugh, and Thorpe's eyelid twitched. "Reet wearing, that lot."

A look of complete understanding passed between them.

11

IT WAS NOT to be supposed that the good spirits generated in Lyme Regis could last through the entire Easter holidays. At first everyone was merry as a grig. Even Lady Meriden acknowledged the season by putting off her blacks and donning instead a perfectly stunning series of purple and grey creations. Jane could not imagine when her ladyship had caused them to be made up.

Almost Jane wrote her father that all was now well, for the thought of missing yet another holiday at home pricked her conscience. Fortunately the crisis that blew up as the twins were being readied for their return to school was so spectacular that Jane could write instead—in guarded terms, of course—of fresh catastrophe. Vincent had been imprisoned for debt.

By the time Aunt Louisa received this news—a friend was kind enough to write her—Meriden had already posted off to London.

To be sure, he had warned Jane, but she was left, with only Miss Goodnight and the girls to sustain her, first to dread, then to cope with her aunt's imaginings in which scandal and gaol fever loomed equally large.

How it was she did not know, but Jane found Lady Meriden's histrionics far less endurable than they had seemed last autumn and winter. Although Miss Goodnight bore her ladyship's inevitable accusations against Meriden with her usual adroit sympathy, neither of the girls was of the least use to Jane. Softhearted Maria could be brought to weep over Vincent's plight, but she would not allow it to be laid at her elder brother's door. Drusilla showed no tact at all. She listened to her mother's recriminations for ten minutes or so, then said bluntly, "It is Vincent who got himself thrown into a sponging-house, Mama, not Julian. Serves him right."

Drusilla was immediately exiled from her mother's presence, in some confusion. Jane thought, however, that the disaster hit hardest at Felix.

He cared not a whit for Vincent's trials, but he endured Meriden's absence fretfully, every morning listening for his brother's step, and every morning cast down.

Jane carried him to Lyme Regis with her when she took the twins to their school, but Felix merely bore the journey; he did not enjoy it. When she returned from that brief excursion, Jane must, for the fiftieth time, hear her aunt's doleful reflections. She managed not to lose her temper, but later that evening in the privacy of her room she poured out her feelings to Miss Goodnight.

"Goody, what are we to do?" she asked at last. "There is some justice in her strictures."

Miss Goodnight said gently, "She is unhappy. Lord Meriden will do as he ought. There is little reason for her apprehension, but she must fix the blame, you know—and on someone other than her late husband. Do not refine too much upon justice and injustice. His lordship will not regard it."

"He is inclined to blame himself."

Miss Goodnight frowned. "Jane, has it occurred to you that your aunt and Lord Meriden should not continue long under the same roof?"

Jane bridled. "He shows her a deal of patience."

"Oh, yes, but she is also hard for him to bear, you know, and he has a great many other things to try his temper."

Jane swallowed. "You think she should remove to the Dower House?"

"No. Farther. To Bath," Miss Goodnight said with gentle inexorability. "She must take the baby, Thomas, and the girls with her. It will not be best for Drusilla and Maria, I fear, but if one considers the good of the whole family.... In her own house your aunt may order things as she likes."

Jane shuddered.

Miss Goodnight had apparently given the notion some thought, however, for she went on to describe the advantages that must obtain from her aunt's move to Bath in such careful detail that Jane was forced to accede to her logic.

How to persuade Aunt Louisa to make the change exercised both ladies for some time. Finally they decided on indirection and subterfuge. Miss Goodnight was to plant the seed, Jane to cultivate it, but Lady Meriden must never suspect the idea was not her own.

Jane thought the plot might bear fruit by autumn. Surely her papa could spare her until autumn.

All the way to London Julian berated himself. The truth was, he had half forgot Vincent after their quarrel, had wanted to forget him. Now there would be more scandal and, of course, more debts. He could only hope he had not lost Vincent irretrievably.

The imperturbable Horrocks had seen to it that Vincent was released. Julian half expected his brother to have run off somewhere—the Continent, perhaps. It was not unheard of. The solicitor was able to reassure him on that head.

"No, your lordship, I have established Mr. Stretton in a decent inn and discharged his immediate debts." The man pursed his lips. "He is, er, rather restive, however. May I say I am relieved to see you, sir."

"You may say it," Julian replied grimly, "but I hope you've not set his back up."

Horrocks looked startled. "I merely instructed him to await your arrival. I was sure you yourself would wish to explain to him the grave nature of his offence...."

Julian swore.

"But, my lord, the scandal...."

"Damn the scandal. He's probably mad as fire."

"So *you* should be, Lord Meriden."

"No, I should not, sir. I've played hob with Vincent's feelings from the first. When he came to me I jawed at him, and the upshot was he wouldn't confide in me in time to prevent this fix." He saw that Horrocks looked stunned and broke off. Wounded him in all his principles at once, Julian thought ruefully. He hoped he should deal better with Vincent. He made himself stand up.

"I'm obliged to you, sir. Will you give me my brother's direction? I should call on him without delay."

Horrocks mumbled something indistinct about whippersnappers but complied.

"Thank you."

"My lord, there's a deal of business—"

"Yes, I know. *You* decide where the next mortgage falls and allow me to come to terms with my brother. First things first."

"My lord—"

"I know. I'm damned unreasonable. I'll wait on you tomorrow."

By the time he found his brother, Julian was wishing Vincent in hell and himself in Yorkshire. His left leg ached abominably, the other throbbed from the punishing ride, and he was not sure he could stand.

The inn, when he found it, was constructed entirely in staircases. The only humour Julian could console himself with as he stumbled after a disapproving maid lay in the inn's obvious unsuitability to a man of Vincent's parts. It was actually *in* the City.

"Dash it, what if one of m'friends should see me!" Vincent moaned.

Julian forbore to point out that Vincent's friends might be taken aback to see him in prison also and that it was highly unlikely that anyone—let alone one of those dashing tulips—should find him at all at the White Rose, for so, improbably, the inn was called.

Content to let his brother air all his grievances at once, he kept silent and sipped at the brandy Vincent had called for and tried to think of what he ought to say himself. He was concentrating so deeply that when Vincent did leave off, Julian did not at once notice the strained silence.

He looked up.

"I suppose you'll ship me off to India."

"Good God, why should I?" He was startled not so much by the silliness of the proposition as by the real fear he saw in Vincent's eyes.

"I daresay you'll want me out of the way."

"If Horrocks has been ringing a peal over you for the scandal—"

"You can't like it."

"No." Julian began to feel some amusement. "I don't, but I shan't be going about in Society, so it doesn't matter to me a great deal. *You* will feel it, no doubt."

"My sisters...."

"Blooming, thank you."

Vincent essayed a small smile.

"These things blow over, Vincent. If you rusticate for a time...."

"Where?"

"Meriden, I thought, if you can bear the company."

Vincent was silent.

"I know," Julian said. "It's dashed dull."

Vincent looked up, and Julian saw with some astonishment that there were tears in his brother's eyes.

"I'd like it of all things."

"Then go home tomorrow, unless you've grown so attached to the White Rose that you can't bear to leave it."

To Julian's relief, Vincent gave a shaky laugh. "They stare so. And the dinners, only two removes...."

"Then by all means go home," Julian said cordially. "Perhaps you can work your way through Cook's plain little dinners. *I* can't."

Another glass of brandy and a pinch of his own blend of snuff—for

Horrocks had caused his traps to be rescued as well as his person—soon restored Vincent's spirits.

Julian's spirits were less volatile. He felt the consequences of his own ignorance. Vincent, after all, was a stranger still. It was easy enough to read the surface, easy to suppose nothing much lay beneath. He thought there might be more to Vincent than high shirtpoints and an exquisite neckcloth, but he wasn't sure.

He decided on bluntness. "Vincent, I'll have to know the full extent of your debts."

His brother flushed. "If you're going to start in—"

"I've no wish to comb your hair with a joint stool. Sneck up." I sound exactly like Will Tarrant, he thought wryly. "When I settle for you, I'd liefer settle everything at once. Billets-doux from Harry's creditors still come in from time to time."

"Did ... was my brother in deep?" Vincent asked shyly.

Julian hesitated. Harry might have been a shocking loose screw and up to his neck in the River Tick but he was a hero still to Vincent.

Vincent took the lead from him. "I'm sorry. It's not my affair," he muttered in hurt tones.

Julian said quietly, "Would you like to know how things are left? I was very surprised when I found that Horrocks had not laid the circumstances before you on my father's death."

"I wasn't a legatee."

"You mustn't refine too much on that. It was mischance, not intent. Horrocks is a letter-of-the-law man, however. If you like, I shall instruct him to show you how things stand."

To his surprise, Vincent leaned forward. "Would you dislike it, sir? Not *knowing* is the devil."

"It is at that." Julian regarded his brother thoughtfully. "I'm calling on Horrocks tomorrow morning. Postpone your escape for another day, and I'll put him to answering your questions."

"Not sure I'll ask the right questions," Vincent said with such unexpected shrewdness that Julian smiled.

"Then we'll both ask. Between us we should devil the truth from him.... Vincent?"

"Yes?"

"I've seen the letter of instruction my father intended Harry to follow. Did you know the provisions?"

"No. That is, Harry happened to mention I was to have Fern Hall. It ain't entailed," he added defensively.

"I know. Did he mention the mortgages?"

"Mortgages?"

"Two," Julian said drily.

"I say, how paltry!"

"Well, I thought so. I considered breaking the Rosehaugh entail—it's not so encumbered and the house is in better repair—but Horrocks says it's impossible as things stand." He hesitated, then said carefully, "Besides, from what little I knew of your interests, I wondered whether you'd care to spend your time overseeing an estate."

"I daresay you think I'm a dashed fribble."

"I don't think that. I didn't know. Do you want to manage land?"

"Oh, if it was mine—" Vincent stammered. His face fell. "I don't know the first thing about it."

"There's nothing to prevent you learning."

"I'm one-and-twenty," he said glumly.

"Past praying for."

"Well, sir, you can't deny I've made a hash of things lately. I'd be a cawker if I expected you to believe I've got a head for figures."

Julian bit back a grin. "There's more to land than ciphering."

"Yes, dash it. What thingummies go in what field and how many sheep to the acre. I'd make a mull of it, sir."

"I think you'd learn soon enough, but that's by the way if you don't wish to. Fern Hall or Rosehaugh—or whatever property I may be able to settle on you—will need a master. If you'd liefer not be tied to land, I'll fix the equivalent in monies on you to do with as you wish. Not just immediately. As soon as may be. But you must tell me what you wish to do, Vincent."

Vincent's beautiful brow furrowed in unaccustomed thought. Watching him, Julian reflected that it must be difficult to grow up so entirely innocent of purpose.

"You needn't decide just now," he said gently.

Vincent started and flushed. "The thing is, sir, if I could just try my hand...."

"Oh, if that's the problem, I've been needing help at Meriden these two months past. I'm my own agent, you know, and my experience is not precisely vast."

"What happened to Peavey?"

"He was milking the estate."

"No! I didn't like him above half, but I'm dashed surprised. I say, sir, you've taken on rather a lot of work."

Julian preserved his gravity. "It would seem so." Since his arrival at

Meriden, he had been up at dawn riding most of the day from one property to the next and rarely cleared his—or rather Peavey's—desk before midnight.

"Well, I don't know what I can do, but I'd like to try."

"Thank you."

Vincent looked down at his shapely hands. "I know very well I should be thanking you. You're dashed generous, Meriden."

There was a bad taste in Julian's mouth. Lord Bountiful. Not for the first time he felt a rush of anger toward his deceased parent. It was bad enough that a grown man like Vincent should be placed in the position of dependent to a brother a mere six years his senior, but that that man should know rather less about making his way in the world than a day-old chick seemed to Julian an equally grave crime. He resolved that the same fate should not befall his younger brothers. Now, however, he said merely, "If that's the way you feel, you can pour me another sniff of your brandy. Gratitude gives me the headache."

Vincent stared. "You're bamming me, I daresay."

"No. I assure you."

Vincent began to grin. "Well, I'll be—"

"Dashed," Julian supplied helpfully.

Vincent returned alone to Meriden within the week. Aside from looking unnaturally pale and subdued, he did not appear to have taken permanent harm from his sojourn in a sponging-house. He said very little about it and even less about his rescue.

Lady Meriden killed the fatted calf. She wept over Vincent in the privacy of her rose-scented boudoir and even exerted herself so far in his honour as to appear at dinner two evenings in a row, once in grey and once in purple. If Vincent expected Felix and his sisters to make much of him, however, he was doomed to disappointment. Maria avoided his eyes. Drusilla stared. Felix, deprived of these expedients, was more forthright.

"Where's my brother?" he demanded.

Vincent looked rattled. "In London. Dash it, Felix, how should I know? Left him in London."

Felix continued to scowl. "It's been more than a week. If he don't come back it's your fault."

So *that* had been Felix's fear. Jane said hastily, "He'll return soon, Felix. His lordship no doubt has affairs in Town that require his attention."

"That's it." Vincent cast her a grateful look. "Left him closeted with old Horrocks."

Felix grumbled into his meat.

"You *were* on terms with his lordship when you left him?" Jane ventured cautiously.

Vincent avoided her eyes. "Oh, yes. Dashed civil when he wishes to be, Meriden. Told me to come on home and do the pretty. Gave me orders for his bailiffs, as a matter of fact."

"Did you execute them?"

"Who, the bailiffs?" Vincent laughed heartily. "Yes, yes. First thing." He sobered. "I say, Jane, I don't know why you should be asking me such devilish questions."

Jane regarded him silently.

He flushed. "Gave him my word. Dash it, a gentleman don't go back on his word."

"Only, I collect, on his debts," Jane murmured and regretted the jibe at once. The old Vincent would have flared at her. Now he merely mumbled something indistinguishable and took to poking at his dinner in a disheartened fashion. No spirit.

Lady Meriden showed no want of emotional vigour, however. She broke into lamentations and gave Jane to understand she was out of grace.

For two days her ladyship did not send for Jane. As Miss Goodnight was capable of coping with her aunt, Jane relished the respite. She took Maria and Felix into Whitchurch and spent a good amount of time finishing the long-deferred green walking dress. It became her charmingly, though it *was* dashing, and she determined to wear it if only to provoke Meriden to satire. If he had been tied so long to his man of business, he would require cheering. Vincent must have got into deep water.

On Tuesday morning she donned the gown and walked nearly an hour in the garden. In vain. Meriden had not returned. Wednesday she repeated the fruitless process and felt such disappointment she began to wonder why it should be so.

Two minutes of reflection showed her the absurdity of her reasoning. Because she had taken pleasure in the moments of conversation she had had alone with his lordship nearly every morning, she supposed he must regard the encounters with the same pleasure, even look forward to them. Whether she wore the green dress or did not made little matter. What was grave, very grave, was that she had insensibly grown to depend upon Meriden's presence for some part of her comfort. Felix, even Maria and Drusilla, must entertain such feelings with justice. They were Meriden's dependents. She could not. She *would* not.

Next morning she came down late dressed in her oldest muslin and, having eaten with Felix, persuaded him to walk with her. As he was cross as crabs she revelled in her mortification. For some little time, for they soon exhausted the weather as matter for conversation, they paced along the low terrace without speaking. As they turned to go in, Meriden came up the first steps.

Jane stopped short.

"I hoped I should find you here," he said, smiling.

Jane swallowed and managed to return the smile.

Unfortunately there was no time for her to respond as she wished, for Felix, his face glowing, shouted, "Julian! I thought you'd never come!" He turned and took an unregarded step forward.

His brother caught at him, laughing a little. "Well, cawker, I've come. You needn't *spring* at me." He gave the boy a hug and listened to him for some minutes, a hand on his shoulder. "Yes, I perceive you've worked like the devil. Not the entire Haydn sonata?"

"Note-perfect," Felix said modestly.

"Splendid, *maestro*, but you must allow me to form my own judgement."

Felix grinned.

Meriden smiled at Jane. "How do you do? We're a rag-mannered lot."

"Yes, I know, and I don't regard it." Jane smiled, too, though her mouth felt stiff, and taking his other arm walked on into the house with the two brothers.

That his lordship was glad to be home, even glad to see her, she could not doubt, and she should have been more pleased than Felix had she not observed the tired lines about Meriden's mouth and eyes and the stiff, betraying gait. He was dusty and windburnt, and she supposed he must have risen at dawn to ride on home.

She said merely, "Have you broken your fast?"

He had been listening to Felix chatter and turned back to her. "I beg your pardon. Yes. In Dorchester. I put up there last night. How is Lady Meriden?"

Jane's heart sank. "I'm not perfectly sure. She has not spoken to me in two days."

Meriden stopped in his tracks and gave her a wicked grin. "This is news indeed."

"Oh, Mama's in one of her pets," Felix interposed scornfully. She'll come about. I say, Julian, you will hear me, won't you? Now?"

"I must sluice off an inch or so of dust first. Give me an hour, Felix. Here's the stair." He laid a hand on the newel and gave his brother a friendly tap in the right direction. "Go on up and limber your fingers. I expect nothing less than mastery."

Felix grabbed the banister and swung up the steps with jaunty assurance. "An hour, then." He called back over his shoulder, "I'm *dashed* glad you're back, Julian," and vanished.

Meriden said ruefully, "I'm tolerably sure Vincent is in residence."

"How, sir?"

"The effect on Felix's vocabulary. Now what is this about my esteemed stepmother?"

Jane told him of Lady Meriden's state, on impulse adding a description of Miss Goodnight's plot to remove her aunt to Bath.

He looked dumbfounded and kept his grip on the newel.

"What should you do with Meriden Place if my aunt were gone?" she asked, teasing, for she wished for a light answer.

He took a long breath. "Close it. No, to be honest, let it to the first nabob Horrocks should unearth for me." He added rather wearily, "Don't look so dismayed, Miss Ash. I'm fairly sure Miss Goodnight's amiable plan will come to nothing."

Jane murmured a polite disclaimer and watched his slow progress up the stairway. In fact, she *was* dismayed, not so much at the prospect of his closing the house as of his feeling the need to do so. She had to remind herself that he was not deeply attached to Meriden Place and that such a course must seem less desperate to him than it seemed to her—or would seem, she thought with sinking heart, to her Aunt Louisa.

As it happened, the Bath scheme received an unexpected advocate in Vincent. Quite unprompted, he one day suggested to Lady Meriden that she remove his sisters to Bath to give them a taste of Society before their come-outs. It transpired that his principal reason for offering the suggestion was to provide himself with a base in that dowdy but undeniably respectable spa. He found Lyme Regis flat. At least in Bath the Assembly Rooms *were* Assembly Rooms.

Lady Meriden was seldom inclined to put anyone's comfort before her own, but she was still compassionate toward Vincent, and, besides, the idea had apparently been working in her mind with greater vigour than either Miss Goodnight or Jane had suspected.

Her ladyship announced with a sigh that she would enjoy a visit to Bath of all things, that a course of the waters must be helpful to her shattered nerves, but to be finding a house so late....

"I'll find a house for you, ma'am," Vincent said, his eyes lighting. "Dashed if I don't."

He was as good as his word. Abandoning his brother to the bailiffs, he trotted off to Bath of a Monday morning and returned on Friday to announce that he had found her ladyship an excellent small house in Laura Place. Somebody's great-uncle had died without warning, and the owners must find a new tenant. Not just anyone, of course, but the Stretton name had worked its way. Lady Meriden had only to instruct her lawyers to see to the lease and the house would be hers in mid-June.

Lady Meriden, appalled by the precipitate course of events, nearly balked at the gate. If Jane or Miss Goodnight had tried to cajole her, she would certainly have scratched. Vincent had greater address, however. In no time at all his charm worked its way, and it only wanted Meriden's disapproval to convince her ladyship to begin at once her preparations to remove.

Jane broached the matter to Meriden next morning at breakfast.

"So you see, sir, if only you will contrive to raise some objections, the thing is done...."

He looked dazed. "Very quick work, Miss Ash."

"Oh, I did little enough. It was all Vincent." She explained Vincent's miracle, and after a stunned moment Meriden began to laugh softly.

"I'm very much obliged to Vincent."

"Then tell him so," she urged. "He wants your encouragement, sir, for he is still a little in awe of you, and he has been so well conducted lately."

"Yes. I begin to think Vincent was meant to be a country squire; he plays the rôle so well. You don't think he'll run amok from an excess of rural virtue, do you?"

Jane smiled but said thoughtfully, "He is country bred, after all, and I believe his recent, er, experience shook him badly. He is glad enough to be home, if only he may escape now and again. To Bath, for instance. Is he a great nuisance to you?"

"No, not at all. He knows the people and they him. I find him helpful." He stared at the dregs of his coffee and grimaced. "He won't like it above half if I let Meriden Place."

"Do you still think it necessary?"

He looked across at her, still frowning a little. "No. It was never necessary—merely expedient. I can't staff Meriden as I ought. The grounds are beginning to look unkempt. And what you so delicately refer to as Vincent's recent experience has put me in a bad road to be making the repairs my tenants need elsewhere." He broke off and said ruefully, "Good God, Miss Ash, I wish you won't repeat any of that to Vincent. His withers are already sufficiently wrung."

"I shall say nothing to anyone," Jane replied, "but I think you underrate Vincent's good nature." And his obligation to you, she added, but to herself.

"He does have a happy disposition, does he not? Well, we shall see. I daresay it would take Horrocks some time to find a suitable tenant. Meanwhile, you feel that I should take up my cudgels to her ladyship's boudoir? I can think of several objections—for one, I don't care to lose Drusilla and Polly so soon. Shall I play the heavy guardian?"

"Excellent, and by all means call Maria Polly, for it is a nickname my aunt abominates, but do *not*, I pray you, drop a word about letting Meriden Place or all is irretrievably lost."

He smiled, a little wryly. "You're a deceitful woman, Miss Ash. A true Machiavel."

Jane flushed. "If I believed my aunt's interests would be better served by staying here...."

"Don't," he said gently. "I know. I shall do my possible with Lady Meriden. This afternoon, do you think?"

"Yes, and I warn you I'll be there, for I'd not miss the encounter for the world."

His eyes lit. "I always perform better for an audience. Shall you invite Miss Goodnight and Vincent as well?"

"No, I prefer closet drama," Jane said with dignity and poured two fresh cups of coffee.

Meriden did not play the heavy guardian. Jane thought he did not play at anything. Instead he attempted to make as reasonable a case against her ladyship's removal as could be made—a disinterested act that did not entirely surprise Jane. He pointed out to her aunt that he intended to supervise his brothers' education and therefore meant to keep Felix by him—and the twins in the school holidays.

Had Lady Meriden's professed need to have her children about her been as sincere as it was dramatic, she would then have abandoned her plan, but she had never intended to take the older boys with her. Little Thomas and his nurse must come—with flashing eyes she dared Meriden to deny her her baby—but she did not attempt any such lionesslike rescue of Felix and the twins. Beyond intimating that her stepson had alienated their affections from her, she seemed ready to Make the Sacrifice.

A few probing questions from Meriden about his sisters' future finally did the trick. Suddenly the move to Bath became a means of rescuing her daughters from his clutches. Jane saw her aunt's resolution harden, and gave a small sigh of relief. Lady Meriden would remove to Bath. She had at last found a Gothic reason for doing so, and nothing would now shake her.

Afterwards in the privacy of the library Jane congratulated his lordship on his adroitness, but he did not seem altogether disposed to be amused by the encounter with his stepmother.

"I'm sorry for Drusilla and Polly," he said bluntly. "They deserve better than to be turned into an invalid's handmaidens."

"Goody and I shall see that they get about and meet other young people."

"If I didn't think so, I *would* kick up a dust. And then, I suppose, Lady Meriden would remove to the Antipodes to spite me."

"Surely not so far," Jane murmured, but he was frowning, abstracted, at his hands and did not seem to hear her.

After a moment he stood up and moved about the room restlessly, coming to a halt once more by his chair. "I suppose I should rejoice, but I wish I could deal with your aunt on a reasonable basis, Miss Ash."

Involuntarily, Jane sighed.

"You don't think it's possible?" He began rubbing the ivory fabric of the chair with one brown hand.

Jane met his eyes. "It's possible, as you, sir, have shown, to deal with my aunt, but she seems to me fixed in unreason."

The lines about his mouth deepened.

"I wish it were not so," Jane said gently.

His hand clenched on the chair back but he seemed to catch himself in the action and after a pause smiled at her. "Sackcloth and ashes. The truth is I shall miss female company. What a delightful prospect—to be mewed up all summer with Felix and Vincent. I'll look forward to the twins' holidays as a composer."

Jane rose, smiling. "Then you must come often to Bath to catechise your sisters on their social accomplishments. A few days in my aunt's company and you'll soon be ready to resume the happy bachelor life."

12

ONE MAY AFTERNOON Jane escaped from the grand packing and sorting marathon and went for a long, solitary walk in the home woods. In spite of surface chaos, the plans for Lady Meriden's removal to Bath were well in hand, and it had been, in general, a pleasant few weeks. Jane was very well satisfied with the world, with the Stretton family, with herself.

The rhododendrons along the avenue that led to the house, the same plantation which had seemed to her so melancholic the previous autumn, now flared with bloom, scarlet and white and pink. On the steep wooded hillside bluebells hazed the ground. She picked a prodigal bouquet, well aware they would wilt before she reached the house again but wanting nevertheless to bring indoors some token of her pleasure.

She was rambling along, humming one of Drusilla's airs and wishing that Meriden would accompany his sister more often on the guitar and thinking that Vincent was being uncommon civil about his rustication and that Aunt Louisa would kick up a fuss when she found Maria down to dinner in that jonquil-hued gown, when a distant crunching and clopping along the drive obtruded on her consciousness. A carriage. She supposed Mrs. Calvert had decided to pay her aunt a call, so she turned as the equipage came bowling into view with the intent of begging a ride.

Papa. Dismay clutched at her. There could, however, be no mistake. Mr. Ash's chaise, rather dusty, pulled up beside her, and her father's florid face beamed down at her.

"Well, Jane, I've come after all."

"So I see, sir. And Jack. What ... that is, I'm glad to see you, Papa. Will you be staying long?"

Mr. Ash looked mysterious. "We'll see. All well here?"

"Oh, yes," Jane said, rather faintly. She was tempted to afflict Felix with the chicken pox or claim an outbreak of typhus in Whitchurch. Why must her father come now when everything was going so well he must see at once that her presence at Meriden was no longer necessary?

"Climb up, Jane, and leave off your chattering," Jack interposed unjustly. "The team's resty."

She obeyed.

"Ah, this *is* comfortable. We did not look to see you so quick." Mr. Ash patted her hand. "You're in good looks, my dear."

"Thank you, Papa." She stared blankly at the bluebells withering in her hand.

"I daresay you're surprised to see us."

Jane rallied. "No. Your room has been prepared these four months, for I was sure you'd come with each letter you wrote me."

Mr. Ash laughed heartily.

They pulled up before the front steps, and Turvey, alert for once, directed a grinning footman to help Miss Jane down and see to the gentlemen's traps.

Jane led her father up the steps and into the small salon. Jack, she perceived, had fallen into earnest conversation with a groom. She turned to the hovering butler.

"Inform Lady Meriden that her brother has arrived, Turvey. Is his lordship at home?"

"No, miss. He's off to the home farm with Mr. Vincent."

Jane found she was relieved. She did not, for reasons obscure to her, look forward to the meeting between her father and Meriden. She directed the butler to see to refreshment for the travellers and to inform Mrs. Pruitt and Cook of the unexpected guests, and sat down, rather uneasy, on an upright chair opposite her father.

"So young Vincent's here, is he?" Her father gave her a shrewd look. "A bad business."

"His debts? How did you hear? I wrote merely that he had got into a scrape."

"Oh, Louisa wrote me, too. Dithering that Vincent would be shipped off to the colonies. I didn't regard it, of course, but I thought I should lend Louisa my support. The corn's doing well," he added to justify his absence from Walden Ash at so crucial a season. "I'd a scheme to lay before you in any case, my dear, so I packed my gear and brought young Jack along for company. Fine weather all the way, though it promised to be wet." He looked so pleased with himself that Jane's sense of foreboding grew.

"What scheme?" she asked baldly.

"Oh, time enough to talk of that later. Here's Turvey back already. Rheumatism better, eh, Turvey?"

Turvey favoured Jane's father with a discreet smile. "Yes, thank you kindly, sir. I hope the season finds you well."

"Tolerable, Turvey, tolerable. Not getting any younger, though. Yes, yes, excellent." This to a glass of wine and a generous plate of thin-sliced bread and butter. Turvey withdrew discreetly.

Some time elapsed in which Jane's father consumed bread and butter, Jack rejoined them—"Had to see my cattle, you know"—more wine was poured from the crystal decanter, and the remaining viands disappeared.

"Ah, that's better. That's the thing." Mr. Ash sighed and loosened his neckcloth. "Meriden should see to that lower drive of his, Jane. Potholes. Now, my dear, tell me the whole. It was very bad in Vincent, a damned scandal, but there's no vice in the lad for all that. A high-couraged young'un. I hope his brother has not dealt too harsh with him."

Jane compressed her lips. Really. In front of Jack, too.

"Lord Meriden and Vincent are on good terms, I believe. His lordship has settled Vincent's debts."

"Has he? Handsome of him, though I daresay he felt obliged to. Should've prevented Vincent from getting into such a scrape in the first place." He eyed his silent daughter warily. "Not my affair, perhaps, but Louisa—"

"My aunt is a little inclined to exaggerate," Jane said in colourless tones. "How does Joanna go on? The baby is strong, I believe."

"Dashed powerful lungs," Jack uttered feelingly.

Mr. Ash gave his son a reproving look and waxed eloquent about his new grandchild, as Jane had hoped he would. This led to other home news, and Lady Meriden's languid arrival—this time she required only Miss Goodnight in attendance, a favourable sign—prevented further cross-examination.

As soon as she might, Jane pulled her brother from the salon and took him off to the stables on the theory that Thorpe could entertain Jack better than Aunt Louisa. He was inclined to be awed by the size of the outbuildings, but she left him happy enough, deep in horse talk, and slipped up to her room to think. She was fairly sure her father meant to take her home with him, and she had no intention of leaving.

Julian and Vincent found Jack just going on the way up to the house from the stables when they returned. Vincent let out a whoop.

"It's Jack Ash, Jane's brother, y'know. I daresay they've come to fetch her home."

He slid from his mount and, tossing the reins to one of the grooms, ran after the young man, a fresh-faced boy with his sister's unruly brown curls. Vincent caught young Ash at the first terrace steps, shook his hand vigorously, and plunged deep into conversation.

Julian dismounted. He had been preparing in his mind to lose Miss Ash to his stepmother and sisters. Bath, after all, lay in Somerset—a mere day's ride from Meriden Place. It had not occurred to him that they would lose her entirely and so soon, however, and he found he disliked the idea very much, so much that he was a little shaken by the strength of his feelings. After all, why should not Jane's father require her at home?

When he had seen to his horse, he walked slowly across the stable yard and found the two younger men in profound discussion of some mill they had both attended. Presently Vincent caught sight of him and looked flustered.

"I say, I'm sorry. Jack, make you known to m'brother, Meriden. Julian, it's Jack Ash, you know."

Julian shook hands. The boy, who bore an even stronger resemblance to his sister close to, stared at him in an unnerving manner. Shy? Julian tried to imagine Jane shy and failed. He made some innocuous remark about the handsome pair of bays he had observed in the far stalls.

The boy's eyes gleamed. "Complete to a shade, ain't they? Short-legged, powerful shoulders. M'father said they'd never pull together, but *I* managed them." He flushed and added shyly, "Your man, Thorpe, says you had just such a resty pair in Yorkshire."

Julian smiled. "Yes, and he was sure I couldn't hold them. Your father is here, I collect?"

Jack nodded.

"Then I'd best go make my bow. I'll talk with you later. Show Vincent your bays."

"Yes, I will. I say, I'm devilish glad to meet you, sir. I was a Volunteer in Belgium, but I didn't see action at Waterloo."

"Then I daresay you joined in the chase afterwards," Julian said in as civil a tone as he could manage.

"Oh, yes. It was famous sport."

"Don't go prosing on about that again, Jack," Vincent interposed.

Jack smiled in a superior manner as if to say, Who is this mere civilian? and went on to deliver the *coup de grâce*. "You, I collect, was with the Ninety-fifth at the centre. I say, I hope you wasn't badly wounded, sir."

Not so deep as a well nor so wide as a church door....

"I've made a fair recover, as you see. Vincent," Julian said rather desperately, "will you ask Thorpe to check Dancer's left fore? I believe the shoe is working loose."

He made his escape, not at all surprised to find that his palms were damp and his stomach tied in a knot. The prospect of edifying Master Ash with a minute-by-minute account of the battle left him feeling more than a little ill. However, to be snubbing Jane's brother was not in order. He made a resolve to introduce the subject of Portugal, which he did not object to recalling, as quick as might be and hoped the boy would succumb to diversion.

It then occurred to him that Vincent had listened to the exchange with a rather set look about the mouth. A moment's thought reminded him that Vincent knew nothing whatever of his participation in last summer's action and that his brother might justifiably feel that *he* had been snubbed.

He wondered whether he ought to go back and make his peace once more with Vincent or, alternatively, flee the country.

In the first storey corridor he bumped into a tear-slubbered Maria.

"Oh, Julian, they've come to take Jane away!" she wailed. "Whatever shall we do?" She clutched at his sleeve.

As he did not have the least notion of what to do, he stood like a stock for a long moment, patting Maria's hand in an idiot fashion. Suddenly the concatenation of disasters struck at his sense of the ludicrous.

"You might contrive to break your arm," he began to laugh.

Maria stiffened.

"I know, I know. I'm the greatest beast in nature. Go wash your face, Polly."

"But Jane—"

"Her father does have a superior claim," he said gently. "But try and see if you can persuade him to let Jane stay. Are you sure he means to take her with him?"

Maria sniffed. "He hasn't said so...."

Julian felt inordinate relief. "Then perhaps it would be best to let sleeping uncles lie."

She gave a watery chuckle. "Best of my brothers—"

"Polly!"

"I only said it to madden you."

"I'm maddened sufficiently without your aid. Go! You're all bleary and blotched."

"You're covered in dust," she retorted.

"And horsehair and muck and other worthy things. I'm persuaded your mother would go into strong convulsions at the sight of me and that, you know, would sink me further in Mr. Ash's opinion than a little delay. Do go down again directly. After you've scrubbed your face."

"Is it so very bad?"

"Revolting."

At that she took herself off with a saucy flirt of her skirts. He reflected in an absent-minded way that Maria showed marked improvement over the watering pot he had met in March. That, in turn, recalled his first encounter with Jane, over cold buttered eggs, and his previous gloom returned.

That evening, sipping at a very tolerable claret, Mr. Ash had leisure to reflect. His daughter, he thought, was looking a little hagged. That must be laid to Louisa's door. Indeed a deal of pother might be laid to Louisa. She was, her loving brother decided, a damned tiresome female. When he considered the crossed and recrossed pages of fustian he had troubled to decipher in the past year, not to mention losing Jane for long months, he found himself wholly out of patience with her ladyship. Let her go off to Bath with Miss Goodnight and her daughters. *His* daughter deserved a kinder fate.

As for Meriden, Mr. Ash could find nothing in him to dislike except a deal of reserve and too little idea of his proper consequence. Lord Meriden's tenants should wait on Lord Meriden, not vice versa. Mr. Ash could not approve this business of his lordship acting as his own agent. Shabby-genteel. Encouraged familiarity. He wondered where the lad had imbibed such radical habits. Not surely in Lord Carteret's household. Old Carteret had been as high in the instep as anyone. The fault couldn't be laid at *his* door that his grandson was to be found in the stables jawing with a common groom and puffing a great vile-smelling seegar. Filthy practice, smoking tobacco. Snuff, now, that was a gentleman's habit. Mr. Ash took a pinch of the finest and sneezed in a satisfying way. Cleared the tubes.

The gentlemen were sitting around the cleared table, the ladies having withdrawn, and Jack was prosing on about France. Although Meriden listened with the appearance, at least, of interest, Vincent looked devilishly bored. Mr. Ash considered diverting the conversation into new channels, decided it not worth the effort, and retired once more into his own thoughts.

He didn't wish to judge Meriden severely. Louisa was too willing to do that. It beggared wonder that, her rackety husband safely dead, she had elevated him to the rank of a minor deity and now wasted energy objecting to trivial changes—such as Meriden's refusal to wear knee breeches to dinner and his practice of riding out before breakfast— merely because her late spouse would not have done so. Nor did Mr. Ash see any harm in sending the twins to school. Dashed sensible idea. Took the brats out from underfoot.

But closing off the better half of the house, now, that was not to be lightly dismissed. And disposing of Harry's racing cattle. And selling up the London house. Cheeseparing. Mr. Ash was glad his sister's portion had been secured to her for her daughters. Otherwise there was no telling what might happen. He was seriously concerned for his nephews.

Young Vincent, as Meriden's full brother, must remain Meriden's affair. At least those shocking debts were settled, but Mr. Ash meant to confront Meriden over Felix and the twins and young Thomas. Their futures must be secured. Accordingly, when a suitable pause in Jack's military narrative ensued, Jane's father asked Meriden the favour of a private interview next evening.

Meriden looked puzzled but acquiesced politely, adding, "I had meant to ride with Vincent to Fern Hall tomorrow on a matter of business. If you and your son care to join us...."

The prospect of escaping Louisa's natter appealed. "Why, yes. Thank you. Civil of you, Meriden."

Vincent brightened at once and began describing to Jack the first-rate fishing to be had in the neighbourhood of Fern Hall, and if Julian should not object, perhaps they might spend an hour or two angling. He knew a pool....

Meriden did not object, but excused himself from joining them. Mr. Ash let out his breath gustily. He was not partial to fishing, a dull sport, and damp besides.

Meriden cast him an amused glance and suggested that they rejoin the ladies. As Mr. Ash wished further talk with Jane, he offered no objection. Unfortunately he could not get her to himself.

Lady Meriden's presence in the withdrawing room dampened any disposition to unseemly high spirits the party might be feeling. Felix, scowling terribly, was made to accompany Drusilla in several songs. Miss Goodnight, too, was persuaded to play, which she did, briefly and sedately. Maria recited a very dull poem. Lady Meriden then rose majestically and announced that, as it was past ten, she must retire. That she expected everyone to follow suit was apparent. Felix, the girls, and

Miss Goodnight complied, nor did Jane object. Mr. Ash wondered if his daughter was avoiding him.

However, after the men had talked a bit longer, after Jack and Vincent had disappeared (gone off to the village, Mr. Ash supposed), and after Meriden had also excused himself and vanished (into the agent's office, so far as Mr. Ash could tell, though it seemed unlikely at that hour), Jane came to him.

"Did you wish to see me privately, sir?" She led him to the library where a pleasant fire glowed and settled him into a chair that was almost as comfortable as his favourite chair at home. What a good girl she was.

"I'm sorry Aunt Louisa required me before dinner."

"Well, well, it's no matter. I felt the fatigues of my journey, you know, and took a nice snooze. Now, Jane, what is this about Bath?"

"Aunt Louisa has determined to take a house there next month. She wishes to drink the waters and also I think to enjoy a little of the Society to be had there."

"How long does she propose to stay?"

"Until Maria's come-out. After New Year."

"Good God!"

"Pray do not say you object, Papa. We were hard put to persuade her."

"Was the plan yours?"

"Miss Goodnight's. I concurred with it, however. My aunt does not deal comfortably with Meriden."

"Very true," said Mr. Ash with feeling.

"And I believe her health must improve if she goes out more. She is sometimes very low."

"If Meriden—"

"No, Papa," Jane said firmly. "It is entirely my aunt's doing. She takes a pet whenever he makes the least alteration in what is, after all, *his* household, or she imagines herself to be ill and takes to her rooms for a week. He has at no time suggested that she remove, even to the Dower House, but she will never act his hostess. It cannot matter now. He must sooner or later desire to receive company, however, and for my aunt to be languishing about like a ghost will, you allow, create difficulties."

Mr. Ash said cautiously, "You take his lordship's part, then."

Jane sighed. "No, Papa, but I am obliged to say that my aunt is a trifle unreasonable. I think the Bath scheme an excellent one. I shall, of course, remove with Aunt Louisa and my cousins."

"No, you will not," Mr. Ash said firmly.

121

Jane stared.

"Your Aunt Hervey has taken a house in Brighton for the summer. She desires you to join her."

"But I don't wish to go to Brighton."

"Jane, you are four-and-twenty. To mew yourself up with Louisa is what I will not countenance. You may say that you'll go about at Bath, but I know Louisa and I know Bath. Show some sense, girl. You must meet young men."

"Not, I collect, younger than I."

"You will mend your tongue with me, miss."

"I beg your pardon, sir, but I *will* not go to Brighton." She bit her lip.

Mr. Ash steadied his temper with an effort. "I am sensible," he said carefully, "that you have shown more than your duty to my sister, but she cannot make you her drudge. I won't allow it."

Jane's eyes shone with tears. "Oh, Papa, it's very kind in you and in Aunt Hervey, too, but truly I'd liefer not go to Brighton. Insipid balls and routs. Card parties. Pic-nicking at Lewes and admiring the ruins for the hundredth time. It is not in my style."

"Jane, you cannot wish to dwindle into an aunt."

"No indeed." She drew a shaky breath. "Marriage is the only comfortable state for a female, as things are. I am not obliged to go out as a governess, however, if I fail it, and I will not marry some puffing idiot merely to escape aunthood."

"That puts me in mind ... young Wincanton has deserted you and fixed his interests with Miss Derwood. Indeed, Jane," he said crossly, "I do not know why you laugh so. Wincanton must have established you suitably."

Jane composed herself.

Mr. Ash eyed her warily. "You're a deal too nice in your notions, miss."

"I could not have borne Edward. If that is overnice in me, then you must be held just in your strictures."

Mr. Ash sighed. "If your affections was fixed on someone, if you'd a *tendre* for Meriden, now, I should not object to your staying. I can't like his nipfarthing ways, but the connexion must be considered eligible."

Jane had gone white. "Papa, do I understand you correctly?"

"Hrmphm. Proximity, you know. Dash it, Jane, I said 'if.' "

Jane said coldly, "I trust Lord Meriden and I are on terms of civility. He is, as you suggest, a most eligible parti. If you suggest further that I have *lurked* about here these last months in the hope of entangling his lordship in my coils...."

"Jane!"

"... you have a very low notion of my character."

Mr. Ash had never been able to deal with his daughter when she took to her high horse. "Here, I say!"

Jane's mouth set in a hard line. "I shall consider Aunt Hervey's kind offer, sir, and give you my decision tomorrow. Good night."

Mr. Ash stared after her. He was wretched, for he doted on Jane, but he was also a stubborn man, and in this he did not mean to be gainsaid. She was a pretty enough young woman, and her means must make her more than eligible. Why she had not fixed on some inoffensive gentleman and established herself years ago he did not know. He did know he wished her safely wed.

Jane spent a miserable and sleepless night. At first she was so angry with her father that she determined to defy him even if it meant a serious breach. She formed wild notions of setting up her own establishment in some remote part of the kingdom, like the Ladies of Llangollen, but she could think of no female friend to join her in exile. Her particular friends had all married.

That thought made her melancholic, and she wept and pitied herself and wondered if she ought not, after all, to have married Edward Wincanton. She must at least then have had her own children. *That* prospect brought Edward's gooseberry eyes and wet hands to mind, and she fell again into a rage, this time at the unkind fates.

Had she been Felix she would have broken every movable object in the room. Being Jane, she contented herself with pummelling her tear-soaked pillow until the feathers flew. She would have laughed at herself at that point had she been less frantic, but she buried her aching head in the covers instead and gradually grew calmer and began to think.

If her father, who was not fanciful, had supposed her to be hanging out for Meriden, what must others be thinking—Joanna, Aunt Hervey, her brothers, the neighbours at home? As for Meriden himself.... She thought of the green dress and the two mornings she *had* lurked in the garden, ready, she admitted, to be private with him, to pounce. And when he did come.... She lay still for a long time and thought.

Meriden was not, à la Vincent, a dashing figure, nor had he his brother Harry's florid good looks. As Miss Goodnight had so reluctantly admitted, he was not romantical. But he had a certain quiet style, and his manners, though not particularly formal, were better than Vincent's. She supposed him to be equal to most situations. That he had contrived to make friends with his brothers and sisters in spite of Aunt Louisa's best efforts argued a deal of address. No, not address. Kindness. At that point she stuck.

At last she brought herself to admit what it was. She liked him very well. In fact, she liked him better than any man of her acquaintance, and, what was even more lowering, she did not like him so particularly because of his kindness to Felix and the others, nor for his common sense, nor for his undramatic acceptance of what must be very heavy burdens, for she had known other responsible, intelligent, kind men. What she liked was his sharp tongue.

She sat bolt upright in the bed and stared at the near-dead fire. No one, surely, formed an attachment from such a flimsy, such an unworthy cause. She prided herself on her judgement. True, she had imagined herself in love with Edward Wincanton's uniform, but that was when she was green and silly. Surely she knew better now. Affection must grow from esteem, not from a shared sense of the ridiculous. To base a marriage on....

Marriage.

I *have* been lurking and laying snares, she thought wretchedly. Papa is right. And Meriden has not shown me the kind of distinguishing notice that would argue any partiality on his part. He enjoys my company, but he also enjoys Felix's company, and Miss Goodnight's, and his sisters'. I believe he is even beginning to like Vincent. Where is the partiality in that? He thinks of me as a ... a useful female. An aunt. Good God, I shall *have* to go to Brighton.

Jane's acquiescence—rather baldly given next morning after breakfast—seemed to her father so unnatural that he brooded over it off and on all day. What could she be up to? He had steeled himself for argument, even half considered giving in to her. Tame submission was the last thing he had expected of Jane. Perhaps she was sickening for something.

During the jaunt to Fern Hall, Mr. Ash managed to remark the decay and disrepair everywhere and imparted a good amount of advice to Meriden on how to set things to rights. It even seemed as if his lordship was listening. But, for once, Jane's father's mind was on Jane, not on agriculture.

Once arrived, Mr. Ash began the interview with Meriden preoccupied and found it hard to fix his attention on the far less immediate matter of his nephews' education.

Meriden offered him a glass of sherry, which he accepted, and a seegar, which he declined with horror, and, the requirements of civility discharged, waited courteously for Mr. Ash to begin.

Mr. Ash cleared his throat. "No doubt you're wondering why I wished for this private chat, Meriden."

His lordship made a polite noise.

"The thing is, I feel I must speak to my nephews' future."

"Which nephew?"

"All of 'em," Mr. Ash snapped.

Meriden was silent.

"Dash it, Meriden, you must admit things was badly left."

A flicker of amusement showed in his lordship's eyes. "Certainly."

"Well ... ?"

"You mean, I collect, to require some assurance of me—"

"Not my place to *require* anything," Jane's father said with dignity. "I'm sensible of your position as guardian."

"Thank you, sir, but I'm not sure you understand the position at all."

"Well, upon my word!"

Meriden ignored the outburst. "Legally, I can do precisely as I please. There was a letter of instruction directed to Harry, however."

"Do you mean to honour your father's wishes?"

"Will you read this document, sir?" He reached into his coat and withdrew a parchment sheet. Catching Mr. Ash's bewildered gaze, he said drily, "I supposed you must want to speak with me either of your sister or of her children, so I came prepared."

"Oh." An unnerving young man. Mr. Ash took the proffered document.

"I wish you will read it with your nephews in mind."

Mr. Ash read. It took him some time, for the letter was couched in flowery and obscure language. When he thought he had grasped most of it, he looked up. Meriden regarded him with raised brows.

"It ain't generous, but it's a deal better than nothing."

"You were assured, I suppose, that I intended nothing."

Light dawned. Lord Meriden, it seemed, was angry.

Mr. Ash leaned back comfortably. "No need to fly into the boughs. I don't scruple to admit, sir, that my sister sometimes shows less than common sense. I presumed you would provide for your brothers in one way or another. Merely I wished to know some of the particulars." He tapped the paper. "This satisfies me."

"Does it?"

Mr. Ash blinked.

"You're easily satisfied," Meriden said bleakly. "It's a damned ungenerous document and so vague as to give me a very dim view of my father's understanding."

There ensued an uncomfortable silence. A dozen contradictory reflections passed through Mr. Ash's mind. "But your father's intent...."

Meriden grimaced and said nothing.

Mr. Ash ran a finger inside his suddenly constricting neckcloth. He had come prepared to deal in form and found he must address himself to substance. Confound Louisa, he thought, with justifiable wrath.

At last Meriden said rather wearily, "Well, I don't mean to devil you, sir, but I've some difficulty understanding their mother's wishes."

Mr. Ash gave a short bark of unamused laughter. "So I should imagine."

Meriden waited.

"Louisa will be brought to accept any reasonable plan," Mr. Ash said firmly. "I shall see to that, Meriden. You may set your mind at rest."

Meriden regarded him silently for a moment, then smiled a little. "I trust we may not disagree as to what's reasonable. I intend to have Felix prepared for one of the universities."

Mr. Ash stared.

"He is uncommonly bright," Meriden explained.

"But his disability...."

"He'll require a companion, of course."

"Even so...."

"I dislike waste, Mr. Ash."

Mr. Ash rubbed his nose. A most unnerving young man. "Louisa will kick up a dust. I don't know the lad well. Musical...."

At that Meriden did smile. "Perhaps I should propose training him in one of the musical professions—conducting would suit his temper. A mere university must then seem gentlemanlike and unexceptionable to his mother."

Jane's father began to laugh rather helplessly. "Dash it, Meriden, I believe you've taken m'sister's measure." Mopping his eyes, he said, still chuckling, "Do as you judge fit. I'll give you what support I may."

"I'm obliged to you, sir."

"You mean to send the twins to Harrow, I collect?"

Meriden nodded. "Next year. They're badly prepared."

"I daresay. Wild as Mohawks, ain't they? I suppose you'll fix 'em in some respectable profession...."

Meriden's mouth quirked. "Respectable? You cannot have made their acquaintance."

"Well, I have," Mr. Ash said, feelingly. "I wasn't here above three hours last autumn but they managed to bestow a hedgehog in my gear. My shirts was a trifle ripe, I can tell you. Ah, well, my Jack was just such a hell-born brat. I daresay they'll come round."

If Meriden viewed the prospect of rearing two Jack Ashes with less than enthusiasm, his expression did not betray him.

Mr. Ash went on obliviously, "It's early days yet to be speaking of young Thomas. My lord, I'm satisfied as to your intentions. Perhaps you'll inform me from time to time of my nephews' progress. And do not," he added with heavy good humour, "ask which nephew."

Meriden smiled politely. "You've not mentioned your nieces."

"But Louisa—"

"My sisters are nominally in my charge also."

"Yes, yes. Leave 'em to her ladyship."

Meriden looked troubled. "Would you, sir, if they were your daughters?"

Mr. Ash stiffened.

"I've no wish to offend you, Mr. Ash. Perhaps you've not observed it, but your sister is become something of a recluse. Maria has turned eighteen...."

"Can't make her come-out in black ribbons."

"No. After September, however...."

"Lady Meriden," Mr. Ash said coldly, "will take her daughters to Bath."

Had he had proper feeling, Meriden must then have dropped the matter. Instead he said in caustic tones, "Bath is not London."

"Upon my word, sir, you have sold your London house."

"Houses may be let. And there are other choices."

Mr. Ash sniffed. "No doubt you suppose I shall spare you my Jane to lend your sisters countenance."

"Miss Ash has been very kind."

"Well, I take leave to tell you, Meriden, you'll have to form other plans, for I am removing Jane directly. She is a good girl and not past her last prayers by any means. I intend she shall join her Aunt Anna Hervey in Brighton for the summer. After that, we shall see. If Anna wishes to take her to London, be that as it may. My Jane is to be no one's duenna. I expect to see her suitably married and soon, too. Then, perhaps, you may think of foisting your sisters onto her." He stopped because he did not like the dangerous look in Meriden's grey eyes. "Well, sir, you must admit, if you've any sense of justice, that I'd be a sad father to consent to any such scheme."

"Your daughter must do as she wishes, of course," Meriden said in a colourless voice. "I had meant to establish my sisters with my cousin Georgy."

"Lady Herrington?" Mr. Ash was startled out of his wrath. That was high flying indeed. A fashionable and by all accounts a pretty-behaved young woman. If Meriden was on such terms with his Devonshire cousins....

His lordship added, still without expression, "Not, of course, against Lady Meriden's wishes."

Mr. Ash said slowly, "I beg your pardon if I misunderstood you, Meriden. The thing is, Jane has been much on my mind. To bury herself in Dorset for eight months...."

Meriden did not speak.

"She's a good girl."

"My sisters are sufficiently in her debt." Meriden rose, the ghost of a smile in his eyes. "Indeed we all are. I think Miss Ash far too young to chaperon anyone, sir. I'm surprised you considered it."

"I didn't," Mr. Ash said, crossly, rising, too.

He retired shortly thereafter, *hors de combat*, having made at least three persons, including himself, thoroughly unhappy, and, though he told himself he was glad to be rescuing Jane from thralldom, his victory tasted remarkably like defeat.

13

A LETTER FROM the Honourable Maria Stretton to her cousin, Miss Jane Ash. Bath. June 1816.

My dear Cousin,

Mama, Drusilla, Thomas, and I have removed to Bath at last—and, of course, Miss Goodnight. Thank you for sparing us Goody, for we should go on very ill without her.

Bath is the strangest, steepest town, but sadly flat without our Jane. Every day we go to the Pump Rooms, and Mama drinks the waters. I must own, Cousin, I think it very Brave in her, for I cannot swallow more than a few drops myself. Even Goody makes terrible faces.

We do not go to the Assemblies. Mama says that would be Ramshackle behaviour. Perhaps she will take us after September. There are a deal of people to watch in the Pump Rooms and the Municipal Gardens. If they are all rather Old, I am sure they are very diverting to look at. Only think, Jane, a lady in panniers.

How do you in Brighton? Drusilla and I make sure you are gay to dissipation. If you wasn't our Best Friend we should be Envious. Do you think my Uncle will allow you sometime to visit us? Mama said we wasn't to ask, but we miss you sadly.

Oh, Jane, the oddest thing. Julian has let Meriden—the house, not the land. He and Felix and Vincent will live at Fern Hall. Mama disliked the Idea, but Felix shall have his pianoforte and a new Tutor, and the twins will go to Julian in their Holidays. Vincent says they live in the stables anyway, so it can't do them an injury to leave Meriden. Fortunately he does not say so to Mama. It is sad to think of strangers at Meriden, but Vincent says it is only for two years.

Vincent is much Improved, Mama says, so I gather he has left off gaming. He visits us every week. Julian came once, but he and Mama had Words. I wish you was here, Jane, for you know how to soothe Mama better than me or Miss Goodnight. Drusilla is no help. She is mad as fire with my Brother, too.

My duty to my Uncle and my cousins, especially Jack, and to your dear Aunt Hervey.

Yours, etc.

Maria

Post Scriptum: *Julian is come, and he will frank this for me. He has took Miss Goodnight and Drusilla to the Gardens. I hope he will talk Sense to her, Dru that is.*

PPS: *Jonquil is* not *a racketty colour, even if Mama does think so.*

Julian missed Jane very much and thought about her too much. He had tumbled into and out of love with the beautiful eyes of the ladies of Portugal with the celerity of any other young officer, but his circumstances had always prevented him thinking of marriage. When, in the first flush of the illusory peace, he had bought Whitethorn, he had thought of it as a place where children might grow up happily, but marriage as such had not presented itself in his thoughts with any urgency.

He had remarked in a vague way Will Tarrant's domestic happiness. If he had followed the observation, he would have laid most of the credit to Peggy's gentle common sense and not to any virtue in the state itself. He did not think of looking about for a bride.

That winter in London his cousin Georgy, of whom he was very fond, had tried briefly to turn him into a social lion. The damsels she strewed in his way had seemed to him universally insipid and fit only for balls and flirting. He did not object to flirting, but he had certainly been unfit for balls. Georgy, to her credit, gave up the game quickly, before their friendship showed strain.

Thinking back, he supposed his boredom with these worthy young ladies had been due in part to his glum daytime sessions with Horrocks and in part to the ladies' extreme youth. They had all spoken pretty inanities with charm, but showed a disposition to stare when he tried less predictable conversational gambits.

With Jane Ash, he reflected, such inanity as she was capable of grew from strategy. Only once had he seen her thrown into confusion, and that had been in the infamous *fandango* episode. He had been miffed enough that evening to try deliberately to overset her and had instead found her chagrin delicious and her swift recover admirable. Nor was she easy to best in a duel of wit. Indeed, he thought, ruefully and sadly, he had met his match in more ways than one—and recognised the fact too late.

Or was it? Sometimes he thought he would abandon Meriden and Fern Hall and Rosehaugh and all the tedious labour thereto appertaining, fling himself on his horse, and dash off à la Vincent to Brighton. Or, less dramatically, write to Jane. But what should he say?

Could he explain that he might very well murder his stepmother if Jane did not at once, with her gift of laughter, come to his rescue? Or that he had a handsome title, a scandalous name, a very large load of debt, and an extravagant number of dependents to offer her, and would she please come at once to his rescue?

Julian was in the habit of valuing himself rather coldly according to his desserts, and in that summer his opinion of his merits had sunk dismally. Partly it was that, like Othello, his occupation was gone, and he was frightened by his lack of qualification for the work he had taken on. And it had depressed him to let Meriden.

He did not regard Lady Meriden's strictures, but he knew his grandfather Carteret would have thought ill of him for leasing his principal seat to a *parvenu*, however amiable. Better to scramble along in gentlemanly debt forever than sink so low. But the money meant he could repair Fern Hall for Vincent and perhaps pay off something of the encumbrances. More significantly, it meant he could repair some of the injuries his father's neglect had wrought in the estates now and not in some dim future when his tenants' trust must be forfeit and his own sense of justice numbed.

He had let Meriden. If Jane, by some quirk, should wish to ally herself with such disabilities, he could hear in his mind Mr. Ash's response—an outrage to his daughter's consequence. And so it must be.

All the same, he was tempted. The thought of some blade of fashion insinuating his way into Jane's regard and carrying her off to a debtless, carefree life in London—such a life as his cousin Georgy led—set Julian's teeth on edge and pushed him almost into action.

It was only consideration of Jane that prevented him. He needed her far more than she needed or could possibly need him. Her father might dither about her unwed state, but it seemed to Julian that she could marry or not marry at will. Surely the gentlemen of England were not grown so dim-witted as to overlook a woman of her worth, and, as for Jane herself, perhaps she had formed a distaste for marriage. There was nothing, he surmised, to prevent her living a pleasant and useful life quite unwed.

And there was also nothing, nothing whatever, to indicate that she regarded him as anything other than an occasionally conversable cousin-in-law. She had gone off with her father meekly, though Jane was not meek. That argued that she had finally tired of Strettons, of Meriden Place, of him.

When he reached that point in his unhappy reflections, Julian usually threw himself into one of the half-necessary tasks of supervision he could have delegated to Vincent, and rode until he lamed himself or, more unforgivable in Thorpe's eyes, his horse. There would then ensue a brangle with Thorpe in which Julian would puff off his fury, come to his senses, apologise, and, leaving his groom to recover equanimity, set about doing whatever real work he should have been doing in the first place.

Visiting Bath was one of the tasks he had willingly sloughed off on Vincent. However, it soon became apparent from Vincent's reports that his sisters were not happy. Drusilla in particular was homesick. Reluctantly he decided he had best make his peace with her. How that was to be accomplished he did not know, but he felt sorry for Drusilla and knew he would have to try.

When he presented himself in Laura Place of a Saturday morning, his stepmother was fortunately still abed. As the girls and Miss Goodnight had breakfasted, he proposed a walk in the Municipal Gardens. Maria had the sniffles and decided to write letters, so he set off with Miss Goodnight and Drusilla, Miss Goodnight chirping and Drusilla sullen.

The day was sullen, too—grey and sticky and vaguely threatening rain. Bad for the hay, he thought absently. They made their way past the abbey and down the steep steps to the gardens.

"And how is Felix?" Miss Goodnight was saying, puffing a little from the steep descent.

Julian forced his thoughts back to Bath. "Well, thank you. He found the remove a little disturbing, but he's tolerably used to Fern Hall now and gets about without confusion. Mr. Thomas still comes to him."

Miss Goodnight nodded. "Excellent. He must not be kept from his music. And Vincent?"

"Working virtuously. I'm afraid it's dull for him. He wishes for the excitement of Brighton at this season."

"Jane don't like Brighton above half," Drusilla said flatly.

Julian could think of nothing to say to that. He ushered the ladies down one of the paths. The roses were in full bloom.

"She writ it," Drusilla went on. "Didn't she, Goody?"

Miss Goodnight assented, fluttering a little.

"I wish Jane was here. It's so dull without her, and besides she can always talk Mama out of the dumps."

"Dear Jane," Miss Goodnight said soulfully.

A constrained silence ensued. Julian began to feel battered. Abruptly Drusilla turned on him, her round face damp and red with the heat. "Why did you let Meriden?"

"Cupidity."

"I don't know what that is, but I want to go *home*." Her face crumpled, and she ran off down the rose-bordered path, weeping.

Miss Goodnight said in her gentle light voice, "I wish you will go to her, sir. She needs you. Do not regard me. I shall sit on this bench quite cosy and await your return."

Glum and guilty, Julian left her and went in search of his sister. He found her on the stone bank of the Avon glaring down at the fish and sobbing sporadically.

"Dru, come along with me." He touched her arm, expecting her to pull away, but instead, to his horror, she turned to him and began to weep lustily onto his waistcoat.

He led her to a near bench and patted her shoulder clumsily.

"Oh, Julian, I'm so unhappy!" She sobbed a few more times and subsided into sniffles.

"Then mop your eyes and tell me why before that gentleman over there with the swordstick decides to run me through."

She gave a hiccuping chuckle.

"That's better. Here, take my handkerchief."

She tidied herself and blew her nose with vigour.

"You know, Dru," he said cautiously, "you couldn't return to Meriden without your mama, and she assures me she intends to keep her household here."

"I hate Mama."

Julian bit back a conventional rebuke and regarded her tear-smeared face, feeling rather helpless.

After a moment she said in a dreary voice, "Oh, I don't, of course. You needn't look so troubled. Jane would tell me to bite my tongue. But, Julian, I don't *like* the Pump Rooms, and there's nothing else. I'm too young for the Assemblies even if Mama would countenance dancing. I miss the gardens and my pony and our musical evenings and Jane. I miss Jane."

"Yes, but Jane has her own life to lead."

Drusilla sniffed. "Catching a husband. It's not *fair*. What does Jane want with a husband? She don't need p-protection. Jane is equal to anything. And besides she's too old."

"No, my dear, she is not," Julian said wryly.

"Oh." Drusilla stared at him. "Well, when I'm grown *I* shan't want a husband. I shall be a great explorer like Lady Hester Stanhope. Or ... or the Rose of the Pyrenees. *You* know. Goody is always jawing about her."

"Lady Wilbraham? She was a widow."

"Then I'll be a widow."

"An excellent plan. Shall you murder the man or trust to chance?"

"You're funning me." Drusilla stiffened. "I hate you, Julian. I thought you was on my side."

"I hope I am."

"Then take me away from Bath. Take me home." Her large blue eyes, just now rather bloodshot, pleaded with him.

He said as gently as he could, "I can't, Drusilla. It's let."

"Did you have to?"

Julian was silent. He had a fair regard for Drusilla's intelligence and did not wish to fob her off with half-truths.

She looked at the toe of her slipper. "Mama says it's just cheeseparing and ... and shabby-genteel economy. I don't believe that, only, Julian"—her voice thickened—"I didn't think you was a *traitor*."

Julian said carefully, "I didn't have to let Meriden. I had a choice, Dru, and perhaps I judged wrong. What do you know about mortgages?"

"Oh."

"There are rather a lot. I'd prefer fewer. I have Vincent and the boys to think of, you know. In a few years, perhaps sooner, Vincent will need his own establishment. My father wished him to have Fern Hall."

"But you've moved everybody there."

"A house that's lived in stays in better order than a house that's left to rot. Because I let Meriden, I can repair Fern Hall and be sure that Meriden is cared for as it should be, too, and not left half closed and understaffed." He took a breath.

"Why didn't you use the Dower House? It's empty, and at least we should be able to *see* Meriden."

Julian hesitated, frowning.

"I know," Drusilla blurted, with uncommon shrewdness. "Mama wouldn't let you have it. Of all the paltry things—"

"I didn't ask," Julian interrupted. "Don't take on so, Dru. Meriden's only let for two years."

"Two years!"

"Lord, you'll be eighteen then and doomed to a season of balls and routs, won't you? It's very bad of me. Can you think of another solution?"

Drusilla sighed. "No. I'm sorry I called you a traitor, for I can see you're being sensible. I wish Mama was sensible. I wish *I* was sensible."

"You're very well as you are."

"Do you think so?" She brightened. "Julian! The very thing! I'll come to Fern Hall and act as your housekeeper." She stared at him wide-eyed, daring him to laugh at her, but he had seldom felt less like laughing. "I know all about it—counting the linen and bottling the soft fruit and keeping the keys to the wine cellar. And I've a head for figures. Everyone says so. I should sing for you whenever you liked and ... and be civil to Felix."

Julian cleared his throat. "It's very kind in you, Dru."

"But you don't want me."

"I'd like it very well. Your mother would have a few objections—"

"Pouf! You don't care what Mama thinks!"

Julian was taken aback by her certainty. "Does she believe that? She's wrong. I prefer to live on good terms with her, and so should you, Drusilla. She's your mother."

"I wish I was an orphan."

Involuntarily Julian grinned. "Do you know, I've been feeling that way myself. If everyone could be orphaned at birth, life would be much simpler."

Drusilla gave a snort of startled laughter.

"We should go back to Miss Goodnight. Be civil to your mother, and try to like Bath, at least for now. I've decided to take the twins to Harrow in the autumn."

"May I come? Oh, famous! Jane took us to London, you know. When you closed the house last autumn."

"Did she?"

"Yes, Maria and me looked like crows, all in black, but we had a splendid time with Jane's Aunt Hervey. Oh, Julian, shall I write Jane and tell her?"

"No!" He spoke more sharply than he had meant to.

Drusilla's face fell.

"You must not be troubling Jane, Drusilla."

"Why do you call her Jane when we talk and Miss Ash when you speak with her?" Drusilla asked, starting a hare.

"Perhaps because she always called me sir," Julian snapped. "Now, attend to me for a moment or I'll rap your knuckles. You're not to say a word to anyone about this. Not even Polly. If, er, anyone got wind of our plot...."

"You mean Mama, I collect."

"You're a deal too quick, miss. Stop giggling. You're confusing the gentleman with the swordstick."

"I wish you had a sword," Drusilla said fervently.

As it happened, Julian did—rusting away in an attic at Whitethorn. "Good God, why?"

"I could swear on it, like Hamlet's ghost."

"Oh. Well, rest, perturbéd spirit, and if you don't stop whooping like that I shan't be able to show my face in Bath again. Come, not a word to anyone." He stole a quick look at her now smiling face. "And I think you'd best try to look downcast. You ran off wailing like a banshee. Miss Goodnight will sniff out our secret at once if you return too cheerful."

Instantly Drusilla's face became a masque of woe.

"Excellent," he murmured. It occurred to him that Drusilla would someday be a force to reckon with. He hoped she would wait a few years to exercise her wiles.

Jane did not like Brighton. She did not like the young men her aunt put her in the way of meeting. They paid her graceful compliments, one danced magnificently; one brought her posies in silver holders; one read her poems of his own composition. She endured their attentions. She was courtesy itself. She even agreed, when the invitation came, to go once again to the Prince Regent's pavilion, there to swelter through a concert of ancient music in toplofty company.

Indeed Jane was conformable, pretty-behaved, docile. She curbed her tongue, she was sweet, and she did not fool her Aunt Hervey at all.

"Are you sickening for something?" her aunt demanded shortly after Jane had been cast into the dismals by Maria's letter.

"No!" She caught herself. "That is, thank you, Aunt. I'm well enough. The weather is a trifle gloomy, is it not?"

Aunt Hervey gave her a strait look. "I must say, you was never used to be dull company. My dear, are you homesick?"

136

Jane essayed a smile. "Aunt, I am sorry. You've been kindness itself, and I'm making you an ill return. I'm not homesick. How could I be? Joanna is so puffed up in her own consequence, I'd liefer keep away from Walden Ash. Truly I'm just blue-devilled."

"If I didn't know it was nonsense, I'd say you was in love."

Jane did not reply.

"Well. Who is it, my dear—Meriden?"

Jane startled her aunt—and herself—by bursting into tears.

Aunt Hervey comforted her, and when she had at last had her cry out, sat next her on the chaise longue regarding her thoughtfully. "What was your father about, I wonder, to drag you home? An unexceptionable connexion."

"Aunt!"

"No need to fly into the boughs with me." Jane's aunt pursed her lips. "I thought John was up to something ill-considered, but I did wish for you, my sweet. Hervey is not the liveliest company these days, and I miss my girls."

"I came very willingly."

"Then the more fool you." Unexpectedly she added, "I met your young man last winter at one of Georgy Herrington's musical evenings. Not just in the ordinary style, perhaps. The limp must be considered a sad blemish...."

Jane said nastily, "Did you examine his lordship's teeth? 'A good horse but a trifle short in the hocks.' "

"Jane!"

"I beg your pardon." The dreary mood descended again.

"I've nothing to say against Meriden," her aunt continued in a milder tone. "He is not a man of his father's stamp, but that must be to the good. Not but what his late lordship was a dashing blade in his day." She frowned and added cautiously, "My dear, this man is so very *quiet*."

Off guard, Jane blurted, "Then he must've been on his best behaviour when you met him in London. He has the most deplorable, ill-timed, sharp-tongued sense of humour. Aunt, what in the world shall I do? He regards me as a ... a cousin."

Aunt Hervey stared.

"I'm besotted," Jane wailed. "No. That's not true. I was besotted with Edward Wincanton. I don't know how to explain .... The thing is, we go on so comfortably, Meriden and I. Lord, that sounds as if he were an elderly uncle, and I don't in the least think of him as an uncle. The thing is ... the thing is," she said, rushing it, "we laugh at the same things."

There was a pause. Aunt Hervey said firmly, "You should never have left Dorset."

Jane swallowed to ease the ache in her throat. "I left because I found out my feelings, and I think ... that is, I know he could not return them, and if I stayed I should have begun to cast out lures, which is what everyone would think I had been doing all along, and he is too good a man to be snared. Aunt, I can't bear it."

"I must say, I had never thought you lacking in common sense," Aunt Hervey snapped, indignant. "This is a fine time to develop scruples. The world is ordered for the convenience of men. They have every advantage. To balk at the few poor weapons available to you—"

Jane broke in upon her without apology. "We aren't speaking of Men and Women. We're speaking of me and Julian Stretton."

Her aunt was unimpressed. "And you're unique, and he's a paragon. Pouf! I'm sure I hope honour will make you a pleasant bedfellow."

"Aunt!"

"And don't take that missish tone. My dear Jane, I am very sorry for you, and I'm sure Meriden is a good kind of man, but you might consider this. You are a handsome, lively young woman of excellent birth and comfortable fortune. All the obligation would not be on your side, if Meriden were the most eligible *parti* in the world. Which he is not. His name is just now under a cloud of scandal, his estates are debt-ridden, he has a parcel of dependent brothers and sisters to look out for, and he is stepson to the most tiresome woman it has been my fortune to meet, even if she is your father's sister." She drew a breath. "Indeed, Jane, he would be fortune's child to win you."

Jane laughed reluctantly. "What a splendid King's Counsel you would have made, Aunt. It's no good, however. I may be hen-witted and a traitor to my sex, but I will not lurk about setting snares for Lord Meriden." She recalled the episode of the Spanish *guitarra* and how rapidly the tables had been turned on her, and smiled a little. "He would perceive my duplicity directly, in any case, for he is quite the *quickest* man of my acquaintance. I should like at least to keep his friendship."

Jane's aunt looked depressed. "Your scruples don't forbid you to write to his sisters, I hope."

"Why, no. They must think it very odd in me if I were to turn the cold shoulder, for we are such old friends."

"And if they was to come up to Town, you would not refuse to see them?"

"No, but I see where your thoughts are tending, best of my aunts, and it will not do. Maria and Drusilla are fixed in Bath. If Aunt Louisa comes to Town I shall certainly visit her. I shall not, however, *use* the girls for my own ends."

Aunt Hervey threw up her hands in despair.

Jane managed a smile. "If I stumbled on his lordship in the park, I'd not cut him. I'm not *bent* on making myself wretched."

Her aunt sighed. "Well, if that is your philosophy, I hope you will at least contrive not to make *me* wretched."

Jane said meekly, "Have I been uncivil? Dear Aunt, forgive me."

"And when you are in that frame of mind, I know very well what to expect. I believe I shall retire to my room and recruit my strength against the coming storm."

Jane gave her an impulsive kiss. "Poor Aunt, what a trial I am, to be sure."

14

IF JULIAN HAD enjoyed anything like a civil state of mind in that wretched, hectic summer, he would have made a push to earn Vincent's friendship. As it was, it took the last dregs of sociability he possessed to shove aside thoughts of Jane and help Felix come to terms with a strange house. With Miss Winchell gone and the new tutor not yet come, Felix had nothing but his music to occupy him, and at times the boy was very crotchety indeed. So Vincent was left often to his own devices.

Vincent's attention to the details of farming showed some steadiness of character, and at times his superior acquaintance with local people was a help, for Julian figured as an unknown quantity to farmers accustomed to Peavey. Except when his devil drove him, Julian was glad to use his brother in the long, wearing rides from one farmhold to the next that had left him stiff and sometimes half sick with pain.

If he did not spend time making Vincent's acquaintance, at least he knew enough not to keep his brother on a leash. He made sure Vincent felt free to go fishing or cubbing or to watch a mill or carouse with the local gentry or run off to Bath whenever he wished. When Horrocks despatched his quarterly allowance and he was once more plump in the pocket, Vincent might, for that matter, have gone in for whatever mild gaming the region afforded. He did not choose to do so, however, and Julian felt relief and some gratitude. He also appreciated Vincent's tact in accepting the leasing of Meriden without demur, but he thought that Vincent was lonely and, at least in the evenings he spent at Fern Hall, thoroughly bored.

Julian wondered how long it would be before his brother's high spirits overcame his determined virtue. To listen evening after evening to Felix play or, worse, to watch Felix and Julian at chess, must drive even the most civil sprig of the *ton* wild. Julian foresaw disaster. He knew the eventual solution—Vincent must have his own establishment—but he was too weary and unhappy and often too preoccupied with the books to find a temporary solution.

He and Vincent came closest to friendship when they talked over matters affecting the estate or Lady Meriden's peculiar household in Bath, but Vincent's reminiscences of the high life put Julian to sleep, and he supposed he was not himself a scintillating conversationalist. At least he avoided lapsing into that most boring of rôles, the old soldier reliving past campaigns.

He would have been astonished to know Vincent's true feelings, for he supposed his brother to be merely marking time.

In fact, Vincent was not often bored that summer. He found the particulars of farming less dull than the fusty rot he had put up with at school, and he took pride in Julian's use of him as an auxiliary. As for missing London, he had been far more frightened by his brush with the bumbailies than he allowed anyone to know. He missed his friends, but he did not miss the sensation of being in over his head with no one to throw him a rope.

Besides that unarticulated but deep sense of relief, Vincent was attached to the neighbourhood as Julian could not yet be. It was no punishment to him to rusticate at home. He renewed acquaintance with childhood cronies, enjoyed his prestige among the daughters of the local squirearchy, and generally had a pleasant time.

True, Fern Hall was not yet fit to receive company—not with carpenters and sweeps and plasterers underfoot—and he did find it a matter for wonder that Julian should bear with Felix every blessed evening, but he supposed his older brother must in fact enjoy listening to a lot of crash-and-tinkle music. As for chess, it was a closed book to Vincent, but, *de gustibus*, he had never believed that everyone must enjoy the same pleasures.

If Vincent felt tranquil languishing in Dorset, toward Julian his feelings were less clear. Harry's ghost stood between the two. Harry had been Childe Harold and Beau Brummel and a high-born Gentleman Jackson and every sort of social hero rolled into one. Eleven years Harry's junior, Vincent had never been his brother's intimate; one is not a crony of the gods. Distance had lent Harry glory, still lent him glory.

If Julian had dared to rail against the dead heir, Vincent must have defended Harry. The hurt was too raw still for the boy to think clearly, but Julian—apart from his one reference to Harry's debts and his single bitter allusion to the duel—didn't speak of Harry at all. True, he had taken what would have been Harry's place, but after the first shock, Vincent could not envy that. He had never seen himself as head of the family, nor, now that he knew how things were left, would he have wished for the honour, not for ten thousand pounds in Consols.

Julian made no attempt to replace Harry, but in a few short months his presence had come to seem reasonable, even a good thing. Vincent no longer hesitated to talk over his troubles with his brother, and that was something that had not happened with either Harry or his father. He could confide in Julian—he trusted him so far—but they were not friends. If his mind had been of a military cast, Vincent would have said he felt like Julian's subaltern.

It was his brother's reserve that baffled Vincent and sometimes hurt him. Julian did not talk about *his* wishes or tastes or troubles. There was no reciprocity. Vincent had been humiliated to find Jane's brother nattering on about Julian's past with greater knowledge than he had himself, and, though it had seemed to Vincent that Julian did not enjoy Jack's prying, Vincent had envied Jack the common experience. His pride was hurt, however, and he was too much afraid of a snub to exercise his curiosity.

So things went: Vincent half confiding, half hurt; Julian withdrawn.

Towards the middle of July, Felix's new tutor arrived, and the company grew rather livelier. When the twins returned from their school, it became very lively indeed.

The tutor came first. Vincent was delegated to fetch the man, whose name was Ned Winters, from Dorchester. The fourth son of a clergyman, he sounded dashed dull. Vincent wondered where Julian had found him.

"I didn't."

"Put a notice in the *Times?*"

Julian looked up from a pile of correspondence he had been buried in and grinned. "'Tutor required for gentleman's household. Must be musician, Latinist, chess master, arm wrestler.' No. My cousin Georgy—Lady Herrington, that is—found the man for me. In general, I trust her judgement."

"Oh, I say, Lady Herrington!"

"D'you know Georgy?"

"Not to say 'know.' Met her once. Famous beauty, ain't she?"

Julian raised his brows. "When she doesn't forget to carry her sunshade, I suppose she's tolerable. Freckles." He bent back to his work, adding, "She's your cousin, too, Vincent."

"I *say!*" The revelation worked powerfully on Vincent's mind, and he formed the intention, if ever he should find himself back in social grace, of pursuing the connexion forthwith. To be admitted to Lady Herrington's salon.... He stared at his ink-daubed brother and tried to imagine

Julian cutting a dashing figure in the elegant company that surrounded the Divine Georgianna, and failed. "Does she ... er, did *you* ... oh, Lord...."

Julian burst into laughter. "Don't look so stunned, Vincent. I grew up with Georgy, you know. She couldn't very well cut an old playmate."

Vincent flushed and grinned. "Dash it, Julian, no one could accuse you of being *tonnish*. I was surprised, that's all."

"Not half as surprised as Georgy's friends. I'll make you known to her the next time we're in Town. You can conspire with her in my reformation."

Vincent smiled uncertainly. He was rather shocked at his brother's cavalier dismissal of a golden social opportunity. To remain outside the higher circles for want of means or connexions was forgivable. To have the choice and decline it ... he wondered if he would ever understand Julian.

"For now," Julian was saying obliviously, "find the right Ned Winters for me in Dorchester. Felix has mated me three times in a row. My self-esteem won't bear many more defeats."

Winters turned out to be a good-natured young man, perhaps a year older than Vincent, who was trying to make up his mind to enter Holy Orders and meantime must support himself. His Greek was good, his Latin excellent, and he had a decided gift for mathematics. To Vincent's relief, he had also an excellent seat on a horse and good, even hands, nor did he seem averse to a day spent fishing.

He played chess very well. That won Felix's grudging approval, for Winters' chief defect lay in a want of advanced musical training. However, Mr. Thomas still rattled over thrice weekly from Lyme Regis. Felix, newly challenged and for the first time made aware of Julian's plan to send him to a university, fairly hummed with activity. Not even the eruption of Horatio and Arthur into Fern Hall disturbed his bliss. All this and a new chess master, too. The twins might put frogs in his boots with impunity. Felix was lord of creation, and what were mere frogs to such an one?

As it happened, the twins gave Fern Hall a cursory look-through, dropped their collections of shells, pebbles, newts' eyes, and bats' toes, and made for the stables. There they found their hero, Thorpe, and a pair of stocky moor ponies. No one had given the boys their own mounts before. Partly from kindness and mostly in self-defence, Julian had bought the ponies and directed Thorpe to instruct his young brothers in proper horsemanship. The twins did not object.

In fact, they vanished into the hills for long stretches of time—Julian's fell design—and when they did reappear on their uncomplaining ponies, Thorpe wore them out currying and polishing, and posting round and round the home pasture. At night they crammed down dinner and collapsed into bed with no strength left to devil Felix or anyone else. Mrs. Pruitt was heard to remark that school had done they varmints a mort of good, and even Thorpe's diminished staff no longer flinched at the sight of them.

It was fortunate that things went well with the boys, for Julian found himself with little time to spare them. That summer rumours of rick-burning and stoning of houses spread throughout the countryside. The weather was bad—wet and dreary—and there was widespread fear for both the corn and hay harvests. Will Tarrant wrote of serious unrest in Yorkshire, though not near Whitethorn. In Dorset, the local gentry nattered about illegal conspiracies among farm labourers, and everyone seemed gloomy beyond reason.

Julian found it hard to understand the roots of discontent. He had seen far greater poverty in Portugal and Spain. In fact, he was looking at England through eyes accustomed to a wasteland, and the placid green countryside seemed to him by contrast almost paradise. But broken walls and leaking thatches he could understand and, thanks to the munificent nabob at Meriden, mend.

It did not occur to Julian that, by using local men to repair Fern Hall, he had prevented some of the want experienced in other areas that year, or that the nabob's careless liberality in Whitchurch redounded to *his* credit. For whatever reason—perhaps because it was his habit to listen when people talked or perhaps because, unlike his father, he was *there*—the Meriden estates suffered little from the unrest.

One notoriously mean farmer attached to Rosehaugh lost out-buildings to incendiaries, however. When Calvert, as MP, begged Julian to call on the lord lieutenant for troops, Julian refused. He wondered in some disgust what Calvert imagined the temper of the countryside would be if it found an army quartered on it.

Though nothing particularly dreadful happened, people required soothing and reasoning with, and that required time and a great deal of jauntering about from place to place. Julian was glad of Vincent's help.

Unfortunately he neglected to say so. Vincent chafed. Through the early dog days, resentment roiled in him like a thunderhead. Finally the storm broke.

Vincent came in late and a trifle bosky, having dined with the Calverts of Rosehaugh, and, deciding it was his duty to apprise Julian at once of the latest rumours of revolution, leapt up the stairs and scratched at the door to his brother's room. No response. The next door, the library, showed a crack of light so he turned the latch and went in.

Julian looked up from the paper-strewn escritoire, frowning. "What is it?"

As he did all too often in his brother's presence, Vincent flushed like a chidden schoolboy. He said sulkily, "Nothing. I dined at Rosehaugh."

"And our esteemed MP persuaded you that the Jacobin uprising scheduled for last Tuesday commences tomorrow instead."

"Something like that. Dash it, Julian, I ain't a fool. Didn't say I believed him."

"Sorry," Julian said in a perfunctory way and dipped his pen in the inkwell.

Ordinarily Vincent would then have withdrawn from the room and gone off somewhere to brood. Tonight, however, he was sufficiently foxed to allow his resentment to fly.

"Thought you wished me t'do the pretty with Calvert, Meriden. No pleasure t'me. Devilish dull cove, Calvert. Prosy. What's more, y'can dash well sh-stop making up tasks for me. Think I can't see through you? Sent old Vincent chousing after Calvert. Send ol' Vincent over to the home farm. Keep'm out of the way. Keep'm busy. Le' the l'il boy play. Jush like the dash twins."

Vincent sat down abruptly. He was sober enough to hear his diction slip and angry enough not to care. "Y'can demned well stop p-patronising me, M-meriden. Not m'father." He eyed his silent brother through a haze of wrath and brandy. "Demned Puritan."

Julian blinked.

" 'f I wasn' unner obligation t'you, wunt stay 'nother day," Vincent concluded. He rose and added with dignity, "Tha's all."

Next morning he woke early with an aching head and a hideously clear recollection of everything he had said.

Whatever his faults, he was not a coward. He sat up resolutely and rang for his man and, when the valet did not immediately appear, even more resolutely dragged himself from the high bed and struggled into buckskins and boots. He was splashing his face with the remains of a pitcher of cold water when his unbelieving and very sleepy man appeared.

"Shave," Vincent ordered.

The stunned valet went into action.

A quarter-hour later, he stumbled into the empty breakfast parlour. There was no sign of Julian or anyone else, but an array of hot chafing dishes and urns reassured him. He puzzled a moment over whether to go in search of his brother or to wait, and decided in favour of coffee.

Just as he stirred his lagging will to action, everyone came in at once—Felix and Ned Winters from upstairs and Julian and the twins from the direction of the stables.

"...and if I hear of either of you riding through standing corn again, I'll have Thorpe nail your ears to the stable door," Julian was saying in dispassionate tones to one of the twins. When he saw Vincent, he stopped short but said merely, "Good morning. Headache?"

Vincent did not respond as he should have liked, for a cackle of general chatter commenced and there was no way to edge in a private word. He mumbled assent and addressed himself to a portion of beef and mustard.

Presently the twins, cramming their pockets with bread, dashed off shouting. Vincent waited. At last Felix concluded the lecture he had been giving Julian on the sappiness of the lesser Latin poets and left on his tutor's arm, not forgetting as they squeezed through the door to extract a promise from Julian to hear the splendid étude he had just mastered as soon as might be. Julian and Winters exchanged grins. The door thudded to.

Vincent cleared his throat. "I say, Julian...."

"We'd best have a talk, hadn't we?"

"Er, no need. Just thought to apologise." He met Julian's eyes and said miserably, "I'm sorry. In my cups."

"You're seven kinds of fool to apologise."

"What?"

"You meant what you said, I collect?"

"Well...."

Julian was not smiling, but there was no rancour in his voice. "We misunderstand each other from time to time, but you know, Vincent, the fault is not always mine. You don't often say what you think."

Vincent stared. "After last night I should hope not!"

At that, Julian did smile. "Come up to the library with me." When Vincent hesitated, he added drily, "The breakfast room is not ideal for privacy. You may enjoy apologising before witnesses. I don't."

Indeed the servants were clanking about in the hall, and so, feeling blank and apprehensive, Vincent went on up to the library with his brother following more slowly. Julian was limping again. Dashed unfair of him, Vincent reflected. Gloom and the residue of resentment stirred in him sluggishly.

"I did mean it," he blurted when they were seated. "What I said about patronising."

"Yes, I know."

"It's true."

"I hadn't thought so," Julian said with evident wariness, "but I don't see things through your eyes. I know it's been dull as ditchwater."

Vincent bridled. "You're wrong there. It's dashed interesting. Old Buford was telling me only last week I've an eye for the land. It was that matter of the Meriden water meadow...." Finding Julian's gaze on him, he flushed. "He *did* say it."

"It was what I should have said. You needn't take to your high horse. I thought you were bored, however. The devil, Vincent, if you like the work, what's troubling you? You've wanted to try your hand, and God knows I've needed your help."

Vincent snorted.

"Why is that so hard to believe? It's true."

Vincent muttered ungraciously, "Good of you to say so, Meriden."

Julian's shoulders sagged. "Oh, very well. I was afraid of this from the first." He took out a stiff sheet of paper. "This is a deed of conveyance. I'll give you your choice. Fern Hall or my Yorkshire property, Whitethorn. You've not seen it. It's small but clear—or will be when the rents come in. Fern Hall's still encumbered. I'll do what I can to help you clear it...."

Vincent stared at him. "Now?"

"Yes, now." Julian began to mend his pen. He looked very tired and very serious.

"Dash it, Julian, you can't do it."

"Why not?"

When Vincent didn't reply, Julian set the pen down and said gravely, "It's not good for you to be kicking your heels here at my convenience. In fact, it's ludicrous. If I were fifteen or twenty years your senior, or if I were someone like Harry whose motives you could trust—"

"I don't mistrust you," Vincent said miserably.

"You trust me enough to know I'll see you established, but you don't trust me sufficiently to go on day after day living and working in my household. I'm sorry for that, for despite what you've been imagining, I do need your help."

"Doing what?" Vincent interjected, torn between shame and exasperation.

"Exactly what you have been doing."

"I've done nothing you couldn't do better yourself."

"I wish that were true," Julian said rather wryly.

Vincent stared.

After a moment his brother shrugged and took up the pen again. "I don't see any other course. You need to be your own man, and I should've admitted that to myself last spring. If it's Fern Hall, I'll fix a rent for the house."

"No!"

"Do you want legal counsel?"

"Dash it, stop talking, will you?" Vincent rose and took an agitated turn of the bookroom. "I was *foxed*, Julian."

"*In vino veritas.*" Julian's mouth twisted in a smile. "Don't refine too much upon last night. I've been expecting some such flare-up for weeks, but I was too blasted lazy to face up to the problem."

Vincent placed both palms on the writing desk. "There's no problem," he fairly shouted.

Julian frowned but said nothing.

"I ain't brainy," Vincent continued, "but I can see a wall when I run into it. You can't go splitting up the estate yet. Dash it, Julian, I don't expect it, and I ain't ready now if I did. It's the trifling bits of work you set me. Riding ten miles over to old such-an-one to find he don't need much more than a plain yes or no, and then ten miles back with nothing to do but watch the leaves wriggle in the wind. What's useful in that?"

"Oh, God, Vincent. Twenty miles...."

"What?"

"I *can't* ride twenty miles of an afternoon."

"Well, dash it, you might've said so earlier."

"I might've, but I don't like to admit it. The stupidity of the world is doled out in fairly equal portions. Allow me mine." He turned the pen, which had begun to look draggled, in his long fingers.

"If I was you," Vincent muttered, "I'd tell me to go to hell."

"No, you wouldn't. Ramshackle manners."

After a moment Vincent grinned. "You're a complete hand, ain't you? I'll wager that paper's a fudge."

"You'd lose. It's exactly what I said it was." Julian pushed the sheet across the desk. "I don't object to admitting I hoped you wouldn't take me up on it, however. You'd've had the devil of a time squeezing the rent for Fern Hall from me."

Vincent examined the document with awe. "Julian?"

"What?"

"Could I keep this by me for a while?"

"Yes, of course." He smiled. "Next time I drive you wild you can fill in the blank spaces." The smile died. "I think I should take you to Yorkshire with me. You'd best have a look at Whitethorn."

"If you're starting in again...."

His brother looked troubled. "No. I don't really mean to force your hand, Vincent, but Whitethorn is clear. This year looks to be rather bad, and I may find it slow going in the next few years in spite of the nabob. I think you should consider taking Whitethorn. You can't want to wait forever for Fern Hall."

"I like Fern Hall," Vincent replied tranquilly.

"Nevertheless I wish you will come with me to Yorkshire."

"Very well. When?"

"September."

"Good God, we can't both be gone then. The harvest...."

"Had you intended to swing a scythe?"

Vincent grinned. "I might've done."

Julian ignored that and returned inexorably to the point. "I think we'll know the worst by then. I'd prefer to leave later, but I must convey the twins to Harrow in September and, in any case, the bailiffs will survive without us."

"Dash it, let Thorpe take the twins."

"That would be wanton cruelty to Thorpe. Besides I've promised to take Drusilla to London, and I suspect Polly will want to come, too."

"A regular family reunion," Vincent said, disgusted. "D'you know your problem? You're too soft by half. Mark my words, Dru will be after you to take *her* to Yorkshire."

"Then I'll definitely need your protection."

Vincent laughed.

"I'm placing the girls with Georgy," Julian murmured.

Vincent sat up. "Say no more! I'll come. Dashed if I don't."

15

My dearest Cousin Jane,

Only guess *what famous news! We are to spend a month in London with Lady Georgianna Herrington!*

She has writ Mama the prettiest letter "desiring to be better acquainted with her Cousin's sisters." We couldn't guess what she meant, but Vincent says she is his and Julian's cousin and Julian's Friend, and she has found a splendid Tutor for Felix.

At first Mama couldn't like the Idea, but Vincent and Goody have talked her round. Oh, Jane, shall you meet us? Vincent says Julian will bring us to Town when he takes Arty and Horatio to Harrow. I fancy that will be in September, and surely you will also be come to London by then if your Aunt Hervey means to return from Brighton direct to her house.

Do say you will come to our rescue. Her ladyship is fashionable and elegant, and I know *I shall disgrace myself, and if I wasn't so much in Alt I should be frightened to Death. Drusilla says Nonsense.*

Mama has brought Papa's niece Lucy Brackhurst—Lady Brackhurst's eldest and a quiz, *besides doing hideous needlework we are obliged to admire—to live with her, and I don't see it, but they deal famously together. Goody will chaperon us to London and sends you her best Love and wishes you will find her netted purse, for she vows she has left an Ear-ring in it.*

How are my Uncle and Cousins? How do you at Brighton? Oh, Jane, write soon.

Yours, etc.
Maria

Post Scriptum: *I have knotted a Fringe.*

After many heart-burnings and some wringing of her hands, Jane showed Maria's letter to her aunt.

Aunt Hervey puzzled over it, from time to time begging Jane to translate a phrase. Finally she set it down. "We shall certainly remove to London in September."

"But the Graingers' rout—"

"Pouf."

Nor did reason move her, nor agitated reconsiderations.

"Pouf," said Aunt Hervey. "You're hen-witted and cow-hearted. London it is."

She was as good as her word. The first of September found Jane in London with nothing to do and the Town thin of company. Maria had not said *when* in September. Jane tried to recall when the autumn session at Harrow commenced. She was rather afraid and rather hopeful that it might be October. She dithered and paced the floor and caught up on all her correspondence and read five silly novels and wondered if she would go mad waiting. Her aunt, however, was possessed of an almost religious calm.

"Gowns," she said firmly.

Jane resisted.

Her aunt brought in a dressmaker.

Jane selected all the fabrics and colours that made her complexion dull, her eyes muddy, and her hair hideous. Aunt Hervey sent the bolts back and chose peach and mint green and the softest primrose, and three bonnets so fetching Jane nearly fed them to her horse.

"I will not turn myself into a man-trap!"

"No point in turning yourself into a Guy, is there? My dear, if Meriden is as quick-witted as you say, he would be very much more likely to notice you in sackcloth than in *crêpe de Chine*. You surely did not go about Meriden Place looking the dowd?"

Grumbling, Jane submitted. She even allowed her aunt's dresser to brush her hair into several startling—and charming—new modes, but she secretly decided that she would shave her head before she would allow anyone to see her so transformed.

By anyone, she meant Meriden. He was too much in her thoughts. She half forgot it was Maria and Drusilla she would be visiting and that the odds were good she might not see his lordship at all. Only surely he would pay a courtesy call.

The girls called first.

Jane had waited so long that she had learnt not to start when a carriage drew up before her aunt's door. Thus she was taken unawares when one afternoon at teatime she returned from a ride in the park to find Drusilla, Maria, and Miss Goodnight in her aunt's salon with Aunt Hervey in beaming attendance.

After the inevitable flurry of greetings and embraces, Maria, who was looking bright-eyed and happy, said with satisfaction, "You see, Jane! We've come after all."

"We escaped," Drusilla announced around a cucumber sandwich.

"Drusilla!" Maria and Miss Goodnight said automatically.

Drusilla swallowed and stuck out her jaw. "It's *so*. My brother is the most complete hand."

"Which brother?" Jane asked feebly.

"Julian, of course. I told him I was hipped as far back as June. So he caused his cousin to send for us."

Maria gave a shriek. "You didn't! Oh, Dru, whatever must Cousin Georgy be thinking?"

"I don't know," said Drusilla with dignity, "but at least Mama ain't thinking anything. I swore an oath not to tell anyone our plot, not even you, Polly."

Maria and Miss Goodnight stared, clearly taken aback. Even Aunt Hervey, whose character in some ways resembled Drusilla's, looked startled at such unabashed duplicity in one so young.

Jane began to laugh. "You're a bad, deceitful person, Drusilla, and your brother—to compound a felony!"

Drusilla smiled seraphically. "He is taking me to Yorkshire."

"Yorkshire?" Jane's heart sank. For some reason she had assumed Meriden would squire his sisters about Town. Absurd.

Oblivious of Jane's apprehensions, Drusilla nodded, and Maria said, "Julian wishes Vincent to see the Yorkshire property, and since Drusilla don't care above half for dressmakers and plays and such, he's taking her with him, too."

"And Goody," Drusilla added.

Miss Goodnight looked martyred and did not meet Jane's eyes. Jane suspected Meriden had cut her a wheedle. Poor Goody. Yorkshire. Jane's gloom thickened.

"It's not fair for Vincent to have all the fun," Drusilla was saying. "I wish to see York. There's a wall and ruins and the minster. And I shall stay with Julian's friends while my brothers conduct their business, and I daresay I'll have a famous time while you're nosing about a lot of tedious cloth warehouses, Polly. Goody don't mind."

"Oh, no, not at all," Miss Goodnight murmured in faint accents.

Jane eyed her former companion with sympathy, and, it must be admitted, envy. To agree to such a journey. She turned back to her cousin.

"Drusilla, does Lady Herrington know you'll be leaving her?"

"Of course. Julian and Cousin Georgy are thick as thieves. It was all arranged ages ago. Oh, Jane, don't you wish you was coming?"

Jane's Aunt Hervey had listened to that interchange with a glint in her eye. Jane scowled at her and said repressively, "I am very happy here with my dear aunt, Drusilla. However, I hope you have a pleasant journey and that you do not try Goody's patience too far. Or your brother's."

"Which brother?" Drusilla's grin was so impudent Jane longed to box her ears.

"Either." Jane turned pointedly to Maria. "How do you go on with Lady Herrington?"

Maria's eyes shone. "Splendidly. She is so elegant, and so kind. Shall you call on her?"

"Certainly," said Jane's aunt.

Jane nodded.

Maria heaved a sigh. "Bath will seem duller than ever when we return, but at least I shall be all the crack in my London gowns."

"Aunt Louisa will be planning your come-out soon," Jane murmured.

Maria forced a smile. "Oh, I'm to make my come-out in Bath. A small dinner party. Mama says I may go to the Assemblies after Christmas."

"Of all the shabby things!" Jane bit her lip. "I beg your pardon, Maria." She looked from her cousins to Miss Goodnight. "I had thought my aunt meant to bring you to Town in the spring."

Maria's eyes welled tears. She shook her head.

"Her ladyship's health...." Miss Goodnight fluttered her hands helplessly.

"Oh, Lord," Jane said, exasperated. "Maria, my dear, we must contrive something." She cast a beseeching look at her Aunt Hervey, but that lady was observing some interesting pattern in the carpet and would not meet Jane's eyes.

Maria swallowed a sob and said, with a pathetic attempt at wit, "I shall be nineteen in the spring. Old cattish."

"Mutton dressed as lamb," Jane said crossly. "Do try not to be mutton-headed, love. Does your ... his lordship know of your mama's intent?"

"No. That is, I'm not perfectly sure. He sees so many things without being told. He may have guessed, but he has been very kind to give us this treat ... and besides the London house is sold. What can Julian do? *He* cannot present me."

"Marry," said Aunt Hervey.

Drusilla and Maria stared, and Drusilla gave a small unsisterly hoot. "Julian?"

Aunt Hervey cast Jane a malicious look. "Well, my dears, he is a young man. Just at the most susceptible age. Eight-and-twenty, by now, is he not? As Lord Meriden he must be considered quite the catch. I daresay, if he were to move about in Society, all the ladies would throw their caps at him."

Maria said doubtfully, "Julian is not very romantical."

For once Drusilla kept quiet.

Miss Goodnight's mild eyes lit, and she said warmly, "I think his lordship would make an excellent husband. Indeed, Mrs. Hervey, a capital idea." Abruptly she descended into incoherence. "Er, that is, poor Lady Meriden, one could not expect her to exert herself ... his lordship with a wife to lend the girls countenance ... living at Fern Hall ... oh...." Her voice trailed off.

Aunt Hervey smiled and said in rallying tones, "Well, Maria, shall I turn matchmaker?"

Maria gave her a shy returning smile. "It would be very obliging in you, dear Mrs. Hervey."

"Of course, Meriden may have plans of his own," Aunt Hervey reflected. "The ladies of Yorkshire ... shall you be going to Harrogate, Drusilla?"

"My dear," said Miss Goodnight gently, "Mrs. Hervey was speaking to you."

Drusilla blinked. "Oh. No, Vincent may, but I don't care to ... that is, I daresay it's quite a distance from Whitethorn to Harrogate, and besides it's no use. Julian don't dance."

There was a constrained silence in which Jane cast her aunt a repelling look. Mrs. Hervey, however, was attending to Drusilla still.

"You said you were to stay with your brother's friends?"

"Yes."

"I believe Mr. William Tarrant was an officer in his lordship's regiment," Miss Goodnight interposed. "Until the peace. That is, the

154

first peace, before that fellow Bonaparte escaped. The estates march. Mrs. Tarrant has writ Drusilla and me a very comfortable letter."

Aunt Hervey smiled at her kindly. "Has she marriageable daughters?"

"Aunt!" Jane hissed.

Miss Goodnight looked flustered. "Oh, dear, no. Quite a young family. A boy in leading strings and his lordship's goddaughter who is scarcely one year old."

Catching Jane's scowl, Aunt Hervey said mildly, "I see I must give up hope of immediate success. What a good plan it was, Maria."

Apparently Maria agreed, for she looked so downcast that only the prospect of a visit to Jane's mantuamaker cheered her.

Lord Meriden did not call, but Jane had the felicity of meeting Vincent in the park. She and her aunt, surfeited with shopping and visiting, were taking a turn in the barouche when a handsome young man hailed them.

Aunt Hervey required the coachman to stop. "It's Vincent Stretton. Shall we take him up?" She greeted Vincent, ignoring Jane's feeble protests.

He returned the greeting in his best manner and climbed up beside Aunt Hervey quite cheerfully when she invited him. Jane allowed her aunt to carry the burden of conversation. In truth, she was surprised out of her self-absorption by the changes in Vincent.

He was, of course, impeccably turned out. Apart from a ruddier complexion, his appearance had not altered since spring, but he seemed, nonetheless, quite different. Confident, grown-up, much less affected.

"You've seen my sisters?" he asked her presently.

"Yes, and paid your cousin, Lady Herrington, a morning visit."

His eyes lit in a way that reminded Jane painfully of his brother. "Is she not splendid, Jane?"

Jane murmured assent. Clearly Lady Herrington had won his heart. She listened to his raptures with a smile and wished she could concur. A half-hour courtesy call had given her very little opportunity to form an opinion of Lady Herrington's character. That she was beautiful—such red-gold hair, such white skin, such brilliant green eyes—there could be no doubt. She had seemed, in a languid way, friendly enough and was on easy terms with Miss Goodnight.

Maria went in awe of her. Drusilla, of course, was not awed by anybody, but once Jane caught her ladyship regarding Drusilla with raised brows, and to Jane's surprise Drusilla subsided. Lady Herrington's languid manner may have been affectation. Jane did not know. She did know that it seemed incongruous to imagine her ladyship and Meriden with anything in common.

Vincent, his raptures exhausted, edified Jane with an account of the move to Fern Hall and Felix's tutor and the twins' ponies, then said rather diffidently, "Jane, your father has writ Julian a stiffish note over his letting Meriden."

Jane's heart sank. Bless Papa.

"I wish you will just drop a word in his ear." Vincent's beautiful brow furrowed. "I'm sure my uncle meant it for the best, but you know, it ain't fair to devil Ju. He is fixing up Fern Hall and mending walls and draining bogs and whatnot, just as my uncle told him he should, and that costs the earth. It's in good hands—the old place, I mean. I've dined with the nabob." Vincent flushed. "He ain't a nabob, really. That's just a joke between me and Julian. He's a ... a Cit, but dashed civil, and his wife was one of the Skeffingtons. They take the greatest care of everything, and they're not encroaching. Will you tell Uncle John that?"

Jane was as much touched as embarrassed. Clearly Meriden as well as the new tenant had won Vincent's allegiance.

She was glad to assure Vincent of her intercession in the matter and even gladder to find him on good terms with his brother. But, Vincent, she thought wryly, the nabob was a joke between your brother and me before you were on speaking terms with Meriden. She cleared her throat. "I trust Lord Meriden is well?"

"Oh, yes. That is, a bit gloomy just now. A friend of his in Yorkshire—Tarrant, you know—has taken a bad fall, and Julian's devilish worried. We mean to drive up tomorrow."

"Tomorrow," Jane said blankly. "But Drusilla—"

"Oh, poor Dru. She's mad as fire, but she can't very well impose on Mrs. Tarrant at such a time. She'll stay with Lady Georgy."

Vincent appeared to regard staying with Lady Herrington as ample compensation for Drusilla's disappointment.

Drusilla did not agree.

Later that day Jane and her aunt paid her ladyship an afternoon call. As soon as Aunt Hervey and Jane had exchanged civilities with Lady Herrington, Drusilla began to pester Jane to take her north. In vain did Jane point out the impropriety of going against Meriden's wishes, the difficulties attendant upon ladies travelling without male escort, the want of a hostess to receive them in Yorkshire.

Drusilla pleaded and begged and stormed and behaved in general so much like Felix in a pet that Jane was very much ashamed of her. Lady Herrington watched the girl without apparent emotion, but her eyes had narrowed to green slits.

Jane said rather desperately, "Drusilla, I am sorry for your disappointment, but you must see that it is impossible for you to go now."

"I don't see it. I should help Mrs. Tarrant. I'm very good with invalids."

"Not with Mama," Maria interjected smugly.

Drusilla's eyes filled. "It's not *fair*. I bore with Mama all summer because Julian asked me to, and now he won't take me north when he goes dashing off to some beastly friend who ain't even family. Mama is right. He is a ... a Villain. I'm his sister, ain't I? He *owes* me...." She buried her head in a sopha cushion and began to weep lustily.

"Drusilla," Lady Herrington murmured, "you are making a vulgar spectacle of yourself. Dry your eyes and cease shrieking, if you please."

Drusilla sat up with a startled sniff.

Lady Herrington rose. "You must understand that your brother owes Mr. Tarrant his life, for it was he who found him so badly wounded in Belgium, and brought him home and cared for him. And that is considerably more than he owes you or any member of his family." She did not raise her voice. "I am very glad to receive you and Maria, for Julian's sake, but I will not hear my cousin abused. Drusilla, you may go to your room. Miss Goodnight, I wonder if you will be so kind as to escort her?"

When a scarlet Drusilla and her fluttering escort had vanished, Lady Herrington turned back to her callers.

"Dear me, how happy I am not to be sixteen. Mrs. Hervey, Miss Ash, I beg your pardon."

Maria, upright and pale, was still sitting on the sopha. A tiny frown formed between Lady Herrington's excellent brows.

"Maria, my love, do not look so downcast. I am very glad to have you visit me, but you do see that I was obliged to give your sister a set-down, do you not? Only imagine what would happen if she were to throw such a tantrum in Lady Jersey's company."

Maria did not smile.

Lady Herrington sat beside her and, quite unaffectedly, gave her a hug. "There, now, don't pull away."

"I shan't," Maria said with dignity, "and I am sorry my sister behaved so ill, but I believe you are unjust. We did not know Julian. Indeed we did not know he was hurt. You, I collect, did, Cousin, and, if that is so, how came it that *you*, who have known him all your life, left him to be cared for by strangers?" She stood up and stalked from the room with quite un-Maria-like dignity.

Lady Herrington gazed after her thoughtfully. "I shall certainly present Maria. Who would have thought the child had so much spirit?"

In the previous few minutes Jane had experienced wild impulses to flight. Aunt Hervey appeared beset with the same feeling and, indeed, bent upon acting on them, for she gave every sign of preparing to depart. Lady Herrington's last remark, however, so intrigued Jane that she placed a restraining hand on her aunt's wrist.

Lady Herrington came to herself with a small shake of the head and startled Jane very much by giving her an engaging grin. Her languor had vanished.

"Forgive me," she said simply. "Do stay. There is a deal I must discuss with you, Miss Ash. Only first excuse me, for I must tell Greave I am not receiving, or who knows how many interruptions we shall have?" She rose and slipped from the room.

Jane and her aunt exchanged glances.

"Well, upon my word...." Aunt Hervey began.

"No, dear Aunt, do *not*. If she will see to Maria's come-out, nothing could be better."

Presently her ladyship returned followed by a servant with a tea tray the sight of which in some sort mollified Aunt Hervey.

"I had not understood Meriden's obligation to Mr. Tarrant," Jane ventured, "or I should have made myself plainer to Drusilla."

Lady Herrington grimaced. "What a coil! I have never even met the man. Maria is right, of course. Only, you know, we were *deep* in Devon and did not have word of the battle until two weeks after it was fought. By the time we reached Town, we had the casualty lists, but things were in such an uproar at the Horse Guards that even Richard could not get word of Julian's whereabouts."

Sir Richard Herrington was an ornamental member of the Opposition. Lady Herrington's faith in her husband's capacity to track down missing cousins was touching but, Jane thought, a little naive, considering the magnitude of the battle and the confusion afterwards. Her father had waited a month for word of Jack.

"I went to Lord Meriden, that is, Julian's father." Spots of colour burnt in her ladyship's cheeks. "He told me," she said indignantly, "not to put myself in a pother."

Jane grinned.

"Yes, you may smile now, but I can tell you it was not amusing at the time. What a ... a toad that man was. I beg your pardon, Miss Ash."

"No need," Jane said warmly. "He was not my kin, and toad is the least of what I should have said."

Lady Herrington's mouth relaxed in a reluctant smile. "Well, in August I had a note from Julian to say he was with his friends in Yorkshire and I was to thank Mr. Tarrant that he did not write to me in the character of Pegleg Stretton. I was very much relieved, I must say, but I cannot help feeling guilty...."

"No one could censure you, Georgianna," Aunt Hervey pronounced.

"*I* could," Lady Herrington said shortly, "and so, apparently, could my sweet cousin-in-law, Maria. Tell me, Miss Ash, if Maria is so lion-hearted, how has she contrived these past few days to appear so hen-witted?"

Jane preserved her gravity. "I believe Maria may have been a trifle in awe of you, ma'am."

Lady Herrington wrinkled her perfect nose. "Could you contrive to call me Georgy? 'Ma'am' is a little daunting."

"If you will call me Jane."

"Very well, Jane. Now, dragon that I am, I have stunned Maria into insipidity."

Jane laughed. "It is surely not so bad as that. As you see, she has spirit, and, given confidence, she shows pretty, funning ways, and her share of the Stretton charm."

"Do you find the Strettons charming? I must tell Julian."

Jane felt herself flush and avoided Aunt Hervey's eye. She was not about to be outfaced by this unexpected and alarming lady, however. "Vincent is quite the most beguiling young man of my acquaintance," she said with a tolerable assumption of coolness, "and Harry, you know, was famous for his address. As for his lordship, his appearance is deceptive, for I think him *capable de tout*."

Lady Herrington gave a crow of delight. "You're perfectly correct. He's outrageous. What fun we had as children, and how many scrapes he got me into! He is quite my favourite relation." She chuckled. "And his abominable twin brothers are exactly like him. Tell me, Miss ... Jane, is it necessary for Julian to mew himself up in the country? I have *longed* to loose him on the *ton*. He would set everyone by the ears in no time."

"No doubt you are right." Jane smiled but rather vacantly, for she was a little stunned by the allusion to Arty and Horatio.

Lady Herrington sighed. "Ah, well, one cannot always indulge one's wishes. He seems bent on turning himself into an agriculturalist. Considering the state in which his tedious father left things, I suppose he believes he has no choice." Her green eyes lit. "Only to think of Julian raising corn. Or mangel-wurzels."

The mention of mangel-wurzels depressed Jane so severely she could not smile. She pictured Meriden slowly metamorphosing into her father and shuddered.

"I was only funning."

Jane forced the smile. "I know. Does his lordship have a taste for Society? I should have said not."

"He might have at one time but had never the means to indulge such a taste, and now I fear he cannot take our frivolities seriously enough to enjoy the game." Her smile turned rueful. "I wouldn't wish him other, but I could wish for his company rather more often than I'm likely to have it."

Jane found herself liking Lady Herrington very much.

Unaware she had just received Jane's stamp of merit, her ladyship gave her head a tiny shake. "Lord, why am I prosing on about Julian? It's these sisters of his we should be speaking of. Maria, now—you think she'll blossom?"

"With proper cultivation."

"What an agricultural turn our conversation has taken. *I* shall prune with a will, and do *you* see if you can root out Lady Meriden's objections, whatever they may be. Maria must stay with me."

"I shall certainly do my best. It is very kind in you, Lady ... Georgy. As for Drusilla...."

Lady Herrington's creamy brow clouded. "I trust I have not quite crushed her spirits."

"It would take more than a single reproof to crush Drusilla," Aunt Hervey interjected.

Both ladies jumped, for they had half forgot her presence.

"Aunt is a little unkind," Jane murmured. "Drusilla behaved abominably, but I believe she had looked forward to the northern journey very much. She has not got over her hoydenish ways, so Bath did not suit her, and she and her mother do not go on, er, easily. I am sorry for Dru. Perhaps I can think of some outing she would enjoy."

"Ah, she's very young," Lady Herrington said indulgently. "I'll leave her to reflect on her sins for a time, then make my peace with her. Do you think she would enjoy a review? Richard might contrive something. He has friends in the Household Cavalry."

"It might do," Jane replied, but she had doubts. Drusilla's was a very tenacious mind.

Next morning Jane did not rise early. She had attended a theatre party the evening before and had retired late to lie awake several hours brooding over the unkindness of fate which, it was clear, was determined to deny her even a glimpse of Meriden.

She breakfasted in bed and made her way downstairs after eleven to find a message awaiting her. It was brief, elliptic, and rather hard to decipher, but it seemed that something grave had transpired, and would she come at her earliest convenience to her obliged friend, Georgy Herrington.

Jane did not await her aunt but caused the doorman to summon a hackney directly, flung on her pelisse, and flung out of the house.

Her sensible self told her Drusilla or Maria had probably broken out in the measles. Her Gothic alter ego, however, kept tossing up horrors. Meriden had been assaulted by rioters, thrown from his bolting horse, murdered by footpads.

She bit back these fancies as best she could, but she reached Lady Herrington's door in an agitated frame of mind and, shown into the salon by a carefully blank-faced butler, was not immediately soothed to sense.

Maria greeted her with a Banbury tale about Drusilla having run off to the border, and Miss Goodnight was too much occupied soothing Maria to present a coherent narrative, so Jane greeted Lady Herrington's entrance with relief.

Her ladyship did not speak but handed Jane a note.

> *Dear Jane,*
>   *I have gone off Alone to Yorkshire. Do not be alarmed for my Safety. I have got Money. Farewell, crule cousin.*
>   *Yours, etc.*
>   *Drusilla Louisa Mary Stretton*

Jane returned the note to Lady Herrington. "What an ill-conducted brat she is. What's to be done?"

Maria wailed something about Scandal.

"Nonsense," Jane said shortly. "She has merely gone off on the mail coach and is probably having a splendid time. I daresay she'll come to no harm beyond the scolding she'll receive when she reaches her brother."

"If she reaches him." Lady Herrington's green eyes were shadowed. "You are too sanguine, Jane. My cousin is at Whitethorn—or will be—and the mail goes no nearer than Market Yeding. I trust she will know when to get down. If she leaves the coach at Malton the distance is nearly thirty miles. She has taken no abigail. I need not tell you the perils attendant upon an unescorted journey in a girl Drusilla's age. Furthermore, my cousin's stepmother will not regard this ... this ramshackle escapade as amusing. The consequences of Lady Meriden's displeasure must be grave for Maria as well as for Drusilla and, I fear, for Julian. *I* had Drusilla in charge. If harm comes to her, her mother will justly blame me and—"

"And unjustly blame Meriden. And our plan for Maria's come-out must go by the board. I see."

"There is another thing." Lady Herrington twisted her rings. "Sufficient scandal attaches to the Stretton name already, what with Harry's duel and Vincent's debts, without tales being circulated of a Stretton daughter wandering unescorted about the countryside."

"Someone must fetch her," Jane said slowly.

All three ladies looked at Jane.

"No. Oh, no. There I draw the line. I will not be bullied by Drusilla...." Her voice trailed off under their combined reproach.

Lady Herrington said carefully, "I am sensible of the burden it places upon you, and if I could hit upon another solution.... Richard cannot leave now, what with the debate in the House, and *I* cannot. I have engaged to be present at a levée honouring the Prince of Orange. I am afraid my absence must be remarked. You are Drusilla's cousin, and she was heard by the servants to be pleading with you to escort her. If you agree to go—Miss Goodnight has kindly offered to companion you—we shall put it about that you finally consented to take Drusilla and she mistook the day of departure and left for your Aunt Hervey's this morning by mistake. I shall lend you my travelling carriage. It's quite comfortable and well sprung. My coachman will serve you admirably. When you return with Drusilla, gossip must be satisfied and no more need be heard of the matter."

"No," said Jane feebly.

Maria began to weep.

Jane rose and walked about the room. "Why should *I* go into Yorkshire? What motive can *I* have?"

"Why, none," said Lady Herrington in some surprise. "None but indulgent good nature."

Jane bit her lip. It was on her tongue to suggest that she might be seen as rackety to be pursuing Meriden into Yorkshire, but such a thought had apparently not entered anyone's head, and she did not wish to put it there.

"My Aunt Hervey will not like it," she objected with absolute hypocrisy.

"I shall go at once to your aunt and explain everything," Lady Herrington pronounced.

Jane's heart sank. "What of *my* engagements?" she shot back. "You are not the only one whose absence from Town might be remarked."

Lady Herrington blinked. "You're right, of course. How stupid of me."

Abruptly Jane saw irony in the situation. She had wished to meet Meriden again, in spite of her noble resolutions to avoid setting snares. Now she would chase him to his lair in his own cousin's splendid well-sprung carriage and with everyone's blessing. So much for heroic self-restraint.

She bit back a chuckle. "Very well. I'll go. In truth, I've nothing so pressing as your levée, Georgy. I was being absurd."

Lady Herrington let out her breath in an undignified "phew."

Jane turned to Miss Goodnight. "Goody, my dear, I shall be glad of your company, but I warn you I shall not hold your head all the way to York."

16

THE JOURNEY TOOK four days. By the time the coach rattled into Market Yeding, both ladies were road-weary and battered. Heroic Miss Goodnight had been ill three times only, but forbearance had told on her.

At the posting inn in York they had inquired after Drusilla. She had indeed passed through that city, changing there for the Scarborough coach, and had caused some comment—ribald, of course—among the ostlers. Jane reflected wearily that Drusilla had spared no pains to make of herself a scandal and a hissing, and that if Meriden had not already murdered the girl, *she* would.

At Malton they learned nothing. At Market Yeding, however—the proper village at which to turn off to Whitethorn and Tarrant Manor—they had word of a girl with a bandbox who had bribed a farmer's lad to carry her in his cart. Jane's spirits revived. She wished she might have seen Drusilla—no doubt fancying herself an aristo fleeing the Terror—jouncing along in a load of cabbages. What a resourceful brat she was, to be sure.

The prospect of explaining Drusilla's aberrant behaviour to Meriden threw Jane again into the dismals, and she was not at all elated when at last the elegant, though by now sadly mud-spattered, carriage drew to a halt and Lady Herrington's coachman announced, "Whitethorn, miss," and threw open the door.

Jane stepped down and looked about her. In the grey afternoon light she saw a pleasantly situated small house—not much larger than a farmhouse—which had been built within the past half-century or so. In its kind it was perfectly proportioned and just beginning to mellow. She liked it, but it looked sadly deserted.

Lady Herrington's man rapped heavily with the brass knocker. No response. He rapped again. Just as he raised the knocker a third time the door swung open and a severe, black-clad woman of middle age required him in carefully genteel accents to state his business.

Jane moved forward. "I am Jane Ash, a connexion of Lord Meriden's, and I would like to speak with his lordship on a matter of some urgency"

The housekeeper—her modest keychain proclaimed her state—regarded Jane with suspicion. "Lord Meriden is not here."

Jane's heart sank. Had Lady Georgy's carriage outrun Meriden and Drusilla as well? "Is Mr. Vincent Stretton here?"

"No, miss."

"Well, Thorpe, then," Jane said desperately.

There was an imperceptible softening of the housekeeper's stiff features. "I'll summon Mr. Thorpe. He's out t'stables, miss. Will you come in?"

Jane gave a heartfelt sigh of relief. "Thank you, Mrs ... ?"

"Bradford, miss."

"Mrs. Bradford. I wonder if my companion may not have a cup of tea. She is sadly overset, for we have had a long journey."

"Yes, miss. I'll see to it directly. Do come in."

Jane and Miss Goodnight were shown into the library in which a small fire burnt. In explanation, Mrs. Bradford said, "T'house is mostly closed, miss, his lordship not being set to receive ladies."

Jane and Miss Goodnight exchanged worried looks, but did not enlighten the housekeeper. Had Drusilla not come yet?

"Perhaps she is with Mrs. Tarrant," Jane murmured over tea and scones. Mrs. Bradford had gone for Thorpe.

"Let us hope so." Miss Goodnight did not look at all well, and Jane regarded her in some anxiety.

"Goody, you must have a lie-down, but I do not perfectly know what to do. Perhaps we should go on to the Tarrants and beg accommodation. I dislike to impose at such a time. The inn at Market Yeding, however, looked decidedly unpleasant."

"Fleas." Miss Goodnight managed a wan smile. "I shall do very well, Jane. Do not be worrying about me."

Thorpe was just then ushered in. Jane rose and shook his hand with a heartiness born of relief. His good eye twinkled at her.

"I'm *glad* to see you, Thorpe. Has Miss Drusilla come?"

His face went blank. "Nay. She was t'stay wi' her ladyship in Lunnon, miss. Did tha not know?"

Miss Goodnight's teacup clattered in the saucer.

Jane swallowed. She explained as cogently and undramatically as she could what Drusilla had done.

Mercifully Thorpe refrained from exclamations and came to the crux. "Saw t'lass at Market Yeding, did un? In a farm cart?"

Jane nodded. "Last afternoon. The host at the inn assured me the cart came this way."

"Did tha think t'ask carter's name, then, miss?"

"I did." Jane took a breath. "I didn't perfectly understand the man, but I believe he said Wicker or Wickart's lad."

"Oh, aye, that'll be Dickie Boggs." Thorpe tapped his forehead. "A mite slow, Dickie, but no harm in t'lad."

"She must be found."

"Aye."

"And ... his lordship must be informed directly. Thorpe...." Her voice trailed off, for he appeared to be deep in thought.

"Us'll just ride on over t'Wickarts'. Like as not Miss Drusilla's safe as houses. Never tha mind, miss."

"You're a great comfort, Thorpe," Jane said gratefully. "Where is his lordship?"

"At Tarrants', think on. Mr. Will's none so bad—broke's leg and took a great knock on t'head, sithee, but looks to be mending."

"I'm relieved to hear it. Shall I put the carriage to and go on to Tarrant Manor? I could give Meriden word of your search."

"Aye, do that, and miss...."

"Yes, Thorpe?"

"Don't fratch. Us'll find un."

Jane blinked hard. "Thank you, Thorpe. I'm obliged to you."

Although Thorpe and common sense reassured Jane in some part, she was very much disturbed not to have found Drusilla's plump self firmly in residence. All phantasies as to how she herself should feel and act in Meriden's presence were driven from her mind as the carriage bowled along the lane that connected Whitethorn with Tarrant Manor, and she could think only of how Meriden must suffer if harm had come to his sister. Miss Goodnight's lamentations did nothing to ease Jane's anxiety.

By the time Tarrant Manor was reached, it was nearly dark, and a wind blew from the east spattering a few raindrops on the dusty carriage. The house, however, was cheerfully lit, and while the maidservant who admitted the ladies scurried off in search of her mistress, Jane settled the exhausted Miss Goodnight into a chair by the fender.

At last Mrs. Tarrant entered. A birdlike little brown woman who must ordinarily have presented a cheerful appearance, she looked just now rather harried.

"Miss Goodnight? Miss Ash? We did not look for you...."

Jane said quietly, "No, and we are sorry to trouble you, Mrs. Tarrant. The thing is, Drusilla Stretton has run off. She came as far as Market Harbrough in the mail coach, and now we ... we cannot find her."

"Good gracious!"

"You see, there is some urgency, and if I may speak with Lord Meriden...."

Mrs. Tarrant looked distressed. "Julian has not yet come in from the home farm. He has been seeing to things for me in my husband's illness.... Vincent is here."

"May I speak to him, then?"

"Of course." She rang a bell, and the maidservant appeared with such alacrity that Jane supposed her to have been glued to the door listening. "Annie, fetch Mr. Stretton from Mr. Tarrant's room directly."

The girl scampered off, and Mrs. Tarrant appeared to collect her wits. "Please, Miss ... Ash, is it?"

"Yes, I am Drusilla's cousin."

Mrs. Tarrant's face brightened. "That Miss Ash. Julian writ us that you had been very kind to his family. Please be comfortable, Miss Ash. And Miss Goodnight?"

Jane said, "I'm afraid Goody is feeling rather ill. She is a poor traveller, and we have not had an easy journey."

"Then she must go to bed at once with a nice bowl of soup and a hot brick."

From that point Mrs. Tarrant took charge, and Goody was whisked from the room, Jane presented with another tea, the fire built up, and orders given to set dinner back an hour—all in the brief time it took Vincent to be summoned and come downstairs.

Jane greeted Vincent in something of a daze.

"What's this about Drusilla?" he asked.

"She's lost, Vincent. Be ... between Market Yeding and Whitethorn. Thorpe has gone in search of her."

"Good God! But how does she come to be in Yorkshire?"

Jane explained.

Vincent's blue eyes glazed. "I'll fetch Julian. No, dash it, I can't. I'm dressed for dinner."

"Vincent!"

"Oh. Well, he should be coming in soon anyway. I'll just run out and find a groom to go for him."

Jane bethought herself of the coachmen. "Vincent, I've kept Lady

Herrington's men out in the chill. Do see to them and the cattle, will you? My wits have gone begging."

He raced off, banging the front door. Jane heard him whooping in the distance. He had looked, she thought wryly, more excited than worried.

She herself was beginning to tremble from strain and weariness. Mrs. Tarrant entered as she tried to pour another cup of tea and took the pot from her.

"My poor dear, you have had a time of it. Whatever can be keeping Vincent?"

Jane explained and drank some tea and began to feel less agitated.

Mrs. Tarrant cocked her head. "That's Vincent outside, and I believe I hear Julian's voice, too."

Without a word Jane jumped to her feet and ran into the hallway. A blast of wind chilled the hall, and Vincent entered, chatting over his shoulder.

"Yes, thank you, Vincent," said Meriden. "I had better see Jane. Ah, there you are." He went to her and took her hands. "I'm glad to see you, Jane. Will you explain? Vincent has spun me some tale about Dru flinging herself into a bog...."

Jane gave him a tremulous smile. "I trust it may not prove so dreadful, but indeed, sir, I do not know where she is." She found she had been clinging to his hands and drew away a little.

Meriden took her elbow and led her to the salon.

"Come into my parlour," said Mrs. Tarrant drily.

"Peggy, I'm sorry to burden you with another disaster...."

"Never mind that, idiot. Don't you think you should hear Miss Ash's story?"

He drew a breath. "Yes. Well, Jane?"

Jane explained as lucidly as she could, considering that she now was, in addition to being frightened for Drusilla, vividly aware of Meriden. He was windblown, mud-spattered, and rather damp from the rain, and she thought he looked splendidly and wondered why anyone would wish him to go about in stiff shirtpoints.

She focussed on the toe of his boot and talked. He did not interrupt. When she had finished, she made herself meet his eyes. In fact he looked more stunned than loverlike.

"Julian, surely your sister is at Wickart's," Mrs. Tarrant interposed. "Thorpe will have found her."

"Very likely. I'll ride over that way now to see if he has. Shall I bring the body here?"

"Body?" Mrs. Tarrant stared.

"I intend to strangle Drusilla," he said apologetically. "I thought I had better tell you."

"Oh, no, you will not, sir," Jane interrupted. "I have been *waiting* to do so this whole week."

His eyes lit. "Yes, but mine is the superior claim. We are closer in blood."

Jane was prepared to argue that point, but Mrs. Tarrant fixed them with an owlish stare. "However you decide to dispose of your sister, Ju, you had better do so here. You cannot have Mrs. Bradford giving notice."

"Very true. Vincent...."

Vincent had followed the interchange with sagging jaw. He started. "Er, shall I come, too?"

Meriden took in his dress. "No, do you comfort the ladies." The teazing glint died in his eyes. "If I've not returned by half-past nine or so, ride over to Whitethorn and tell Mrs. Bradford what has happened. I'll come for you there."

He made for the hall with Vincent trailing after, uttering protests.

"No, halfling, I can't wait for you to change."

The door thudded.

The ladies exchanged looks. Presently Mrs. Tarrant smiled.

"Miss Ash, you look as if you might like a rest."

"No," Jane said firmly. "I couldn't be still. I should not object to tidying myself, however."

"Very well, and then perhaps you and I and Vincent should dine. There's no point pacing the floor and dithering." A horror-struck look crossed her face. "Dithering! Good Lord, Will will have run mad."

Jane deduced that Will was Mr. Tarrant. "Is he very ill, ma'am?"

Mrs. Tarrant sighed. "No, very crotchety. An abominable patient. Julian was far more civilised."

Jane said hesitantly, "You cared for his lordship after Waterloo, did you not? I believe we—that is, the family—are very much in your debt, Mrs. Tarrant."

"I believe you are," her hostess replied with a hint of coolness in her voice. "For without Will and Thorpe, Julian must have died in Belgium, and it took very careful nursing in Brussels and here, when Will brought him home, to save his left leg. Julian owes us nothing, for he is Will's friend. But Julian's family...."

Jane felt ready to sink. Indeed she was torn between shame and horror, for she had not thought Meriden's injuries to have been so severe, nor did she know how to explain the Strettons to this brisk, kind little woman. Clearly, however, *some* explanation must be given Mrs. Tarrant.

"Has Meriden told you anything of his father?" she asked after a moment.

"I gather they were not on good terms."

Jane sighed. "It is not so straightforward." She explained the late baron without roundaboutation, adding with less frankness an account of the family's ignorance of the then Major Stretton's circumstances.

Halfway through this recital Mrs. Tarrant sat down. She regarded Jane with a fascinated gaze and in the end merely shook her head. "Thank you for telling me, Miss Ash. I can't say I understand, precisely...."

"No more do I," Jane said with feeling.

"You believe Julian's brothers and sisters have learnt to value him as they ought?"

"And he them," Jane said gently.

Mrs. Tarrant gave her a sidelong glance. "This sister...."

"Drusilla!" Jane's apprehension returned. "Lord, I had almost forgot Drusilla. The poor child, how frightened she must be!"

"I daresay Mrs. Wickart has set her to churning butter for her keep," Mrs. Tarrant said prosaically.

Jane managed a smile. "The devil has work for idle hands?"

"Precisely. A frugal and godly household." She jumped up. "I had best take you up and see to Will while you refresh yourself. He'll be in a fine stew."

"Mrs. Tarrant."

"Yes?"

"May I help you? I have some experience of crotchety invalids."

Mrs. Tarrant flashed a grin. "Lady Meriden?"

"I see his lordship *has* spoken of his family," Jane said with resignation. "I should not call my aunt crotchety, exactly. Something altogether grander, perhaps. However, I was thinking of my father. When the gout troubles him, he is not by any means easy to bear with, and I fancy I have learnt to divert him with tolerable success."

Mrs. Tarrant smiled. "Do you know, I believe I'll take up your offer. I had very nearly decided to enter a nunnery."

"Then by all means let me help."

The evening passed with surprising swiftness. Dinner was excellent. Mrs. Tarrant kept up a light flow of conversation that prevented Jane and

Vincent from thinking too much about Drusilla's absence, and afterwards they all visited the invalid.

Mr. Tarrant turned out to be so much like Jane's elder brother Tom that she soon felt quite at home with him. A big, good-natured, rather slow man, he was, like others of his kind, inclined to fret at confinement. Jane soon had him laughing and relating military anecdotes, and she took satisfaction in freeing Mrs. Tarrant to visit her nursery.

When she returned, she surveyed her crotchety husband in mock surprise.

"I should have suspected. He is always pretty-behaved with *other* females, Miss Ash."

Tarrant gave his wife a slow grin. "Now, Peggy...."

She bent to kiss his nose. "No more frolicking, Will. You may delight Miss Ash with your tall tales tomorrow. It's half-past—"

"Good God!" Vincent sprang from the chair in which he had been viewing the conquest of Will Tarrant. "Julian's not come. I must go at once."

Abruptly the lighthearted mood dissolved.

"Tell Ju to call out my people," Tarrant rumbled from the bed. "And Earnshaw. He'll need the dogs."

Vincent went white. "The moor...."

"Yes. He'll want to mount a search party to cover the wild ground between the Wickarts' and Whitethorn. Go *on*, lad."

Vincent vanished.

Jane spent a wretched night of inaction. She tried to sleep and failed. The pleasant bedchamber allotted her gave over the kitchen garden, but she could see nothing at all beyond. She strained her eyes to catch the flicker of torches, and her ears after the voices of men and hounds, but she saw and heard nothing.

The fire in her room grew sullen and, as dawn came, ashy. Finally, impatient of fruitless imaginings, she dressed, shivering, and slipped downstairs as quietly as she could in search of the kitchen. She found it quite empty, but the banked fire in the hearth gave off some warmth.

She found candles and lit them, poked the fire, and set the kettle on the hob. A newfangled iron stove stood next the fireplace, and she contemplated wrestling with it, but gave up. A pantry yielded bread and cheese and the remains of a ham. She sliced the bread and cut her finger slightly. The kettle boiled over.

When she had made tea and eaten a piece of the bread, she felt less stupid and had almost decided to run up for her pelisse when she heard dragging footsteps on the flagway. Fumbling in her haste, she unlatched the heavy door.

Meriden had been walking toward the main entrance around the corner of the house. When he heard her, he stopped short.

"It's me—Jane. No one is awake. Please come here, sir. It's warm, and I've made tea."

He came back, stumbling a little on the uneven flags, and entered the kitchen without speaking.

"Drusilla?"

He shook his head. "She didn't go in to Wickart's farm. Decided to walk from the lane, I suppose." He was hoarse and grey with weariness. "Jane, do you have something of Dru's? A sash or a muff, perhaps?" His eyes when they met Jane's were dark with worry. "For the dogs."

Jane swallowed hard. "I ... yes, I have her trunk. I'll fetch something directly, but first, sir, please sit down. There's hot tea and meat and bread. I think you did not dine last night."

He obeyed, sitting heavily on a bench by the door. "Very well. Only please be quick. They should start as soon as may be."

Jane brought him food and ran up the stairs and down the hallway to her room. Drusilla's trunk perched jauntily on its side. She tipped it down and wrestled it open by main force, taking no care to be quiet. Gowns, petticoats, slippers blurred before her eyes and she shook away her tears impatiently. She pulled out a pair of jean half-boots and darted back down the stairs.

Meriden was sitting as she had left him, staring at the floor.

"My lord." She held out the boots.

"I ... yes. Thank you. Jane...."

"What is it, sir?"

"I should have left her in Bath with her mother."

There was such misery in his voice that Jane could have wept, but his lordship did not require a watering pot. He required bracing.

She said as acidly as she could, "Yes, indeed, the very thing. She would then, no doubt, have run away to Bristol and shipped out as a cabin boy. My dear sir, it is Drusilla we are speaking of, not some mythical, docile female who does as she's bid and stays put. And if you do not drink your tea, I shall pour it over your head."

After a moment he smiled. "I believe you would."

172

17

It was Thorpe, not the dogs, who found Drusilla. About ten o'clock he came across her stumbling down a gorse-dotted hillock and sniffling loudly. She was wet, muddy, frightened, and hungry, but otherwise quite unharmed, and had spent the night in an empty shepherd's cot. The previous day and a half she had apparently wandered in widening circles west of Whitethorn and sustained nature with a bag of boiled sweets.

This much Jane learnt from Drusilla later. Thorpe's arrival at the Tarrants' with his charge—heralded as it was by a whooping, hallooing Vincent who had ridden on ahead to spread the good news—was the occasion for more farce than drama.

Drusilla looked so ridiculous riding pillion behind Thorpe, with her faithful bandbox bumping the horse's rump, that every dignified reproach Jane had rehearsed went by the board, and she dissolved into unladylike snickers.

"Lady Hester Stanhope, I presume. Or is it the Rose of the Pyrenees?"

Drusilla gave her a look of loathing and slipped to the ground on Vincent's arm.

Jane composed herself. "Mrs. Tarrant, I must make Meriden's younger sister known to you. Her fame has, of course, preceded her."

"How do you do, Drusilla?" said Peggy Tarrant kindly.

Drusilla stood looking up at her from the bottom step. Her lip began to quiver. "I meant to be a help to you, ma'am, and instead I have been a trial. I'm sorry." She burst into tears, and Mrs. Tarrant enveloped her in a warm hug.

She glowered over Drusilla's head at Jane and Vincent and Thorpe. "Poor baby. I suppose Julian has been jawing at you, too."

"N-no," Drusilla sobbed, "and I would feel so much better if he had."

Mrs. Tarrant made soothing noises. "It's very inconsiderate of him, to be sure. Come in with me, Drusilla, and I'll see if I can persuade your brother to give you a good scolding later." She bustled the girl into the house.

Jane and Thorpe exchanged glances, and she could've sworn Thorpe winked.

"If that don't beat the Dutch," Vincent said wrathfully. "*I'll* give her a scolding she won't forget. Dash it, she's my sister as much as Julian's."

Jane sat on the step and laughed so hard she disgraced herself.

Julian spent some time dispensing largesse and gratitude to the searchers. By the time he reached Whitethorn, it was nearly two and he had got beyond tiredness and floated, or seemed to float, into the house and down to the kitchen where he supposed he should find Mrs. Bradford and something to eat.

He found Mrs. Bradford, and Thorpe also, deep in speech by the great kitchen table. When they heard his step, they leapt apart like guilty things surprised.

He was a trifle surprised himself but said merely, "Did I thank you, Thorpe? I'm in your debt. Again."

Thorpe flushed and mumbled, which was not his style. Puzzled, Julian looked from his groom to his housekeeper.

"Something to eat, me lord?"

"Thank you, Mrs. Bradford. Don't trouble with a meal. I'm too tired. Is that bread and cheese?"

He helped himself to a chunk of bread and leant against the wall, chewing.

Thorpe cleared his throat. "Me lord...."

"What is it?"

"Me and Ellen Bradford, sir, is wishful to marry. With your permission, sir."

Julian stared. Thorpe, the married man. From Thorpe's highly unnatural diction he could only suppose the speech to have been rehearsed. Premeditated.

"Not if you dislike it, me lord," said Mrs. Bradford firmly, revealing the source of Thorpe's language. "I'm sensible Thorpe has been serving of you many years now, and if you're bent on keeping him in foreign parts I'll not interfere."

Julian recovered his wits. "Good God, what a pair of idiots you are. Of course you must wed if you wish it." He frowned. "Had you thought of this before I dragged you off to Dorset, Thorpe?"

"It was on me mind," Thorpe admitted.

"Well, damn your eyes for not telling me. I'd not have taken you away."

"Nay, then, I know it," Thorpe said comfortably. "Tha needed one of thy own by thee, lad. Sneck oop."

Julian was silent, chagrined at his own obtuseness and selfishness, and more touched than he could have said by Thorpe's loyalty. "Jem—"

"Never the mind."

Julian shook his head hard. "Mrs. Bradford?"

"Sir."

"Is there a bottle of champagne in the cellar?"

"There's the one Mr. Tarrant brought over last Boxing Day," she said doubtfully.

"Fetch it, if you please."

When she returned, he shot the cork and poured three prodigious portions, for she had brought mugs and he didn't wish to send her scuttling off again after glasses. He managed to propose a toast to their happiness.

Presently they were all very merry, and Julian, owing partly to exhaustion and partly to bemusement, was as drunk as a wheelbarrow.

"Drunk as a lord," Thorpe said benignly.

Mrs. Bradford startled the two men and herself by laughing heartily, and Thorpe helped Julian stumble up to bed.

Mrs. Tarrant—whom Jane now thought of as Peggy—chased Vincent off to Whitethorn to catch up on his sleep and, if possible, tie his brother to the bed also.

"For Julian will certainly have lamed himself," she said with resignation, "and we don't need another invalid here. Mrs. Bradford can minister to him. More bread and butter, Drusilla? My dear, what is it?"

Drusilla was heard to mutter guilt-stricken *mea culpa*s for having crippled her brother.

"Nonsense. You didn't mean to lose yourself, did you?"

"N-no."

"Surely you're used to Julian by now. It's his own fault. He could have left the search to Thorpe and Earnshaw, at least long enough to rest his leg, but he can never bear to be sitting and waiting."

"I thought he was a good patient," Jane interposed somewhat indignantly.

"Very civil. At what cost I don't care to contemplate, for he was repressing all his natural inclinations. Julian has a very short fuse."

Jane bridled. "His lordship has been very patient with his family."

Drusilla burst into tears.

Jane and Peggy exchanged chagrined looks.

"She must go to bed at once," Jane said remorsefully. "What a dim thing for me to say. And not true, either, for Meriden bit Vincent's head off.... Dru, darling, don't cry. Oh, dear, I wish Meriden were here. He would know how to make you laugh at this, love."

Peggy said nothing, but took charge of the weeping girl and soon had her settled in a truckle bed in Jane's room. They both sat with her until she had gone off into exhausted sleep.

Peggy raised a finger to her lips and led Jane into the hall.

"Now, do be sensible, Jane, and have a rest also. I'll see to Will. Miss Goodnight—"

"Goody! I had forgot her!"

"She was very much relieved to know of Drusilla's safe return, and I have ordered her to remain in bed until dinner." She smiled ruefully. "Indeed it would be very much better if everyone would contrive to sleep for several days."

"Oh, dear, we have put you to so much trouble."

"Hush. It will do Will a world of good once things have settled down. So diverting. He slept like an infant last night."

"You're very kind, Peggy."

Peggy smiled. "I am an excellent creature and full of benevolence. Off to bed with you."

Jane complied and surprised herself by falling asleep. She roused herself for dinner, however, and tiptoed out so as not to disturb her lustily snoring cousin.

Neither of the Stretton brothers appeared, and Peggy and Miss Goodnight and Jane ate a quiet dinner and spent several hours delighting Will Tarrant by losing to him at whist. Drusilla still slept.

In fact she did not waken until the next morning when the sprightly maid brought in their tea. When Drusilla woke, Jane must perforce wake also, for her cousin at once began to chatter and question her and describe what, after a hearty sleep, now seemed a splendid adventure.

"And I'm dreadfully hungry," Drusilla announced in piercing tones just as Mrs. Tarrant and Annie entered with two laden trays.

"How fortunate. I thought you might be." Peggy smiled at her and left the cousins to eat and dress. It was clear she had been bustling about for hours.

Drusilla fell on the food like a locust—or do I mean plague of locusts,

Jane thought, eyeing her cousin in sleepy revulsion. It was wonderful how revived Drusilla was—full of enthusiasm and vitality, ready, no doubt, to think up yet another devastating escapade and, so far this morning at least, utterly wanting in contrition.

"I don't know why you should be jawing at me, Jane," she said simply when Jane ventured to bring up the subject of her adventure. "Julian did not, and he is my guardian."

"Probably he had not the energy," Jane said drily. "But Drusilla, you must allow Lady Georgy would have every right to censure you, and I am here in her stead."

Drusilla looked mulish.

"What if you had taken some injury?"

"But I didn't."

Jane gave up.

The cousins had dressed and visited Miss Goodnight, who promised to come down presently, and been shown Peggy's babies by the time Vincent and Meriden arrived—in Vincent's phaeton—with a visibly mellow Thorpe following on horseback. Vincent was dressed for riding; his brother was not.

They stood outside for some moments in conference. Then Vincent tooled off towards the stables with Thorpe trotting along behind. Meriden came slowly toward the house.

"I was right," Peggy said glumly. "He's using the stick again. I hope he may not have torn something."

Jane did not reply. In fact she was momentarily so shaken with rage at Drusilla that she could not have spoken.

Peggy went out to greet Meriden and left Jane and Drusilla together.

Drusilla said timidly, "I didn't mean to get lost, Jane."

Jane gritted her teeth.

"At least you're here," Drusilla ventured.

"I had no wish to be here," Jane said coldly.

"I thought if I went off alone, the odds were *you* would be the one to follow," Drusilla said in a small voice.

A horrible suspicion crossed Jane's mind. Her cheeks flamed. "What are you saying, miss?"

"Nothing." Drusilla's eyes dropped. "We ... that is, I missed you, Jane."

Jane was not moved by this exercise of pathos and set herself to pursue the matter further, but she forgot it altogether when Peggy and Meriden came into the withdrawing room.

Drusilla flung herself at her brother, who fended her off good-naturedly enough, as if she had been a rather large puppy.

"Yes, yes. You're thrown into transports at the sight of me. Sit down, Dru, and stop making a cake of yourself."

Abashed, his sister sat.

Meriden turned to Miss Goodnight and Jane with a half-smile. "How do you do? Miss Goodnight, I hope you have recovered. I understand you were a little overset by this business."

Miss Goodnight flushed. "A trifle. I do not regard it."

"I do," he said ruefully. "I'm very much obliged to you both. If you had not set off with such despatch, I'm afraid Drusilla would not have escaped harm. She strayed very far afield and would have fetched up in Tanner's Bog."

"Should I?" Drusilla appeared taken with the notion.

"Yes, and you'd not have liked it. How came you to be such a greenhorn?"

Drusilla looked blank.

"I take it you aspire to become an explorer. If so, why did you wander off without taking your bearings? The merest Johnny Raw would know better than to set off across open country without a guide. You had only to follow that stone wall to come in sight of Whitethorn." Having withered Drusilla, he turned back to Jane and Miss Goodnight. "I take it Georgy sent you, since you have her carriage."

"Oh, yes. So obliging of her and such a comfortable ride ... that is, not comfortable, precisely ... the roads...." Miss Goodnight dwindled into incoherence.

A smile flickered in Meriden's eyes, but he forbore to teaze. "Miss Ash, what did Georgy propose you should do with my sister when you came upon her?"

"Bring her back, sir." Jane collected her wits. Yesterday she had been Jane; now she was Miss Ash. Although his manner was not unfriendly, she felt as if she had been struck.

"Why did she not come herself?"

"There was Maria...."

"Lady Herrington had engaged to be present at a levée in honour of the Prince of Orange." Miss Goodnight interposed. "She was at some pains to avoid unnecessary gossip. Her absence—"

"She bullied you and Miss Ash into taking on her duty. I see." Meriden's mouth set in hard lines. "What very obliging relations I have, to be sure."

Jane said quietly, "She did not coerce us, sir. Her wish was to silence the tattlemongers. Drusilla is my cousin, too, and we agreed that it made a more credible story for me to absent myself from Town at this season than for her ladyship to do so."

"Georgy is entirely too puffed up in her own conceit," Meriden snapped. "I daresay Slender Billy wouldn't know her from Miss Brown of Bristol."

The picture of the elegant Georgy in the character of a provincial nobody tickled a grin from Jane. Meriden did not smile.

"You are unreasonable, sir," Jane said after a moment.

"Am I? I placed Drusilla in Georgy's charge."

Jane raised her brows. "And not in mine? Lord Meriden, I believe my consequence sufficient to lend Drusilla credibility."

"*Touché*"

"I did not have pressing engagements, and even my Aunt Hervey saw at once that my cousin's need for me was superior to her own claims." Even Aunt Hervey, she thought wryly. Aunt Pandarus.

"You are very good-natured to allow yourself to be imposed upon, Miss Ash. Your father will view the matter with less complaisance."

"Oh, I daresay he'll never know of it if some busybody doesn't tell him."

"*I* shall tell him."

Jane stared. "You take too much on yourself, sir. I am not your sister or your ward or even your c-cousin. What I choose to do is my own affair." She bit her lip and gave an unwilling chuckle. "What a harebrained thing to say. If he finds out from someone else, he will blame you. I beg your pardon. I shall write him myself. At once."

Meriden was silent, and she could not read his expression.

After a moment Peggy said drily, "Perhaps you should neither of you write Mr. Ash. Cause Drusilla to do so. Julian, I wish you will either sit down or leave. It is most uncomfortable to be cricking one's neck at a looming man. Drusilla, pull out the wing-backed chair for your brother."

"I'm quite capable of pulling out my own chair." He frowned. "Peggy, what do *you* say?"

"To what?" She relented. "Well, I wish you will go in to Will and allow Miss Goodnight and Miss Ash and me to come up with a plan. I daresay we shall contrive something, and you are just now a great nuisance." She smiled. "Beat Will at chess. He needs a set-down."

"Peggy...."

"It's all *right*, idiot."

Meriden took his leave with wooden civility and clumped off looking grim.

"I must say," Peggy remarked in considered tones, "patriarchy does not become Julian." She did not allow anyone the chance to reply but went on briskly, "Now we shall sort the matter out in peace. Drusilla is here. What do we do with her?"

"Take her back to London at once," Jane said in tones as glum as her feelings.

Drusilla's speedwell blue eyes brimmed tears, but she said nothing to defend herself.

Peggy gave her a measuring glance. "That would defeat your purpose, Jane. Would it not?"

Jane gathered her wits. "How should it?"

"Lady Herrington will put it about that Drusilla has come to Yorkshire for a visit. If you return with her directly, everyone will know at once that is not the case and suspect the worst."

Jane frowned. "True."

"You cannot put up at Whitethorn. *That* is out of the question."

"Meriden is Drusilla's brother...."

"But not, as you pointed out, yours." She smiled. "Besides, Whitethorn is largely under holland covers and not, in my estimation, very comfortably furnished even if Julian were to cause Mrs. Bradford to open the house. No. I propose that the three of you stay here for several weeks and go south again when Drusilla had meant to leave originally."

"That is very kind in you, Peggy, but you already have a deal of trouble on your hands."

Peggy smiled. "You mean I have Will on my hands. Very true, and I shall not be able to entertain Drusilla as I planned. What I mean to do is use the three of you ruthlessly to my own ends.

"Jane, you and Miss Goodnight may take over the cossetting of my beloved spouse. I shall put Drusilla to work in the nursery. For myself, I intend to become a leisured lady and shall expect to be regaled with all the latest *on dits* and crim. cons. And, Jane, you will please allow me to copy the gown you wore to dinner last evening for it would become me excessively."

Jane could not help smiling, but she felt Peggy was making the best of a bad bargain and said so. Peggy, however, would not be moved, and in the end, Jane consented.

"Splendid!" Peggy beamed.

"But Lord Meriden...."

"Julian will not come the lord with *me*," Peggy said firmly.

Peggy was not altogether displeased with the company that had thrust itself upon her so melodramatically.

Will's temper improved as if by magic. The vital work of overseeing the estate, which she must have done in her husband's stead, fell to Julian and Vincent. And her dinner table had seldom seen livelier company. She could have used the services of a few more servants, but Jane and Miss Goodnight did not require to be waited on hand and foot and, indeed, insisted upon helping her with such tasks as mending linen and marketing. Miss Goodnight knit young Margot a cap. Drusilla sang for them and was very good with the children. Even Nurse, inclined to resent intruders, took to her.

At first Peggy stood somewhat in awe of Jane, for Jane was used, clearly, to move in high circles, but she also showed herself to be fully aware of the intricacies of running a household and not at all contemptuous of the plain style of life at Tarrant Manor. They soon became friends.

In one thing, however, Jane would not be drawn out. Peggy judged her to be some four- or five-and-twenty years old, and she was unwed. She had means, wit, taste, a pleasing appearance, good health, excellent manners, and yet she was not married. Madness.

Peggy was too wise to teaze when her first tentative attempts to pry received a playful but definite rebuff. She watched Jane, however, very curiously. Julian she watched less closely or she would have perceived the connexion between what was troubling him and what occasionally seemed to sink Jane into abstracted reverie.

It took Drusilla to enlighten her.

18

PEGGY DROVE WITH Drusilla into Yeding on market day, for the girl had been oppressively well conducted, and it seemed to Peggy that she needed a small treat.

They had a jolly time, and presently, as they drove homeward, Drusilla grew confiding. She described life in Bath with Lady Meriden with such candour that Peggy wondered why Julian's sister had not run away sooner, and was so incautious as to say so.

"Oh, Julian asked me not to," Drusilla said in matter-of-fact tones. "So, of course, I didn't."

That baffled Peggy and amused her. She said lightly, "I collect he forgot to tell you not to run away from London."

Drusilla flushed. "I wasn't really running away. I asked Jane to come with me to Yorkshire, but she would not, so, of course, I had to pretend to run off. I knew she must follow, for Cousin Georgy never leaves London in the Season, and who else would?"

"Miss Goodnight?" Peggy ventured.

"Goody can't travel alone. Casts up her accounts."

Peggy shook her head to clear it.

"I planned it all so exactly," Drusilla mourned. "And then I had to lose myself on that stupid moor. It spoilt everything."

Peggy stared into the ambient air. "My dear, if you weren't really running away, what *were* you doing?"

"Bringing Jane to Julian, of course."

Peggy digested that. "Why?"

Drusilla cast her a sidelong look. "It was Jane's Aunt Hervey who gave me the idea. She said Julian must marry, for then his wife could present Maria, and none of us need stay with Mama in Bath—except Thomas. One sees that it wouldn't do to deprive Mama of her baby, and I daresay he's too young to mind. Why are you laughing?"

Peggy shook her head. "Go on, my dear. Jane's Aunt Hervey...."

Drusilla eyed her suspiciously. "Well, *she* said Julian should go about in Society and all the ladies would throw their caps at him and he'd be wed in a trice, and of course I was horrified. Only think what sort of dismal female he might be trapped by. I was quite cast down. Then all at once I saw what a good idea it would be if he were to marry Jane."

"Good for whom?" Peggy managed.

"Oh, for everyone."

"For Drusilla?"

Drusilla stiffened. "Yes. And Maria and Felix and the twins, and Vincent, even, but especially Julian. He *needs* Jane."

She spoke with such conviction that Peggy was startled out of laughter. "My dear, you can't know that."

"Yes, I can. He's been blue-devilled ever since Jane left us."

Peggy was silent. At last she said slowly, "Even if that were so, Drusilla, what of Jane herself?"

"You mean, I collect, that we should be a nuisance to her? You sound like Julian."

"You haven't discussed this with Ju!"

"No, but he kept saying we were not to be troubling Jane forever and that she had her own life to lead."

"He may be right."

"He's not. She loves us and had the greatest care of us before Julian came. She ... she even took me to the tooth drawer."

"That does argue devotion"

Drusilla nodded emphatically.

"But my dear," said Peggy, who now felt decidedly in over her head, "even if she *is* devoted to you, that doesn't argue she's devoted to Julian. A man and woman don't marry to make their brothers and sisters comfortable. At least," she added cautiously, "I've never heard of such a thing."

"I suppose you think Julian's not romantical or dashing like Vincent. Jane don't care for that. She *likes* my brother. They was always joking together and ... and looking for each other. And besides, if she can't love him, she's *paltry*, for Julian is—"

"I'm fond of Julian," Peggy interrupted. "You needn't catalogue his virtues for me, but, well, tastes differ. A woman can like a man without wishing to be married to him."

"I wasn't bent on *forcing* them to it," Drusilla said in a small voice. "Only how could they find out whether they were suited if they never saw each other? Oh, if only my Uncle John had not come for Jane. We were

183

all so happy...."

"I'm sorry, darling." When Drusilla had composed herself, Peggy added, "But you know, Dru, I don't see much sign that they're in the grip of overwhelming passion. They're both very polite—"

"Polite!" Drusilla looked glum. "It's my fault. Julian was never used to be so ... formal with Jane. I expect he feels *obliged* to her."

On that dismal note the discussion ended, and Peggy drew Drusilla off onto other subjects before that intrepid damsel should create further conspiracies. Nevertheless the seed was planted, and she found herself watching her new friend and her old friend.

From watching, it was a short step to contriving to set them occasionally in each other's sole company. For, she told herself, echoing Drusilla unawares, how can they know they're not suited if they never see each other?

By the time a week had passed, some of Julian's appalling formality had melted, and Jane showed less constraint in his company. Peggy saw what Drusilla must have observed. Friendship. Whether the attachment was more than that, Peggy could not judge, but she decided to put the matter to the test. Shamelessly she set about to contrive the proper circumstances. Lambs to the slaughter.

Mrs. Ellen Bradford was set on marrying a foreigner from off to Huddersfield, one Jeremy Thorpe, by special license in St. Jude's, Harbrough. It was rumoured, though not widely credited, that the groomsman was to be a real lord.

For once rumour had the truth of it.

Mrs. Bradford's dour sons and Methody daughter had not welcomed the prospect of an ex-trooper, ex-poacher stepfather with complaisance. Indeed, for a time it seemed that the marriage must founder on the rocks of their overweening pride, and the kitchen at Whitethorn rang with lamentations, and Vincent complained of a cold breakfast.

When it became apparent that Mrs. Bradford and Thorpe wished to remain in his service, Julian had contrived the happy plan of leaving Whitethorn—house, stables, bog, sheep, and all—in their joint charge for as long as they should wish to keep it for him. Thus there was no financial impediment to their bliss. Mere pride. Julian had racked his brains for days trying to come up with some suffocating degree of consequence to bestow on Thorpe, but it was Peggy who suggested the special license. Nothing like *that* had ever occurred in St. Jude's, Yeding.

184

Once Peggy had suggested the license—Vincent was despatched to York Minster to secure it—it occurred to Julian to offer his service as groomsman. He made the offer rather tentatively. For all he knew, Mrs. Bradford would be offended and Thorpe embarrassed. Not so. They leapt on the idea, Mrs. Bradford with uncharacteristic and appalling glee and Thorpe with a sort of amazed delight that made Julian feel small and silly. And glum.

He did not wish to lose Thorpe, and he definitely did not wish to dance at anyone's wedding—but if Thorpe could make an heroic sacrifice for him, he did not see that he could do less in return.

When Peggy began to compose the groom's party, however, Julian drew the line—or tried to.

"Good God, Peggy, he's *my* friend."

"Will has known Thorpe for years."

"That's not to the point and you know it."

She raised her brows.

"Dru may come," he grudged.

"And Jane."

"I hope I may attend Thorpe's wedding, in proxy for Arty and Horatio," Miss Ash murmured with a delightful gleam in her eyes.

He assented. Indeed it would not have been in his power to refuse her anything when she looked at him like that.

Miss Goodnight assured him that she loved weddings of all things and felt she might dare to represent Lady Meriden.

"Now, that is doing it rather too brown!" Julian began to feel flustered. "I beg your pardon, Miss Goodnight, but if you come, it must be in your own right. My esteemed stepmother—"

"Lady Meriden stands very much in Thorpe's debt," Miss Goodnight pronounced. "Whether she knows it or not."

He regarded her helplessly. He was by now sure some sort of conspiracy was afoot and resented it on Thorpe's behalf. When Vincent announced his firm intent to come, too, Julian exploded.

"I won't have Thorpe's wedding turned into a May game for your amusement."

Vincent blinked. "No, I say, dashed obliged to Thorpe. Found m'sister, didn't he? Never knew a better man for doctoring horseflesh either. And," he finished triumphantly, "*I* fetched the license. Dash it, Ju, you can't stop me."

"Oh, can't I? Peggy, this is your doing...."

She said gravely, "Will and I should come in any case, Julian. We are so well acquainted with the bride and groom that it would be Will's duty as squire."

Julian felt his neck go red. He had forgot that Will, as head of one of the oldest families in the region, must command far solider deference than a mere newcomer to Whitethorn.

"True," he muttered, "but I swear you're up to something. Perhaps Will should stand Thorpe's groomsman."

She gave him a tranquil smile. "No. Thorpe is your particular friend. No one disputes that. But he is a very good man, and you must allow the rest of us to felicitate him properly. He does not have any family, I believe, and Mrs. Bradford has too much. He will feel safer with an impressive contingent on his side of the aisle."

"Your staff work is beyond reproach, General Tarrant."

"As usual." Will laughed heartily.

Peggy bridled and grinned.

Julian looked from one to the other.

"We *like* Thorpe," Peggy said gently.

"Very well. *If* he agrees. And if anyone—" he glared at his brother and sister—"causes Jem Thorpe the least embarrassment, I will personally fling him—or her—into Tanner's Bog."

19

AT PEGGY'S REQUEST Jane rode to and from Thorpe's wedding on horseback, with Meriden and her cousins. The carriage, it seemed, would be too crowded. Will was free of splints at last, and Jane, however suspicious, did see that he mustn't be jostled. After some hesitation she agreed to the plan.

In fact, only Vincent rode with Jane and Drusilla to the inn to change for the ceremony, for Meriden had gone on ahead to make some arrangement with the vicar. On the return, however, he joined the party.

Drusilla and Vincent were in tearing high spirits, chattering and laughing—probably because they had behaved with stultifying decorum at the wedding. They rode ahead. Meriden accompanied Jane, but said very little. Jane thought he regretted losing Thorpe to wedlock, though there had been nothing of regret in his public manner.

The ceremony, far from degenerating into a bear-garden affair, had been perhaps over-solemn, for the vicar seemed inclined to regard the license as not quite proper, and Mrs. Bradford's numerous kin were dour by nature, but the wedding breakfast had turned downright jolly.

As was his duty, Meriden had toasted the bride, who bridled, and, less conventionally, the bridegroom, who had been looking a trifle dazed but who broke into what Jane could only consider a devilish grin in response to some obscure military allusion in the toast. His lordship had also led Mrs. Bradford, or rather Mrs. Thorpe, through the first dance with aplomb and a few winces while Thorpe, by now a little bosky, partnered a beaming Peggy Tarrant. It was all very respectable, however, and Meriden had had the tact to remove the Nobs before the promising aura of goodwill emanating from Mrs. Thorpe's softened kin should be clouded from too much gentility.

It was, Jane supposed, an index of Meriden's kindness that he had kept his sense of humour—and everyone else's—strictly curbed, but Jane could have done with a spot of comedy.

She cast her escort a sidelong glance. He was watching Vincent and frowning a little. Jane chuckled.

Startled, he looked over at her with the beginning of a smile. "What is it?"

"What a Friday face! A wedding, sir, is a festive occasion, as opposed to funerals which, in general, are not." She added in gentler tones, "You look as if you had lost your best friend."

"It's not quite that bad. I'd have preferred them to come to Dorset, but Mrs. Bradford—that is, Mrs. Thorpe—would not like to live so far from her family."

"Besides," Jane said dulcetly, "only consider what must ensue if Mrs. Thorpe and Mrs. Pruitt were thrown together."

"Good God!"

"You are a humbug, sir."

He smiled. "Your exquisite reason, ma'am?"

"You once assured me you had a way with housekeepers."

"Hasty generalisation."

He looked so rueful that Jane laughed aloud. "Do I take it Mrs. Pruitt has proven less than biddable?"

"She didn't care for the remove to Fern Hall." His horse started at a hare, and he steadied it with absentminded competence. "Nor did your father."

Jane bit her lip. "Papa never knows when to let well alone."

"Do I take it *you* do not dislike the move?"

Almost Jane retreated into courtesy. Almost she said it was not her right to censure his judgement. She caught herself, however, for she was weary of setting up barriers.

"I think it a very sensible course, sir. Meriden is a ... a devilish house to run, as I know. Not but what I enjoyed my brief fling at domestic authority."

"Did you?"

"Yes," she said firmly, "and it has been very difficult returning to guest status, especially among the snakes and crocodiles."

"What!"

"My Aunt Hervey has succumbed to the Egyptian mode of decoration. It is all the crack, but I'm afraid I find it difficult to dress under the gaze of basilisks."

He laughed at that but said merely, "So I should imagine."

They continued for a time in silence. Drusilla and Vincent, impatient of their dawdling pace, had now disappeared from sight. Jane stole a glance at Meriden, but as he was bending over his horse's neck she had only a view of his shoulders—excellent shoulders but not expressive.

She cast about for something further to say. They had reached the stone wall that formed the southeastern boundary of the Whitethorn property, and beyond the wall stretched the bleak expanse of gorse-dotted hillside upon which Drusilla had so nearly come to grief.

"My lord," she said without thinking it through, "what made you settle on this country?"

He straightened and looked at her with raised brows.

"I beg your pardon. It's ... interesting but not, well, prosperous."

"Neither was I," he said drily and, after a constrained moment, "Whitethorn is small, but it has possibilities. I expect I thought it would be pleasant to live near my friends."

"Will ... Mr. Tarrant says you would have gone very far in the army."

"Will has an excellent imagination. I would have sold out in a few years."

"Oh. Why?" Jane asked timidly.

He was silent for some time. At last he shrugged. "Indolence."

"Well, of all the Banbury tales!" Jane snapped. "I collect you had had your fill of campaigning and had made up your mind to cultivate your cabbages. Indolence, indeed."

He pulled up short and, grasping her bridle, caused her horse to halt, too. "Jane," he said in tones of exasperated amusement, "will you marry me?"

Jane blinked. "Yes."

They stared at each other.

Meriden had gone rather pale. Jane felt strange. Detached. Only it was difficult suddenly to breathe, and she did not see very well.

Presently he let her reins drop, and they rode on some way in silence.

Jane cleared her throat but found she could not articulate.

"This is not very loverlike," Meriden said abruptly. "I beg your pardon, Jane, but are you sure?"

"Yes."

He drew an audible breath. "Then come along. If we stay in this lane we shall shortly find ourselves in company."

"Good God, the carriage!" Without further ado Jane set her mare at the wall and, clearing it, called back laughing, "Come along yourself."

They were very soon over the brow of the hill and out of sight of the lane. The country dipped and rose again, and at the top of the second rise lay another wall. Jane eyed it.

Meriden shook his head. "No. This is not a rout, my love. We will dismount in good order and go for a little stroll. If you have no objection."

"I'd like to take the wall, sir," Jane said wistfully. She met his eyes, which were very bright, and laughed. "Very well, a stroll. Un ... unexceptionable."

Presently they found a stile. Meriden slid to the ground and tied his horse. When he came to her side and looked up at her, smiling, Jane's heart turned over.

"Julian ..."

"Good God, at last! I thought I should be sirred to death."

"Be serious."

"If you insist. What is it, *mia*?"

"Are *you* sure?"

"Yes, of course."

"I had scruples, you see."

"Do you mean doubts?"

"No! Scruples. I was afraid I might be thought to have entrapped you."

For a moment his face went quite blank; then he leaned his forehead against the offended mare's neck and began to laugh helplessly.

Jane sat still, looking down at him. What a deal of time to have wasted. If Drusilla had not run away ... it didn't bear thinking of. She reached down and touched his hair and, with the beginning of a smile, gave a tug.

"Ouch!"

"I was attempting to twine your locks about my fingers. It is said to be a loverlike act. Unfortunately your hair does not twine."

He grinned. "Shall I put it in curlpapers for you, wretch? Are you coming?"

"Yes, please." She slid down and, finding her hands conveniently upon his shoulders and his conveniently about her waist, initiated an embrace.

Her mare whickered and nudged them.

"Damned animal," Julian said rather breathlessly. He tied the horse to a bush. "Well, shall we suit?"

Jane nodded.

"Good." He helped her over the stile and scrambled after her.

"Where are we going?"

190

"Do you know, I've no idea. Would you like to see Tanner's Bog?"

"Of all things. Perhaps we can contrive to get comfortably lost."

They walked along, skirting an occasional gorse bush, in happy silence.

"Jane?"

"Yes."

"I should've chased off to Brighton after you. I wanted to."

"Why did you not?" she demanded, indignant. "It was the longest, most miserable summer of my life."

Unfortunately, before he could satisfy her with a suitably loverlike explanation, he stumbled on a clod and sat down hard on his biscuit-hued breeches.

"My dear, have you hurt yourself?" Jane bent over him.

"Yes," he said crossly. "I've sat on a bit of gorse."

Jane stifled a giggle.

"You may laugh, madam."

"I'm sorry."

He looked up at her. "I meant to fling my debts and encumbrances at your feet, but I've flung myself instead. Very romantical, as both my sisters would say."

"S-so it is."

He did not rise.

"Shall I help you up?"

"Not just yet."

"Oh." Wild notions of racing for help flashed through Jane's mind. If he had lamed himself again.... On the other hand.... She gathered up her skirts and sat beside him.

"Mind the gorse."

"Yes. Julian?"

As he turned to her, she leaned over and kissed his nose, which as usual displayed a pink patch where the skin had peeled. "I have wished to do that for a long time."

His eyes gleamed. "Well, I have wished to do this for a long time." He kissed her very thoroughly on the mouth and, proximity working its way, they proceeded to become better acquainted.

Presently, Julian, his mouth against her loosened hair, murmured, "Jane, are you sure you have no objection to my encumbrances?"

"Mmmm. Positive."

"Excellent. I only mention it because one of them is just now leaping over the stile and will be upon us directly."

Jane started and made to draw back.

"I thought you had no objection."

"Julian!"

"Hush." He kissed her eyebrow and straightened in a leisurely way, keeping an arm about her shoulders.

Purposefully Vincent strode toward them, his romantic black curls tumbling over his perfect forehead *au coup de vent* and his shirtpoints flashing in the light.

"How handsome he is," Jane murmured.

"Fiend."

As he drew near, Vincent's stride slackened. "I say, Julian, when you didn't come, Will sent me to find you. I was sure you'd hurt yourself. Dash it, what do you mean worrying people like that? It's downright irresponsible."

Julian grinned.

"What are you doing ... oh." Vincent flushed scarlet. "I say. That is ... good God, Jane, you look like a dashed wanton."

"Sir, you are speaking of my affianced wife."

Vincent closed his mouth with a snap. "I say...."

"Well, if you won't go away, help me up, halfling."

Speechless, Vincent offered his hand and pulled his brother to his feet.

Julian winced and steadied himself on Vincent's shoulder. "Wanton indeed. You know, Vincent," he said thoughtfully, "you're no better than a dashed Puritan."

If you have enjoyed this book and would like to receive details of other Walker Regency romances, please write to:
Regency Editor
Walker and Company
720 Fifth Avenue
New York, N.Y. 10019